GET ALL

WITH JUST ONE PROOF OF PURCHASE!

$50 VALUE

◆ **Hotel Discounts** up to 60% at home and abroad ◆ **Travel Service -** Guaranteed lowest published airfares plus 5% cash back on tickets ◆ **$25 Travel Voucher** ◆ **Sensuous Petite Parfumerie** collection ◆ **Insider Tips Letter** with sneak previews of upcoming books

You'll get a FREE personal card, too. It's your passport to all these benefits– and to even more great gifts & benefits to come!

There's no club to join. No purchase commitment. No obligation.

Enrollment Form

☐ *Yes!* I WANT TO BE A *Privileged Woman*.
Enclosed is one *PAGES & PRIVILEGES™* Proof of
Purchase from any Harlequin or Silhouette book currently for
sale in stores (Proofs of Purchase are found on the back pages
of books) and the store cash register receipt. Please enroll me
in *PAGES & PRIVILEGES™*. Send my Welcome Kit and FREE
Gifts -- and activate my FREE benefits -- immediately.

More great gifts and benefits to come.

NAME (please print)

ADDRESS   APT. NO

CITY   STATE   ZIP/POSTAL CODE

PROOF OF PURCHASE ONLY

**NO CLUB!
NO COMMITMENT!**
*Just one purchase brings
you great Free Gifts and
Benefits!*

Please allow 6-8 weeks for delivery. Quantities are limited. We reserve the right to
substitute items. Enroll before October 31, 1995 and receive one full year of benefits.

Name of store where this book was purchased_____

Date of purchase_____

Type of store:

☐ Bookstore   ☐ Supermarket   ☐ Drugstore
☐ Dept. or discount store (e.g. K-Mart or Walmart)
☐ Other (specify)_____

Which Harlequin or Silhouette series do you usually read?

Complete and mail with one Proof of Purchase and store receipt to:
   U.S.: *PAGES & PRIVILEGES™*, P.O. Box 1960, Danbury, CT 06813-1960
   Canada: *PAGES & PRIVILEGES™*, 49-6A The Donway West, P.O. 813,
             North York, ON M3C 2E8

SSE-PP5B

▼ DETACH HERE AND MAIL TODAY! ▼

"This can't be happening," Andie whispered. "This kind of thing doesn't happen to me.

Men don't act crazy around me." She was grasping for some shred of sanity, even as Eli nuzzled her neck. He was so warm, so solid, so... "I'm the sister type, the girl next door, the faithful friend—"

Eli gave a growl of frustration, and his eyes filled with desire. "Oh, Andie, you might be a faithful friend, and you might live next door, but you are definitely not my sister."

His mouth covered hers, and she cried out at the sweet, raw sensation. She lifted her hands to his head and slipped her fingers through his hair.

He aligned her intimately to him. *"This* is how you affect me, my faithful friend...."

Dear Reader,

September is an extra-special month for Special Edition! This month brings you some of your favorite veteran authors, three dynamite series and a celebration of special events! So don't miss a minute of the fall festivities under way.

Reader favorite Christine Rimmer returns to North Magdalene for the latest JONES GANG tale! THAT SPECIAL WOMAN! Heather Conway meets her match—and the future father of her baby—in *Sunshine and the Shadowmaster*. Gina Ferris Wilkins's new series, THE FAMILY WAY, continues in September with *A Home for Adam*, a touching and poignant story from this award-winning author. Diana Whitney's THE BLACKTHORN BROTHERHOOD continues with a story of the redeeming power of love in *The Avenger*.

And this month, Special Edition features special occasions in three books in our CONGRATULATIONS! promotion. In each story, a character experiences something that will change his or her life forever. Don't miss a moment of any of these wonderful titles: *Kisses and Kids* by Andrea Edwards, *Joyride* by Patricia Coughlin, and from a new author to Silhouette, *A Date With Dr. Frankenstein* by Leanne Banks.

But that's not all—there's lots in store for the rest of 1995 and Silhouette Special Edition! Not to give away our secrets yet, but safe to say that the rest of the year promises to bring your favorite authors in very special books! I hope you enjoy each and every story to come!

Sincerely,

Tara Gavin
Senior Editor

Please address questions and book requests to:
Silhouette Reader Service
U.S.: 3010 Walden Ave., P.O. Box 1325, Buffalo, NY 14269
Canadian: P.O. Box 609, Fort Erie, Ont. L2A 5X3

LEANNE BANKS

A DATE WITH DR. FRANKENSTEIN

Silhouette®

SPECIAL EDITION®

Published by Silhouette Books
America's Publisher of Contemporary Romance

Special thanks to Jean Randolph, PICU night nurse, and Dr. Warren Nance, head of Human Genetics at VCU/MCV.

This book is dedicated to my father, Thomas Minyard, for passing on his persistence gene to me; my mother, Betty Minyard, for teaching me the joy of the Three Little Fishies; and last, but not least, my husband, Tony Banks, for explaining scientific stuff and loving me.

 SILHOUETTE BOOKS

ISBN 0-373-09983-5

A DATE WITH DR. FRANKENSTEIN

LEANNE BANKS

is a national number-one bestselling author of romance. Recognized for her sensual writing with a Career Achievement Award from *Romantic Times* magazine, Leanne likes creating a story with a few grins, a generous kick of sensuality and characters that hang around after the book is finished. Leanne's favorite hobbies include hugging her children, dancing with her husband in the privacy of their home, and going out to dinner...any night will do.

Congratulations!

Dear Readers,

Congratulations! The word conjures up dozens of special memories. Major events like graduation, marriage, two babies, a new house and first book. But one of the quirky things about life is how the small moments stick with us.

When I got my driver's license, my father shook my hand to congratulate me. Then, with the resigned wisdom of a man who'd nurtured two other daughters, he paid the insurance premium and prayed. The prayer was justified considering I backed over three mailboxes that first year.

As a parent, one of my most thrilling moments was when my three-year-old son finally decided he would use the potty after all. We celebrated with M&M candies.

The images come fast and furious—my husband winning a tennis match, my daughter's first time on the honor roll, my son earning his brown belt in karate, a friend getting the news that the lump was negative.

In most of these instances, there was a struggle involved, a challenge to be met, and sharing the victory multiplied the joy. Perhaps the best part of all of these moments is that they were shared celebrations. And I'm of the opinion that life is too short to waste an opportunity to celebrate. It doesn't have to be big. It can be as simple as making it through another day.

Leanne Banks

Chapter One

Wallowing in the sensation of crisp, clean sheets against her just-bathed skin, Andie Reynolds buried her nose in her pillow and sighed. The pediatric intensive care unit where she'd just pulled a twelve-hour graveyard shift might as well have been located on the other side of the world. More than food, more than money, more than the multiple orgasm she'd yet to experience, *more than anything,* Andie wanted sleep.

A delicious lethargy took over, and with the shade pulled down to shut out the encroaching sunlight and spring day, she was wooed like a lover toward blissful oblivion. Her breaths deepened and sweet silence reigned ... for a moment.

A persistent buzzing filtered through her barely cracked bedroom window.

Her eyebrows twitched. *It will go away,* she promised herself.

It got louder. A percussion rhythm gave the buzzing sound form.

She frowned. Loath to entertain the idea of opening her eyes, she groaned and shoved her head under the pillow. The sound, however, got louder. Screaming, high-pitched, unhuman voices contorted a popular song. If she'd been asleep, Andie would have suspected she was smack-dab in the middle of a nightmare played out in stereo.

She was *not,* however, asleep.

And someone with a death wish was blaring out Alvin and the Chipmunks' latest musical collection on the other side of her new neighbor's hedge.

Again.

Just in case it was her imagination, she counted to ten, as she had often done in the past two days. Maybe it would go away. When the assault on her ears continued, she tumbled out of bed and slammed the window closed.

Heaven help her, she could still hear it.

Her eyes half-closed, Andie fought her way out of her nightgown and pulled a cotton dress over her head. Stepping over her sleeping dog, she grumbled about his selective hearing, pushed her hair out of her face, and stumbled toward the front door.

She'd done this two other days—gotten dressed, marched around the perimeter of her neighbor's property and walked through the wrought-iron gate.

On both occasions, the music had abruptly ceased as soon as she walked through that gate, and she had stopped midstride, waiting to see if it would begin again. It didn't. By that time, she was awake enough to realize how foolish she would feel complaining about the loud music when there was none. So she'd returned to her bed, stared at the ceiling for two hours and eventually fallen asleep.

Today, she vowed as she strode past the ominous hedge, she was going all the way.

The old neighbors whispered that the reason her new neighbor hadn't trimmed his hedges was that he had something to hide—bodies in his basement. After all, wasn't he some kind of scientist doing experiments at the research facility in Raleigh, North Carolina? He probably cloned people in his home laboratory.

Even in her sleep-deprived state, Andie snorted at the ridiculous notion. As she opened the creaking gate and made her way up the cracked walkway, however, the back of her neck prickled with unease at the sight of the eerie Addams family style house.

Dismissing the unwelcome feeling, Andie rubbed her neck and pushed the doorbell. It made a deep gonging sound. She heard the approach of her sleep thief as the volume of the Chipmunks increased. He'd obviously hidden inside the house after waking her. Within seconds the heavy, battered door opened and a small child appeared, holding "My First Boom Box" as the speakers shuddered under the strain of the maximum decibel level.

Andie shuddered, too.

The little boy with sandy brown hair and a solemn face regarded her intently with his remarkable green eyes. He seemed to arrive at some decision and moved one of his stubby fingers toward the Stop button.

Alarm shot through Andie, and she acted instinctively. "Oh, no, you don't!" This was the only evidence she had that the Chipmunks were disturbing her peace. She reached for the boom box at the same moment she heard a man's voice.

"Fletcher!" Concern and exasperation warred in his tone. "Fletch, I told you not to open the door to people you don't—"

The man stopped directly behind the boy and stared at her. Sandy brown hair, solemn face and remarkable green eyes.

Andie blinked. She wondered if the cloning rumor was true. The grown-up version was about six feet tall with a lean, muscular build. He wore a white open-neck shirt that emphasized his broad shoulders and had a spray of chest hair that she technically shouldn't be noticing at this particular moment. She technically shouldn't be noticing the way his jeans fit, either.

The man's gaze fell to the boom box.

Andie saw that his earphones rested around his neck. No wonder he hadn't heard. She punched the Stop button and began to explain herself. "Hi. I'm Andie Reynolds, your next-door neighbor, and I really wish we could have met under other circumstances. I just got home from my night shift at the hospital." He was looking at her so intently that she felt nervous, and when she was nervous, her sentences ran together. "I'd love to go to sleep, but I keep hearing the Chipmunks right outside my window and..."

The man frowned in confusion. "Chipmunks?"

Andie hit the Play button for a few seconds.

Realization crossed his features. He looked down at Fletcher and sighed. "We better keep the boom box inside the house, Fletch." He glanced back at Andie and his lips twisted in irony. "At least until we master the concept of volume control."

Fletcher's lost expression tugged at her heart. "Here's your boom box," she said, handing it to him. She tried to think of something nice to say about the Chipmunks, but Andie didn't like to lie to children.

She cleared her throat. "Well, thank you." Feeling the curiosity in the man's gaze, she began to back away. "I really appreciate—"

"I didn't introduce myself," he said abruptly, as if he had to remind himself to perform the social courtesy. He extended his hand. "I'm Eli Masters, and this is my son, Fletcher."

"I know." Andie allowed his warm hand to enclose hers.

Eli frowned. "You know my name? We haven't met before."

Andie shook her head, thinking that he had a great voice for a man the neighbors called Dr. Frankenstein. It was smooth and very masculine, the kind that would send ripples through a woman when he spoke close to her ear.

"No," she said, as she dismissed the idea of ripples. She didn't need this kind of ripple in her life. "I meant that I can tell Fletcher is your son. He looks so much like you."

"My dad's a lot older than I am," Fletcher interjected, extending his own hand. "He's a lot taller, too. His face is hairier, and he's got bigger arms." He gave a little shrug. "Everything on his body is bigger."

His gaze caught hers at the same time that he muttered, "Thanks a lot, Fletch."

If she were a different woman, she would have tossed back a flirty, mischievous gaze at Eli and said something scandalous like *Is that so? Everything's bigger?* But Andie knew she wasn't vamp material.

She'd learned that lesson the hard way. She slid her hand from Eli's to Fletcher's smaller one. "I was thinking of your hair and green eyes."

Fletcher's face deepened with sadness. "I got a dimple from my mom."

Wondering at his forlorn expression, Andie felt another tug at her heartstrings. "You did? I haven't seen it yet. You can only see people's dimples when they smile."

Fletcher grimaced, and sure enough the dimple came into view.

"There it is," Andie exclaimed, gently touching the indentation. "I hear you get a dimple if an angel kisses you before you're born."

Eli watched Andie Reynolds work magic with his son and felt the bite of envy, failure, and reluctant admiration. She'd met Fletch less than three minutes ago and was completely at ease and natural with him. Eli was not at ease with his son, even though he'd had the advantage of knowing Fletch since birth, with joint-custody visits after the divorce and full custody since his ex-wife's recent death.

"My dad says dimples are determined by genetics," Fletch told her.

Andie shot Eli a mildly disapproving glance that amused him. He gave his next-door neighbor a second assessing look. Mid-twenties, he estimated, with chin-length auburn hair and sleepy eyes the color of caramel. She was appealingly mussed from her failed attempt at sleep, yet she still looked fresh and young.

That struck him immediately, because in contrast Eli felt old, far too old for a thirty-four-year-old man. Her loose cotton dress didn't cling, but he suspected her body was lean and compact beneath it. She wore no makeup or bra, he noted, when he saw the outline of her nipples against the dress, which billowed in the soft morning breeze.

Natural and warm, with a subtle hide-and-seek sensuality that would make a man look. And wait. And look some more.

In the middle of his looking, Eli abruptly recalled that when it came to women, he had the judgment of an amoeba.

She was a neighbor, though, he acknowledged, the first one to darken his new doorstep since he and Fletch moved in two weeks ago. Though social niceties had never been his forte, he would have to make the effort now. "Would you come inside for a few minutes?" he asked. "I think I can manage to make a cup of coffee."

Andie shook her head. "I really shouldn't. If I don't get some sleep, I'll—"

"Just a few minutes. We haven't met any of the neighbors yet."

She sighed, looking from Fletch to Eli. "I..." She gulped, feeling a sinking sensation. It would be downright unfriendly to walk away, but there was something about Eli that unsettled her. Strength and purpose were stamped on his masculine features. He wasn't the least bit fidgety, yet there was a compelling energy in his gaze that reminded her of those tropical drinks with the little umbrellas. At first taste, they went down smooth and easy. It was only after you were fooled into drinking two or three that you got hit with a big bang.

Still, Fletch looked like a little lost waif. It was just a cup of coffee, she promised herself. She smiled weakly. "Do you have decaf?"

"Sure."

Within three minutes, however, Eli was searching through his bare cabinets while Andie stared in dismay at the kitchen. Moving boxes lined the walls, some opened, some not. The counters were covered with five, no, six pizza boxes, a jar of peanut butter and a bag of Oreo cookies. A box of Marshmallow Frosties cereal and a book, facedown and open, perched on one end of the square table. She glanced at the title—*Parenting the Preschool Child*.

A threatening sense of déjà vu came over her. Her emotional reaction was so powerful it became physical, and Andie felt her throat close up as if she were having an allergic reaction.

Her problems had started long ago and innocently enough, but Andie remembered the date and time when her life veered off course. At thirteen she had come home from school to learn that her father had been injured at work. Like platelets shifted during an earthquake, so had the very foundation of her family shifted. Her mother got a job, and since Andie was the eldest child, she had been left in charge of her three uncivilized younger brothers. For the next six years, she nurtured.

Those six years had shaped her personality, affected her occupational choice and, most deadly of all, etched out her identity with men.

She was the sister, the pal, the woman a man called when he was in a jam. She was *not* the woman a man called because he was so in love and lust with her that he couldn't last another minute without her. And Andie had her own secret wishes about that scenario, wishes that she knew were painfully futile.

With her mind bumping along a familiar route that she usually tried to avoid, her thoughts turned to Paul and his little girl, and the family they might have been.

The memory was a splinter in her heart. She absently rubbed her hands together. She should have gotten over it by now. The hurt should have waned, and Andie did her best to conceal it. But she knew what had gotten her into trouble. It was this damn overdeveloped nurturing gene. It would ruin her if she didn't control it. *Ruin, destroy...*

Eli poked his head out of the cabinet. "Excuse me. Did you say something?"

Fletcher looked up at her, his eyes inquisitive.

Andie blinked. She hadn't realized she'd voiced her thoughts aloud. "Oh, no," she said, smiling weakly.

He turned to the refrigerator. "I could have sworn I had some decaf. We have apple juice and Coke. Don't suppose you'd want a beer at this time of day."

How about a straight shot of whiskey? "Apple juice would be nice."

He poured three glasses, and Fletch took his into the den. Joining her at the table, Eli marked the page and closed the book. He glanced at her, his face subtly shadowed. "Fletch's mom died six weeks ago," he said.

It explained a lot—Fletcher's sadness, Eli's weariness. Her heart went out to both of them. "I'm very sorry."

He hesitated, his eyes flickering with regret and bitterness. "We were divorced," he finally said.

"Oh." She couldn't think of anything else to say, and an uncomfortable silence stretched between them. Andie told herself not to wonder about the story behind the flat tone of his words. She took a sip, set down her glass and rubbed her thumb through the condensation.

Eli cleared his throat as if he wanted to expunge a dark memory. "I think Fletcher will be okay," he said. "The Realtor mentioned that there are plenty of kids in the neighborhood, but we haven't seem them yet."

Andie tried to think of a tactful way to tell him that the neighbors feared being drafted into participating in his experiments. She took another sip. "Well, have you thought about trimming the hedges? They can be a little intimidating."

He looked at her. His gaze was intent, very masculine. And focused directly on her. Andie felt a punching sensation in her stomach.

"You're not going to believe this," he said in a low confiding tone that turned the punch into a flutter, "but I've been so busy sorting through the boxes I haven't even noticed the hedges."

She would believe the world was flat if he said it in that same sexy voice. Her self-defense mechanism kicked in. *Oh, no, she wouldn't.* Andie sat back in her seat. "Have you thought about getting some household help?"

He nodded. "I've signed up with two agencies and interviewed two women, but when they saw the house, they weren't interested." He looked around. "I know it's a relic, but I needed something fast, so I bought it for the space and neighborhood. Everybody said Cary, North Carolina, is a great place to bring up a kid."

Andie opened her mouth and almost volunteered to put the word out at the hospital for Eli. She stifled the urge because it wouldn't end there, she told herself. She would get sucked into Eli's and Fletcher's lives, and pretty soon she would be covering for Eli when

Fletcher got sick or the baby-sitter didn't show. After a while, Eli would see how convenient it was to have Andie around, and he would confuse convenience with some deeper, more dangerous emotion.

Andie knew she was blowing this out of proportion, but she also knew helping people was as natural to her as brushing her teeth. It had gotten her into more emotional messes than she cared to think about.

"I'm sure you'll find someone to help you soon," Andie murmured and wondered why she felt like such a slug.

Eli shrugged philosophically. Then, pausing, he turned his head toward the hallway and stood. "Hear that?"

Silence filled the house. Baffled, Andie shook her head and came to her feet too. "I don't hear anything."

"That's the problem," Eli said darkly and walked toward the den. "Fletcher," he called, "Fletch, what are you—" He broke off. "You found another clock," he said, exasperation leaking through his tone.

Andie rounded the corner and saw Fletch on the floor of the den with his hands in the guts of an anniversary clock and his small face filled with guilt. "I got bored and didn't wanna bother you."

Crouching beside him, Eli sighed. "You're not bothering me, but we've got to keep a couple of working clocks in the house." He wondered if Fletcher had inherited more than the Masterses' green eyes and brown hair. Eli's mother had possessed a genius IQ. So did Eli and one of his brothers. Eli knew, however, that genius intelligence could be a mixed bag, particularly at Fletch's young age. "If you're bored, we can look into a preschool where you can be with other kids and—"

"No!" Fletch threw down a tiny spring and stood. "I don't wanna go to preschool. Or day care either. I wanna stay at home." Green eyes full of accusation, he looked as if he were ready to cry. "You promised me you wouldn't make me go." He picked up his boom box and turned to leave.

The tremble in his son's voice wrenched at Eli. He snagged Fletch's arm, bringing him to a stop. "I said I wouldn't make you go during the first month or so that we're here in Cary," he gently corrected. "Later, we'll have to see."

Fletch's shoulders slumped in relief. "But not now."

"Not now," Eli reassured him and pulled Fletch's small body into his arms. "Now promise not to take apart any more clocks today."

"I promise." Rubbing his eyes, he snuggled closer to Eli. "I'm going up to my room for a while."

"Okay. Tell Miss Reynolds goodbye."

Fletch looked up at Andie. "G'bye. Sorry I played the Chipmunks so loud."

Andie smiled and ruffled his bangs. "That's okay. It was nice meeting you." She watched him go upstairs and wished she hadn't witnessed that heart-tugging scene. It revealed too much about both of them. All her nurturing instincts screamed into overdrive.

"His schedule's still messed up from the move. He'll probably take a nap," Eli explained and shook his head. "Although he would die before he admitted he was sleepy."

Andie smiled. "My brother was like that. Five years old and so afraid he would miss something."

"Fletch will turn five in two weeks." He frowned as if something had just occurred to him. "I'll need to do something about a birthday party."

Andie bit her tongue. She would not offer to help. Eli was a grown man, fully capable of arranging a birthday party for his son, fully capable of hiring a housekeeper and arranging his life. She refused to think about how awkwardly tender he'd acted toward Fletch. She refused to let that quality attract her. "Well, I'm sure you'll have a blast. Thanks so much for the apple juice."

Feeling his gaze on her, she backed down the dark hall, narrowly missing a stack of boxes. If she hadn't known better, she would have sworn the man was staring at her chest. "You trim those hedges and I'm sure you'll be meeting the rest of the neighbors in no time." She extended her hand. "Welcome to the neighborhood."

His warm hand engulfed hers. "Thank you. After we get settled, maybe you can come over for something more than apple juice."

Her breath hitched. What a ridiculous reaction. She blamed it on his voice. He meant *wine,* Andie told herself. "Sure," she managed, and slid her tingling fingers from his. "'Bye now." Andie stepped out the front door and walked swiftly down the cracked walkway.

Eli leaned against the doorjamb and watched his new neighbor as she left. No need to wave. After all, the woman was practically running. He supposed he could be insulted.

Instead, he chuckled.

It was a dry, rusty sound, like the hinge on a door that hadn't been opened in a while. It made him realize *he* hadn't laughed in a while. He hadn't felt like laughing. Between his divorce, his research and his ex-wife's death, life had been god-awful serious.

The wrought-iron gate clanged shut behind Andie, and the last he saw of her was her skirt whipping around her calves as she rounded the corner. He pictured her face with those wide eyes and that mobile mouth that had slipped so easily from a playful scowl to a generous smile.

She'd made it look so easy.

A flicker of curiosity started inside him. He could almost feel the scratching of steel against flint, the score of heat from the flame of a lighter. It wasn't an objective, scientific kind of curiosity, he realized. He'd been acutely absorbed by the shape of her breasts beneath her dress. He narrowed his eyes slightly. The front of her dress had looked a little strange, though he couldn't exactly say why.

He thought of her mouth again and an erotic image sprang to his mind. The tangle of tongues and the brush of feminine thighs, a wispy sigh, nipples thrusting against his chest and womanly heat enveloping him.

His pulse pounding, Eli sucked in a breath of morning air. He was fully, achingly aroused.

He'd obviously been in the lab too long.

Disconcerted, he shook his head and decided the cold pizza he'd eaten for breakfast must have affected his brain enzymes. He didn't even attempt to understand his body's response. Dismissing it, he stepped back into the quiet house, pulled the door shut behind him and glanced up the stairs.

Fletch.

He made his way up the wooden stairs to the first room on the right, where Fletch lay sprawled on his bed, one hand wrapped around the boom box, the other curled over his flushed cheek. Eli eased the boom box away, so Fletch wouldn't roll over and hurt himself with it.

Then he just looked, and his heart swelled at the sight of his son. The familiar heaviness descended on him. There was no room for caramel eyes and sexy smiles since his son's heart had broken. Mending broken hearts was serious business.

By the time she made it inside her home, Andie was exhaling in relief.

She'd done it. She'd escaped unscathed. She hadn't volunteered.

Resting against her closed door, she told herself not to feel guilty or any of the other assorted feelings she was experiencing. It didn't matter that Eli Masters had the most intelligent and intently masculine green eyes she'd ever seen. It didn't matter that he had a to-die-for sexy voice and that Andie was a sucker for a man with a sexy voice.

It didn't matter that he'd looked at her with a flicker of masculine interest. She'd probably imagined that, just as she'd imagined him staring at her chest.

Andie glanced down at her small breasts and hooted with laughter. No wonder he'd been staring at her bodice. She was wearing her dress inside out.

Chapter Two

"His name is Stud." Andie answered Fletcher's ninth question as she pressed the dirt around another tomato plant. She frowned at the stinging sensation on her thigh.

"Stud?" a deep, male voice repeated.

Andie paused, staring at her Big Boy tomato plant. Either Fletch had quantum-leaped past puberty or Eli...

Turning, she squinted into the late-afternoon sun and found Eli watching her. Fletch had wandered off to play with her dog. Dressed in slacks, pin-striped shirt and club tie, Eli must have just arrived home from work. He looked just as good in dress clothes as he had in jeans. His hair was slightly mussed as if he'd put his hand through it several times today. Andie thought he looked like someone needed to loosen that tie for him, maybe undo a few buttons and do something about turning that frown into a smile.

Someone. But not her.

As he continued to study her, she felt her cheeks heat. She didn't want to think about how she looked. Her clothes were smudged with dirt, but at least they were on correctly this time. Using her hand to shield her eyes from the sun, she waved her spade in the direction of her black lab and addressed Eli's question. "My brother Sean named him Stud," she said, feeling inordinately self-conscious from the curiosity in Eli's eyes. "Sean was eighteen when he got him and he was going through a stage when he was trying to prove himself. His hormones were raging. He was in a permanent state of..."

"Horniness," Eli supplied without missing a beat.

Andie hesitated, confused. Was he flirting or—? She dismissed the notion. "I think it was more a delusion of grandeur." Andie stood and brushed the dirt off her hands. "When Sean took a trip to California, he asked me to dog-sit. That was four years ago. Sean's still in California, and I've got a dog named Stud."

Eli heard the mild disgust in her tone. "And is Stud all his name implies?"

Andie's laugh rippled out of her throat. "No. Ever since the operation, he thinks he's a lapdog."

Eli nodded, her laughter winding its way through him. "I wonder if he knows what he's missing," he murmured.

Andie did a double take, her gaze surprised and curious. Then, like lightning, her expression changed. Her eyes flickered with sensual amusement and she shook her head in playful reproof. "Stud's not the kind to brag. He hasn't told me all his secrets."

He felt a kick in his gut, a life-giving heat to his blood. It was odd how discussing the absence of a dog's sex life made Eli acutely aware of his own lack in the same area. But then, for some reason, just looking at Andie Reynolds made Eli think about what he was missing. He pushed aside the thought, deciding it was the effect of long-term abstinence, and shoved his hands into his pockets. "We found a housekeeper two days after you came over to the house. The woman I hired said she heard about us at the hospital. Thank you for putting the word out."

Andie shrugged. "No problem. I hope she works out well."

"Fletch seems to like her," Eli said, glancing at his son as he petted the dog's head. "He seems to like Stud, too. Maybe after we get settled in, I'll get a puppy for him."

She put her garden tool in a small basket. "Hey, if you need a dog, I'll be happy to donate Stud."

"You'd miss him."

Andie put her hand over her heart and feigned sadness. "I could always visit."

"Speaking of visit," he began.

Andie glanced at her leg and made a muffled sound of impatience.

Eli moved closer. "What is it?"

"I think it's an insect bite. A couple of them." She ran her finger over the pink bumps on her thigh. "Guess I'd better put some ointment on it later."

"Better do it now," he said, the advice from the first-aid book he'd scanned last night still fresh in his mind. Since he'd gotten full custody of Fletch, his reading extended beyond scientific journals. "I can help you."

Her eyes widened in surprise. "That's okay," she said quickly and shook her head. "I know what to do." She hesitated, then started toward the house. "I am a nurse, you know."

Eli nodded and followed her. "Which means you probably think the regular treatment applies to everyone but you." He called to Fletch to stay in the yard.

"But a bug bite?" Disconcerted by his assessment, she pushed through the screened back door into the kitchen.

He glanced around the room. "Where's that ointment?"

"I keep some in the cabinet over the refrigerator, but—" Incredulous, she broke off, staring at him as he opened the cabinet. The man had a one-track mind. "I can get it myself. I—"

Eli frowned as he scanned the instructions. "You don't think it was a poisonous spider? Fletch was probably distracting you."

"Not really. He—"

"We need to cleanse the area first."

We? "Eli," she said firmly, wondering why she suddenly felt nervous, "I can do this myself."

His gaze met hers, and Andie had the odd sensation of looking at a bulldozer.

"It's my understanding that health care professionals sometimes have a tendency to downplay their own injuries because they're accustomed to focusing their energy on taking care of others."

She blinked. He'd nailed her personality in one decisive stroke. Bemused and disturbed, she took a washcloth from a drawer and dampened it. "Well, I guess that's true," she admitted as she wiped the stinging spots on her thigh. She extended her hand for the ointment. "As a nurse, I'm usually busy...."

Instead of giving it to her, Eli spread a dab over the bumps. Andie went still, watching him perform the task with a gentle, competent hand. She breathed in his scent, a mixture of musky after-shave and masculinity that underscored the fact that he was a man. He was close enough that she could have touched his hair or rubbed her finger over his eyelashes. She lifted her hand and stopped, alarm shooting through her. What was she thinking?

Confusion swirled inside her. Andie wondered if her feelings stemmed from the fact that she was unaccustomed to having anyone *care* for her, even in this small way. Before she could get her bearings, Eli glanced up, his face mere inches from hers. She saw traces of a five o'clock shadow on his firm jaw. She suspected he'd gotten the expression lines between his eyebrows and at the corners of his eyes from a fierce, all-absorbing concentration. At the moment his fierce concentration was totally centered on her. His gaze traveled a blazing path from her bangs and eyebrows to her nose, cheeks and mouth, where it seemed to linger, until he locked onto her eyes.

Her breath just stopped. She remembered having the same sensation once when she'd tried to break up a fight between her brothers and one of them had socked her.

"You smell like apricots." His voice was rough.

She swallowed. "It's my shampoo."

He glanced at her hair, then her lips again. "I like it."

The wailing of a siren went off in her head. It was so loud she wondered if Eli could hear it, too. She took a quick shallow breath and backed into her butcher-block kitchen counter. "I like it, too," she managed to say. "Listen, thanks for helping with the—"

"My pleasure," Eli interrupted, and meant it. His blood was pounding through his veins faster than when he took his daily run. "Come over tonight for a glass of wine. I'll make up for the apple juice and Chipmunks."

Rattled, Andie immediately shook her head. "Thanks, but you don't need to. Really." Sliding alongside the counter, she took a few steps farther away from him. "Besides, I need a bath." She gestured toward her worn, smudged shorts. "I look like a mess."

"You look—" Eli paused and corrected her "—earthy."

"I'll assume that's a pun that correlates with all the dirt."

It wasn't, and Eli was just about to correct her again when she mentioned Fletcher. He swore. Guilt shot through him and he immediately looked out the window. Fletcher was playing with Stud. He exhaled in relief. "I should have been watching him," he castigated himself as he moved toward the door. "I'm still not used to having him around all the time."

Andie followed him to the back porch. "You don't need to beat yourself up about it. He's okay."

But for Eli, it wasn't okay. He wanted to be a good father. He wanted to make everything better for Fletcher, even though he knew that wasn't possible. "I wonder how long it will take me to climb to the level of mediocrity at being a father," he muttered darkly.

Watching Fletcher, he felt overwhelmed, as he had so many other times, at the prospect of raising his son by himself.

He felt the barest touch of Andie's hand on his arm. Her hand was there one second, gone the next, but a warm concern remained in her eyes. "How's it going?"

He paused. No one else had asked him that question. "I don't have a clue what I'm doing," he replied with brutal honesty. "All my life, I've been told that intelligence is a gift and that I should stretch mine as far as it will go. I've got degrees, but they're useless with Fletcher. I'm finally in a position where I'm researching something that I think is worthwhile." He shook his head at the irony. "Hell, I'm researching the genetic origin for seizure disorders in children. *Children.*" He swore again. "And I can't help my own son with his grief and confusion."

A moment of silence followed, long enough for Eli to wonder what had possessed him to drop his worries on Andie. "Forget I said that. I don't know where—"

She held up a hand for him to stop. "Please don't. Taking care of children isn't something you learn overnight, but they somehow manage to reach adulthood despite their parents' mistakes. You and Fletch will be okay." She must have sensed his doubt. "You will," she insisted. "This is a rough stage and it's just going to take some time." She clasped her hands together briskly. "So what have you got planned for his birthday party?"

A fragile sense of hope pulsed inside him. Later, he would have to figure out how she'd managed to give him that hope with so few words. Later, he would think about the three seconds that he'd touched her leg and how he'd ridiculously wished she had a few more bug bites. Hell, he'd wished the damn bug bites covered her whole body. Eli shook his head at himself. Andie was looking at him expectantly—waiting for a response. *Birthday party, Masters.* "I was thinking about having it in the backyard."

"Uh-huh. And if it rains, do you want a bunch of five-year-olds running around your house?"

The idea held little appeal. "Any suggestions?"

"Chuck E. Cheese's. You pay one price and bring the cake. They provide hats, pizza and entertainment." She wore an expression of great wisdom. "And they clean up."

"That sounds livable," Eli said. "How long do these things usually last?"

"Not more than two hours if you're smart. Write the time the party will begin and end on the invitation. But..."

"But?"

She gave him a look of pure pity. "You might want to hang on to that wine."

"I'm convinced that Dr. Kent was one of Genghis Khan's thugs in another life. He was such an idiot that a priestess killed him with a knife," Samantha French said as she slid into the hospital cafeteria chair opposite Andie. With curly brown hair and big blue eyes, Samantha looked like a sweet, mild-natured woman. Andie knew that beneath that sweet demure appearance was a card-carrying liberated woman who believed she was the reincarnation of Cleopatra.

"I take it you want to assist him into his next life," Andie said with a snicker.

Sam's eyes gleamed with malicious intent. "I was in the operating room. I held the knife in my hand."

Andie made a tsking sound. "What did he do this time?"

Samantha closed her eyes as if in pain. "He forgot he was supposed to be performing an appendectomy."

Andie winced. Dr. Kent had once been a talented general surgeon, but within the past several months he'd developed a drinking problem. "He wasn't drunk, was he?"

Sam shook her head. "No. That's what saved him. I think he was fighting one hell of a hangover, though." She poured low-fat dressing on her salad. "Enough about Kent. Why are you advertising for a housekeeper?"

"I'm not, really. My new next-door neighbors need one, so I thought I'd pass the word along." Andie reminded herself she had given in on this one because it could be accomplished from a distance.

Samantha munched on a piece of celery. "Married couple?"

"Not really," Andie evaded. Sam was generous up to a point, but she refused to be made the fool, and it seemed to Andie that Sam had made it her mission to teach Andie how to say no. Andie wasn't sure she could explain Eli and Fletch and what she planned to do for them, so she changed the subject to Samantha's current flame, a resident at a different local hospital. "How's Brad doing with those megahours he's pulling in O.R.?"

Samantha's lively features muted a bit. "He's tired, but this O.R. rotation won't last forever." She gave Andie a shrewd glance. "Who's your neighbor?"

Andie shrugged. "He's some kind of research scientist. He's got a little boy, and they seemed overwhelmed, so—"

"Oh, no." Samantha put down her fork and shook her head. "You haven't had them over for dinner yet, have you?"

"No, I just—"

"You didn't offer to help out if they needed anything?"

Andie sighed in exasperation. One of the miseries of having a longtime friend was that she knew your weaknesses, and Samantha knew all about Andie's disastrous engagement last year. "Not really. You would have been pleased. I only met Eli Masters for a few minutes, and I didn't offer him anything. Not my food, not my vast experience with children, not my body." Although she'd thought about that last one a few times. The invitation to the barbecue she was having tomorrow night didn't count because it was a neighborhood affair.

Samantha gave a low whistle. "Eli Masters. Isn't he the one who'd doing genetic research on seizure disorders?"

"I believe that's what he said," she said, keeping her voice v-e-r-y casual. Sam had the uncanny ability to ferret out any secrets.

Samantha nodded. "There was an article about him in the paper yesterday. The big boys at the Medical Center had to work hard to lure him down here. He's got degrees out the wazoo and a reputation for never giving up. Even Brad knew about him."

Although Andie stayed abreast of medical discoveries, she kept her focus on the here and now. Her job required it. When one of her young patients was struggling for his next breath, however, she couldn't help praying for a medical miracle. She remembered Eli's fervency when he'd told her about his research. It touched her now as it had then. "I saw the article, too. He feels very strongly about researching something worthwhile, but I think it might take him and his son a while to adjust to all the changes they've been through lately."

"Changes?" Samantha's eyebrows shot up. "This sounds like more than a five-minute conversation."

"His little boy plays with Stud sometimes. Eli stopped by after work once." She took a sip of her Coke. "Just neighborly conversation."

"And Eli Masters doesn't appeal to you in the least?"

Andie shook her head. "Not at all."

"Uh-huh," Samantha said, her voice brimming with disbelief. "And Mel Gibson's a dog. I saw Eli Masters's picture in the paper. Is he better or worse in person?"

"Both," Andie immediately replied. "He looks like this attractive, yet calm man except for his eyes. They're green and—" Andie waved her hand in frustration. She felt strange trying to explain Eli. "Well, it sounds silly, but his eyes remind me of liquid nitrogen. You know, if you shake it up, you better make sure you run for cover. And then, there's his voice—"

"Oh, no." Sam's face was full of disapproval. "You swore that you were giving up these mercy missions. No more deadbeats who need to be rehabilitated. No more single fathers. You promised. Remember—"

"Don't," Andie cut in, then softened her voice. "Don't say his name." It was an unspoken rule between Samantha and Andie that neither brought up

Paul's name. She'd discussed her breakup ad nauseam until the time came that Andie decided the discussions weren't helping. Some wounds just didn't heal as quickly and cleanly as one might want them to. This was one of them. Her appetite gone, she dropped her sandwich to her tray.

She took a deep breath. "It's true. Eli Masters needs a woman's touch." She held up her hand when Sam started to speak. "But I'm not going to be the one to touch him." The announcement tripped off a restless sensation inside her, and she ignored it. "I'm having a neighborhood barbecue and I'm including Eli and his son."

Samantha covered her face and groaned as if Andie had just confessed to committing a bank robbery.

"I'm also inviting Daphne."

Samantha dropped her hands and went abruptly still. "Daphne the decorator?"

Andie nodded.

Samantha's eyes lit with amusement. "Daphne the diva, who's been divorced four times?"

"Yes."

"She's a—"

"Man-eater." Andie lifted her chin. "Perfect for a man who needs a little touching, wouldn't you say?" She felt the faintest doubt, however, buzzing inside her like a bee. "The only thing that worries me is Daphne's steel-plated heart."

Sam let out a whoop of laughter. "Andie, Andie, Andie. When men look at Daphne, the last thing they're interested in is her heart."

She wore a little skirt. A very little skirt, Eli amended. He watched in fascination as the crinkly fabric bobbed around her long slim legs while she directed, like a maestro, men operating gas grills, women piling dishes onto one of three picnic tables and a couple of kids playing tag.

Eli hated social gatherings. They required small talk, and to this day he still wondered what the hell small talk was. If it weren't for Fletch, he would have avoided this one. Standing at the edge of Andie's backyard with Fletch, he just looked and thanked the Lord for the latest fashion trend. It distracted him from the suspicious stares he was receiving from the neighbors.

Besides the little skirt, Andie was wearing a long sleeveless vest and Eli couldn't help but wonder if she had on a bra, too. That skirt was driving him insane. He caught flashes of her thigh with her every movement. He'd remembered what her skin felt like long after he'd touched her the other day. He was remembering now. A surge of heat swelled in his groin and he swore under his breath. His brain had plunged into his jeans. He'd definitely been in the lab too long.

Fletcher tugged at his arm. "There's a lot of kids here," he said, sounding nervous.

Tearing his eyes from the skirt, Eli quickly counted the number of little people. "About twelve. Maybe you can find someone to play with, now."

Fletch moved closer to Eli's side. "But I don't know *any* of them."

Eli rubbed his son's silky hair through his fingers in a comforting gesture. He could identify with what Fletch was feeling. He'd always been lousy at large gatherings. He sure as hell didn't want that for Fletcher. Frowning, Eli spent the next full minute racking his brain for a successful way to approach a passel of new kids.

Just when he felt the edge of frustration creep in, Andie glanced up from her consultation with one of the cooks and smiled. Eli would have sworn the sky got brighter, but he knew it was scientifically impossible.

"Hey, you guys!" She moved toward them, and Eli noticed her skirt and the legs beneath it again. "I wondered when you were finally going to get here."

"Dad was late from work."

Andie shook her head in commiseration. "I know. Isn't it a pain that big people have to make money? Well, at least you're here now. Got any dimples for me?"

Fletch grimaced to produce a dimple.

Andie laughed. She took Fletcher's hand in one of hers and motioned Eli with the other. "Okay, come on over and meet Curtis and Jason."

Eli watched Andie perform the introductions and noticed the hesitancy that remained on Fletch's face.

"I'd like you to meet Mrs. Grandview. She lives on the other side of me, and if you ever need a sitter, she would—" Andie abruptly stopped. "Is something wrong?"

Eli slid his gaze away from Fletch. "I'm just watching Fletch. It's been a while since he was around kids and he seemed a little uneasy. I want to be there if he..."

Her gaze softened. "If he needs you," she finished for him. "Sounds like you're catching on to this parent thing."

Eli recalled how Fletch had cried himself to sleep last night, and how he had tried, without success, to comfort his son. He shoved his hands in his pockets. "One step forward, two steps back."

Andie opened her mouth to comment, but a middle-aged man armed with a spatula broke in. "I'm Ben Hammond, three doors down in the blue Cape Cod. So, are you the guy they call Dr. Frankenstein?"

Andie cringed. She'd tried to do a little PR for Eli and Fletch, but the neighbors were still giving them a wide berth. "Eli is a researcher at—"

"Dr. Frankenstein was a fiction character who used dead human specimens in his experiments," Eli interjected.

Still eyeing Eli warily, Ben lifted his head. "Yeah. So?"

"I study genetic material and chromosome abnormalities collected from blood samples. It's a process involving X rays and hours and hours of studies that..."

Andie watched Ben's eyes glaze over at Eli's technical explanation of his research. When Eli finished, Ben narrowed his eyes. "I just wanna know if you use dead people for these experiments."

Eli cocked his head to one side. "It's possible to use blood drawn from an autopsy, but..."

Ben began to fidget.

"The lab technicians don't haunt the morgues," Eli said in an attempt at humor that went straight over Ben's head. "And we haven't robbed any graveyards lately."

Ben paled. "Lately?"

"It's a joke, Ben," Andie said. "A joke." She wondered if this barbecue was a good idea, after all. Stifling a sigh, she turned in another direction. "Look, there's Mrs. Grandview."

So began a seemingly endless round of introductions. Usually Eli could keep track of the names and faces with no trouble. With his attention partly focused on Fletch and partly drawn to Andie, Eli found he had to work at it.

Andie talked to everyone there, he noticed. All the neighbors seemed to like her. She was a part of them. The men joked with her. The women chatted easily with her. And the kids tried to lure her into their play.

Eli downed the rest of his canned drink and watched his new neighbors. Ben Hammond sold insurance and followed stock car races on weekends. Margie Winfree, a pencil-thin mother of five, suggested two local preschools. Eli didn't think Fletch was ready. Off to the side a foursome of men were having an intent discussion that Eli suspected centered around golf.

For a moment, the familiar isolation seeped in again. He'd spent too much time in the lab this past year, too much time with test tubes and computers, and not enough time with human beings. He might as well be an alien.

Maybe he was expecting too much too soon, he told himself. For Fletch's sake, he hoped the situation would change. He hoped he could help Fletch get past some of his pain and isolation. But for now, Eli felt as if he were in a foreign country.

Except with Andie.

The notion made him feel strange. Eli raked his fingers through his hair. Hell, the notion made him feel like an idiot. Dismissing it, he tossed his can in a recycle bin and checked the yard to find Fletcher playing with a little girl.

Hearing a burst of animated voices, he turned back. Andie was being urged toward him by a young woman with curly brown hair. Andie tossed a warning glance at the young woman, then turned to Eli. "Eli, this is my friend—" she lowered her voice "—and the bane of my existence, Samantha French. She read about you in the paper and wanted to meet you."

Eli extended his hand.

"A Viking explorer," Samantha said, her bright eyes intent and serious. She shook his hand. "Andie, you should have been able to pick up on this. His aura is so—"

"Sam," Andie interrupted. "You promised you would leave your aura evaluation service at home. Do you know how long it took Mrs. Jeter to recover from being told she was a gunslinger in a past life?"

Samantha shrugged. "The idea behind finding out where you've been is so you'll function better in your present life."

Intrigued by Andie's response, Eli watched her sigh in frustration as she glanced heavenward. This was an entirely different side to her.

"Stick to food and the weather," she muttered, then turned back to Eli. "Samantha and I work together at the hospital."

"It's good to meet another one of Andie's friends," Eli said.

Samantha smiled and glanced knowingly at Andie. "You were right about the voice and eyes."

Andie's cheeks turned scarlet. "There are some people," she said in the softest, most dangerous voice he'd ever heard her use, "who belong in a pit of vipers."

Samantha gasped. "Okay, okay. I get the message. I'll go get my hamburger." She shot a grin at Eli. "Nice to meet you."

Eli nodded. "And you." He turned back to Andie. "I don't suppose you could translate that conversation for me."

Andie laughed. "I guess I can try. During the past year, Samantha has been on a reincarnation kick. Just recently, she has been applying it to almost everyone she meets."

"I was a Viking explorer?"

"Of course." Andie nodded. "But surely you already knew that," she said, biting her lip in amusement.

"I can't say that thought ever entered my mind." He imagined holding a similar discussion with the men in his lab and shook his head. They would think he'd sniffed the ether bottle one too many times. "I don't know whether to be flattered or insulted. Why did she get so upset when you mentioned snakes?"

Her caramel eyes glinted with mischief. "Samantha thinks she was reincarnated from Cleopatra."

Eli grinned slowly, appreciating Andie's playful retribution. "That was brilliant."

"Oh, no," Andie demurred, shaking her head. "Just a well-developed survival instinct."

"Who does she think you were in your past life?"

Andie shook her head, this time more vehemently. "Samantha is crazy. You can't take her seriously. Look, everyone's lining up for the burgers." She gestured toward the people crowding around the grills.

His curiosity wouldn't wait, however. Andie had a secret. His pulse thudded in his chest. It was similar to the feeling he had in the lab when he was getting close to a breakthrough. This time, the rush of discovery mingled with a lick of arousal. "Who?" he repeated.

Eli watched her face heighten with color again. "Nobody famous," she said, dismissing his question. "Nobody you would recognize from history class. Besides, it's not as if she's accurate."

Eli cocked his head to one side, focusing intently on the woman in front of him. It was rare for him to be able to read someone. He felt as if he were catching a wave of emotional vibrations from her. "You're embarrassed. You don't want to tell me."

Andie's glance skittered away. "I'm not embarrassed," she protested, squaring her shoulders at the same time. "It's not that important. And the food—"

"Then tell me."

She dampened her lips and sighed. "It's pure fiction," she said, her words crisp with emphasis. Her gaze finally met his again, and if her eyes could talk, they would have said, "Don't you dare laugh." She crossed her arms over her chest impatiently and looked away. "Sam says I was the favored courtesan of a French king."

She said it quickly and with no inflection, but Eli's quick, quick mind had no trouble visualizing Andie naked and hot beneath— To hell with the French king.

Naked and hot beneath *him*.

Chapter Three

She wondered why Eli's silence suddenly seemed louder than her neighbors' chatter. Determined to break the thread of tension pulling her toward him, she lifted one shoulder in a shrug. "So you can see that Samantha isn't exactly accurate. No one would picture me as the courtesan type and—" She glanced up and the smoky intensity in Eli's eyes stalled her words.

"I'm sure," he said in a voice that belonged in a darker, more intimate setting, "plenty of men have no problem picturing you that way."

He left little doubt that he could picture her that way. Here was a man who wasn't thinking of her as a pal. *Was he?* Her mind denied it, but her stomach twisted in feminine apprehension. The sensation wasn't entirely unpleasant.

"Crazy," she muttered, and wasn't sure she was talking about Eli or herself. She cleared her throat. "I really need to check on the hamburger buns," she said and abruptly turned. Andie didn't like the speculative expression on Eli's face. She could imagine what he was speculating, and it made her pulse race and those sirens inside her head start screaming.

The back of her neck drew into a tight knot. Flustered, she felt his footsteps directly behind hers and said a quick little prayer. Her gaze caught on a dark-haired voluptuous woman nearly spilling forth from the cups of her sundress. Muffling her chuckle of relief, Andie whispered a word of thanks, delighted with the Almighty's sense of humor. "Daphne," she called. "Come on over. I'm so glad you could make it." Daphne would never know *how* glad.

Moving in a slinky gait that had every male salivating, Daphne walked over to Andie and air-kissed her. "It was nice of you to include me. These neighborhood gatherings are so charming. I'm glad I wasn't booked tonight." With the sure instinct of a predator scenting its prey, Daphne looked beyond Andie and gave a delicate shimmy of pleasure that drew attention to her assets. "Please do introduce me to the gorgeous man behind you."

Andie stole a glance at Eli. He was looking, but he wasn't instantly besotted. *Give him time.* She made the introductions and gestured toward the food. "Eli just bought the house beside me. I bet he would love to hear some of your decorating ideas. Why don't you two get your food—"

"Where's Fletch?" Eli asked, looking around the yard.

Daphne raised a dark eyebrow. "Fletch?"

Andie felt the slightest tinge of nervousness. Daphne wasn't known for her way with children. "Fletch is Eli's son," Andie explained. "He's over there by the hot dogs. Isn't he adorable? Look, why don't I look after him and make sure he gets some food while you two eat?" she asked, and made to leave.

Eli stopped her by encircling her wrist with his hand. "You don't have to."

Oh, yes, I do. His thumb skimmed over the sensitive spot where her pulse skipped at an alarming rate. "It's no problem. I like him." She pulled her hand away at the same time that she saw Daphne wrap her hand around Eli's arm. Andie felt a different twinge, but ignored it. "Enjoy yourself."

She walked toward Fletch and nearly brushed her hands together at the done deal. Some things never changed. The sun rose in the east, rivers ran to the ocean, and Daphne Sinclair seduced men.

Samantha joined her and shook her head. "You're shameless. She'll have her claw marks on his bedpost within a week."

"Better she than me." Andie waved Fletch toward her.

"I don't know if this is going to work, Andie. Eli's still watching you."

Andie resisted the urge to look around. "He's watching Fletch, not me."

Sam smiled. "Denial is a powerful psychological tool. I only have one question. This is the first time I've actually seen Daphne in the flesh." She lowered her voice. "Are they real?"

Andie just laughed.

Two hours later, the barbecue broke up. As Andie tossed paper plates in the trash, Eli appeared at her side. "Thanks for inviting us. You'll have to let me take you out for dinner in return," he murmured in a low voice that skimmed over her skin.

"Oh, no. You don't have to do that," she told him and felt his gaze measuring her. "Did Daphne have any suggestions for your house?"

"She made some suggestions," Eli said dryly.

"I hear she's very talented."

Eli gave a noncommittal shrug. "Possibly. She reminds me of my ex-wife."

Andie stopped midmovement and met Eli's gaze. She saw masculine cynicism in his green eyes and struggled with an urge to soothe.

Fletch walked toward Eli and leaned against his leg. "My stomach hurts," he announced forlornly.

Eli glanced down at his son. "Too much ice cream, maybe?" he muttered and brushed his hand over Fletch's hair. Hauling the boy up into his arms, he sighed. "Bedtime for you. Thanks again, Andie."

Her heart caught at the sight of them, and something twisted at the way he said her name. Feeling a sinking sensation, Andie hoped she hadn't cause Eli any pain. "I—uh—" She cleared her throat and lowered her voice. "I'm sorry about Daphne. I didn't know she would—"

Eli's lips twisted bitterly. "No big deal. She reminds me of a lot of women. Big on beauty, short on logic. Somewhere down the line, I end up out of luck." He nodded briefly. "'Night."

"Get some sleep, Fletch."

Fletch sighed and nodded. He watched as his dad

paused at the door and said, "Call me if you need anything."

"Okay. G'night, Dad." His dad closed the door and Fletch heard his footsteps on the steps. Wide-awake, Fletch stared at the ceiling of his bedroom. As it often did when Dad turned out the light at night, his mind began to spin and reel. He thought about clocks and numbers.

Tonight his stomach interfered with his usual thoughts. It felt really full, like it was going to burst. Dad had told him it wouldn't, though. Fletch flipped over on his stomach, hoping that would make it stop hurting. He lifted his hand and touched the soft hair of his stuffed llama. His mother had brought it back from one of her trips. His stomach hurt worse when he thought about his mom.

He missed her.

She was pretty and she smelled nice. He remembered that she had smiled at him a lot. She used to touch his hair when she put him to bed. Just like the way Andie stroked his hair and talked with him, he thought. It made him feel good inside to play in her yard with Stud.

But at night after the light was out and he was too tired to think about numbers, he thought about his mom and his stomach and head would hurt. Sometimes he cried.

Fletch squished his eyes shut and tried to swallow past the big, hard lump in his throat. He wrapped his arm around the llama and wished he could call his dad. He was afraid to call him. He was afraid Dad would find out the truth about his mom and not like him anymore. Then Fletch wouldn't have anybody and he would be lonely all the time.

His nose was running, so he sniffed. His eyes felt hot like they always did right before he cried. Fletch rubbed them hard, then hugged the llama and tried to think about clocks.

"Okay, okay. I feel guilty," Andie confessed when Samantha wouldn't let up. Folding some dollar bills into her pocket-sized purse for a girls' night out, she stole a glance out her window. She wasn't really in the mood to go to a bar tonight.

Leaning back in the blue wing-back recliner, Samantha rolled her eyes. "He's a big boy, a Viking in a past life, for Pete's sake. He can take care of himself. Although I'm sure Daphne will do her best to wear him out for a while."

Andie shot Samantha a reproving glance. "His wife recently died."

Samantha shrugged. "*Ex*-wife. He probably hated her guts."

"Your compassion astounds me."

Samantha sat up, whipping the recliner into the closed position. "You're stalling. We've got to meet Donna and Yvette. You know how cranky they get when we're late." She craned her neck to look out the window. "What are you staring at?"

"Nothing." Andie felt Sam's skeptical glance. "Sometimes he goes running about this time."

Samantha shook her head in disapproval and stood. "It's definitely time to get you out of the house."

Andie twisted the strap of her purse. "You know, I'm a little tired...."

Samantha shook her head again, more vehemently this time. "What are you going to do? Stay home and do needlepoint?"

Andie should have known Sam wouldn't let her back out. "I don't do needlepoint. And what's so wrong about enjoying my home? I work hard. If I want to relax here, who's to say I should be doing something else?"

"*I'm* to say. You'd cloister yourself like a nun if you could. Since Paul—"

"This has nothing to do with Paul," Andie cut in, although there were still times when she felt like licking her wounds. "I just don't like bars that much. I don't like the kind of men I meet at them."

Samantha nodded sagely, then extended her hand and pulled Andie to her feet. "All men are jerks. They're only good for one thing. You can't trust them as far as you can throw them."

Andie's lips twitched as Sam dragged her to the front door. "You sound like Yvette." The older woman had recently gone through a difficult divorce, but was determined to keep her social life alive.

"That's right. And if Yvette can brave the prospect of close encounters with the opposite sex, then you can, too."

Andie opened her mouth to correct Sam's convoluted logic. "But—" She stopped herself just before she plowed into her friend.

Samantha stood in the doorway, shaking her head. "My, my, my," she exclaimed.

Andie followed the direction of Samantha's gaze. Her stomach gave a strange twist. She watched Eli walk toward Daphne Sinclair's house. Even from this distance, she could see the purposefulness in his long stride. The waning evening sunlight glinted off his hair. His broad shoulders outlined by a stark white shirt, he lifted his wrist to glance at his watch. He was probably concerned about being late, she thought and felt another twist.

Daphne would ply him with food and soft music. Andie's imagination took the scenario a couple steps further. Daphne would learn what pleased him, and she would be the recipient of all the passion Andie sensed was brewing just beneath Eli's surface.

The image of Eli's eyes, full of male need, his naked body aroused, made her skin hot. An ache, secret and insistent, began to build deep inside her. She swore under her breath. Brushing her hair back from her face, she took a mind-clearing breath. Her plan had worked. She should feel triumphant, relieved at the very least. She felt neither. Andie realized she should have known better. She wasn't a schemer. She had neither the heart nor the knack for it.

"Looks like Daphne didn't waste any time," Samantha said with a broad grin.

For some reason, Andie didn't share her friend's amusement. "Looks like Eli overcame the fact that she reminds him of his ex- wife," she managed dryly.

Sam made a tsking sound. "Don't be too hard on Daphne. She's got a lot to make up for."

"What on earth are you talking about?"

Sam got that mysterious knowing glint in her eyes. "Daphne was once a nun."

Eli slowed to a jog as he noticed his red-haired neighbor bent over the open hood of her car. Dressed in loose-fitting pants and top and white nurse's shoes, she was obviously headed for work. Or, at least trying to go to work, he amended. He didn't get much closer before he heard her swearing at the machinery. The feminists would probably kill him for thinking it, but Andie Reynolds was damn cute when she was mad. "You have the nerve to call yourself transportation. A horse would be more reliable," she grumbled.

"The feed and vet bills would be too high," Eli pointed out.

Andie jerked her head up, and the color instantly rose to her cheeks. For the moment she just looked at him, clearly torn between frustration and embarrassment. Her gaze swished over him from head to toe, making him return the favor and wish that someone would redesign nursing attire. It was a crying shame her legs were covered by loose pants.

Her color intensified and she blinked, fixing her gaze somewhere around his chin. "I was having a private conversation with my vehicle," she explained as if it were the most rational thing in the world to do.

Eli's mouth twitched. "And what does it have to say?"

Andie shook her head. "It made a rude noise when I first tried to start it. Now it just clicks."

Eli frowned. "Mind if I take a look?"

Andie shrugged. "Feel free. I think it's ready for the great junkyard in the sky." She looked at him curiously. "What do genetic engineers know about ten-year-old Ford Mustangs?"

"Most probably don't know much," he said, checking the fluids and the battery. He checked her oil and shook his head. Talk about thick sludge. "How long has it been since you changed your oil?"

"A while," Andie hedged. "How do you know so much about cars?"

Eli glanced up. "My father required my two brothers and I to learn automobile mechanics. We were..."

He hesitated, and eliminated the words that had been used to describe him—genius, gifted, major egghead and, once or twice a very long time ago, geek. "Academically inclined. Dad said all the book knowledge in the world wouldn't help us if we were stranded on some highway with a broken car. So every Saturday morning, he dragged us down to the service station he owned and made us learn about cars." Eli chuckled, remembering the mess they used to make. "My middle brother resented it, so he takes it out on the cars he owns now. He probably changes his oil about as often as you do."

"I resist getting maintenance done on my car," Andie confessed. "It's not rational or responsible, and I usually end up regretting it, but I hate going to the service station and putting up with the mechanics calling me 'little lady'."

Eli nodded thoughtfully. "Would you rather they call you 'big woman'?"

"No," she told him and laughed past her disapproval. "My name would be just fine."

"I haven't thought about it much, but I guess women have to put up with a lot in male-dominated service areas," he said and slid behind the wheel of her car. He adjusted the seat to accommodate his longer legs. "Men get their hassles in other areas."

She stood beside the open door. "Like when?" she asked doubtfully.

"Enforcing visitation rights." Eli was certain the reason he was having such a tough time with Fletch now was that his ex-wife had constantly dodged his efforts to spend time with his son. Glancing up, he saw Andie's face shadowed with sympathy. That annoyed him. He didn't want sympathy from her. He turned his attention to the ignition and heard the same clicking noise she'd described.

His gaze caught on a small square sign hanging from her rearview mirror. It was the kind of sign many drivers displayed in their rear windows. Eli suspected she'd purchased it for her own enjoyment instead of sending a message to the world. He wondered what that meant. "Nurses do it with care," he read aloud, and studied Andie. "My mind is filled with... questions."

"Which will remain unanswered. What do you think is wrong with my car?"

Eli sighed and got out of the car. "Either the starter or the alternator. I can get the parts tonight. Depending on how much Fletch wants to *help,* and I use the word in its loosest form, I can fix it tomorrow morning. If you'll give me a minute to get my keys, I can take you to the hospital now."

Andie blinked. "N-no. I don't expect you to fix it," she said, sounding appalled at the notion. "I just thought you were looking at it to tell me if it *could* be fixed." She slammed the car door and ran a hand through her auburn hair. "And you certainly don't have to take me to work. I can call—"

"Why?" Eli cut in.

Disconcerted, she shook her head. "Well, you probably have plans tonight, and—"

"I don't."

Her warm brown eyes widened. She hesitated, tilting her head to one side. "It's an imposition for you to—"

Impatience flared. "It's not." He studied her, trying to understand her reaction. "You have a problem. I can solve it."

She watched him silently for a full moment, and Eli felt the hum between them start up again. "Just like that?" she asked, a faint smile tilting her lips. "I have a problem. You can solve it, so you will."

It was eminently logical to him. "Yes."

Eli was oddly loath to leave her at the moment. He sensed her approval and for once, she wasn't trying to bolt away from him. His car, however, was not going to magically appear. Eli cleared his throat. "I'll get the keys and pick you up in a minute," he told her and jogged away.

Andie stared after him. She'd never met anyone quite like Eli before. He obviously possessed a formidable intelligence and appeared impatient with social protocol, yet he was deeply concerned about his son and was determined to be a good neighbor to Andie.

Neighbor. That little light feeling inside her chest dulled. She'd do well to remember that Eli's interest in her was just neighborly. She'd do well to forget how those running shorts had emphasized powerful thighs and the bulge of his masculinity. If she had any sense at all, she would pretend she hadn't noticed the way his broad shoulders stretched that old T-shirt and wondered what it would be like to be held by him.

By the time Eli had pulled his sporty sedan into her driveway, Andie had reined in her thoughts. She opened the door and slid into the seat before he had a chance to get out. His proximity made something inside her tighten. "This is very nice of you, but I don't want you to feel obligated to fix my car."

"I don't feel obligated," he said in a tone that rang with finality. "Since I'm new to Cary, you'll need to give me directions."

Andie did, and for the next few minutes, Eli drove quietly. She looked out the window, focusing on the coming night's work.

"Is this what time you usually go to work?" he asked, breaking the silence.

"I was going in a little early, because it's my baby's birthday. He'll be—"

Eli jerked to glance at her, then quickly looked back at the road. "Your baby!" His hands tightened on the steering wheel. "I didn't know you had a child."

Andie laughed. "No, no, no. I work in the pediatric intensive care unit, and we tend to get a little possessive with our patients. When I say 'my baby,' I mean my patient."

"Oh," he said, still sounding slightly confused. "So you're in PICU." He lifted his eyebrows. "Sounds tough. Working with seriously ill children all the time."

"It can be," she agreed. "I like it because there's a lot more one-on-one care. We have a small unit, so I have time to give my kids—" she smiled and corrected herself "—my *patients* the attention they need."

"Do you always work night shift?"

"Most of the time. I like it," she confessed. "At night it's quiet. I feel like I have a little more control over my own responsibilities." Andie thought about the time last year when she'd considered quitting so her schedule would mesh better with Paul's. She stiffened her spine. "Since I'm single, my time is my own. It's not as if it interferes with family life."

Eli silently digested that. "And this baby with the birthday," he said. "What's his problem?"

Andie paused, thinking of the little boy under heavy sedation in the PICU. Her heart tightened. She wondered how Eli would respond to her patient's history. "He's two, with cerebral palsy. He has problems with chronic seizures, so he's in a lot."

Eli winced, and swore softly. "Are they sure it's CP? There are other causes for seizures. And there are some new drugs—"

"They're pretty sure," Andie said, sensing the reason for his tension. Eli took his work seriously and understood that there were human beings hanging by a worn thread while they waited for a breakthrough. She saw a hint of turmoil darken his eyes to forest green. That quality of caring burrowed past her defenses and touched her heart. She lifted her hand to touch his arm, then self-consciously pulled back. "How do you handle it," she wondered aloud, "when you hear about children suffering from chronic seizures when you're trying to find the cause? It would drive me crazy."

"It used to," he admitted in a weary voice. "I'd read something in the paper about a child with seizure problems and bury myself in the lab. But I've learned it doesn't help. Research takes time, patience, persistence." His lips lifted in an ironic grin. "And funding," he added. "What really made the difference for me, though, was Fletch. Something about having a child who relies on me to be my best when I'm *not* in the lab has given me a different perspective."

They stopped at a traffic light and he looked at her, his green eyes intent and thoughtful. "I have a hard time picturing you in such a high-pressure setting every night. You don't come across like a cool, tough woman. What do you do when one of your babies—" He frowned and broke off as if he thought better of asking the question, and accelerated when the light turned green.

He'd nailed her on that one, Andie thought. She didn't have a cool bone in her body, though she'd spent years trying to acquire one. Her training afforded her the ability to be calm in a crisis, but Andie wasn't cool about her job. She cared about those kids as if they were her own. "You wonder what?"

"It's not important."

"C'mon," she coaxed, her voice full of curiosity. "I'm fair. You answered my questions. I'll answer yours."

Reluctant, Eli pulled into the hospital parking lot. He should have kept his mouth shut, but his own curiosity about Andie grew with every new thing he learned about her. "What do you do when one of your babies doesn't make it?" he asked, watching her.

The glow in her eyes dimmed. "You mean, when they die?"

He nodded.

She met his gaze with pure honesty. "I cry," she said simply.

An image, clear and unflinching, flashed in his mind of Andie alone, weeping, her slim shoulders shaking in grief. It disturbed him deeply. He fought the urge to touch her skin, filter his fingers through her silky hair, feel her heartbeat. She was warm and so real it shook him.

A long moment passed while he stared into her eyes and she stared into his. Then her gaze skittered away, and she cleared her throat. "It doesn't happen very often."

"Good," he said gruffly. "I'm glad."

Andie smiled and shrugged. "Thanks again for the ride."

Eli nodded, still wondering what had hit him just a moment ago. "I'll pick you up in the morning. Eight o'clock?"

Andie hesitated. "You really don't have—"

"We're not going to do this again, are we?" he asked, impatience threading through his tone.

"Guess not. Eight o'clock. This entrance will be fine." She opened the door, then bent down with a determined expression on her face. "I want the receipt for the starter or alternator or whatever it is. I pay for parts," she said with emphasis.

"Deal," Eli said.

The next morning Eli picked up Andie at the hospital. After she changed clothes, she made a pitcher of lemonade and brought it outside. While Eli fixed her car, Fletch drank lemonade and played with Stud.

"Thank heaven for small favors," Eli murmured as he wiped his hands on a rag after he finished. "Stud and lemonade." He downed his own cupful. "I would change your oil, but I don't want to push my luck with Fletch."

Andie shook her head. "You've done plenty." Grease was smeared across Eli's cheek and T-shirt. He wore a white handkerchief tied around his forehead to keep the perspiration from his green eyes, which were squinted against the bright sunlight. She shouldn't have found him attractive, but she did.

"Speaking of Fletch, I've made arrangements for his birthday party. It'll be Saturday after next. Are you working?"

She refilled his cup. "Well, no, but—"

"Fletch wants two girls to come to his birthday party. One is the little girl who lives down the street and wears a tutu all the time—Jennifer." Eli's mouth lifted in a grin. "The other is you."

Taken aback, Andie felt tugged in different directions. She felt a rush of pleasure that Fletch wanted to include her, but sensed this situation was the equivalent of emotional quicksand. "It's really sweet of him to want to include me," Andie said, and felt Eli's gaze grow more intense. Her heart thumped erratically. "I—uh, I don't really know what I've got planned that day."

Eli continued to watch her with his unnerving gaze. "We'd both like you to come," he said, in the low voice that threatened to turn her resolve to liquid.

Glancing away, Andie flipped her hair behind her ear and bit her lip.

Eli narrowed his eyes. "You like Fletch, don't you?"

Startled, Andie jerked to look up at him. "Of course I do. You know I think he's adorable. He's a precious little boy."

Eli nodded slowly and his jaw hardened slightly. "Then it must be me," he concluded, and tossed the dirty rag in his tool chest. "You don't like me."

Chapter Four

Andie gaped at Eli. "No!" she nearly yelled, then glanced at Fletch and lowered her voice. "I don't not like you," she said, her mind so scrambled she wasn't sure her last statement made any sense. "What in the world made you say that?"

Just this side of slamming it, he closed the lid on his tool chest. She couldn't tell if he was angry or frustrated, only that his energy level had jumped off the Richter scale. There was something very sexy about this controlled display of temper from Mr. Cerebral.

"You fought me every inch of the way when I offered to drive you to work and fix your car," he said, circling her like a jungle cat.

"I didn't want you to feel obligated."

"I've invited you to come over for wine, and you refused," he pointed out, setting his unfinished glass of lemonade on the hood of her car.

"There just hasn't been a convenient time, lately." Feeling her argument plunge down the credibility scale, she waved her hand and switched the subject. "What about the barbecue? I introduced you to all my neighbors."

"Like Daphne," Eli said in a dry, knowing tone.

Andie felt her cheeks heat, but didn't look away.

"And there's one other thing," Eli said, taking a step closer to her and meeting her gaze.

Acutely sensitive to his effect on her, Andie moved backward. The back of her knees met the chrome bumper of her car. "What?" she asked, her heart picking up again.

"What you're doing now." He took yet another step closer and Andie resisted the urge to climb on the hood of her car. "Every time I get within touching distance of you, you move away."

"I don't. I'm not now. I—" Her throat closed up and with Eli near enough to press his mouth to hers, her mind went blank. She took a breath and his aftershave wove its way into her bloodstream. Inside her body pure bedlam reigned.

Andie tried to think of a way to fix this situation. She couldn't deny his accusation. She did avoid getting close to him. Without sounding like a nutcase, how could she explain she found him attractive and disturbing? How could she explain her insatiable curiosity to kiss him and those diametrically opposed sirens that went off in her head when he was around?

She couldn't. Distressed, she realized her only option was to prove him wrong. And now was the time. It couldn't be that bad, she told herself. It wasn't as if she had to cling to his broad shoulders or crush her breasts against his chest. For that matter, she didn't even have to kiss him.

All she had to do was touch him.

Slowly, she lifted her hand and curled her fingers around his clean-shaven jaw. She felt him stiffen. Eli's gaze locked onto hers with the power of a heat-seeking missile, and a miniature explosion went off inside her. Her heart skipped every other beat, and the sirens started blaring. If she hadn't known better, she would have said the world changed in that moment and would never be the same again.

She shook her head. Certain she *was* a nutcase, she cleared her throat and rubbed her thumb over his cheek. "You've got a little grease, here," she managed faintly.

"Yeah," he said in a rough voice, but he didn't move a fraction of an inch. "I've probably got it everywhere."

"Not everywhere." She rubbed a spot on his biceps with the fingers of her other hand. "Just here and there."

His biceps flexed beneath her touch. Unwillingly fascinated by his response, she resisted the urge to wrap her hands around his arm. "You know, I never realized genetic research was such a strenuous job. Those test tubes must be pretty heavy if you're getting this kind of muscles from lifting them," she quipped in an effort to get past the near-paralyzing effect of his closeness.

"Fletch is responsible." Eli tried to joke, wondering how he could hold a semi-intelligent conversation when he was in physical agony. The sun beat down on them, but Eli still didn't move. She couldn't know it, but Andie was torturing him with the butterfly-light touch of her fingertips. "The only way I can get him to bed at night without screaming is by playing a game where I lift him up over my head and carry him upstairs."

How long had it been since he'd been touched with such care? The question filtered easily through Eli's mind, but the answer was jarring. He couldn't remember the last time.

Andie's mouth tilted in a tentative smile. "Hope he grows out of that bedtime game by the time he's a teenager."

Something inside him eased and tightened at the same time. He let out a harsh breath. "Me too." When she lifted her hand from his jaw, he instinctively reached for her. "Any other places where I've got grease?"

For a long moment, Andie looked at their joined hands. Her soft breath drifted over his skin, and while he was wishing he could see her eyes, she turned Eli's wrist over and rubbed a streak on his forearm. "Just here and maybe a few on your legs."

He thought about asking her to take care of those. He thought about asking her to take care of some other needs, but sanity and Fletch prevailed.

"Dad, you're all messy," Fletch said as he bounded to his side. "Can I have your lemonade?"

Reluctantly, Eli pulled back and gave Fletch the drink. "I was just talking to Andie about your birthday party."

Fletch brightened. "We're gonna have pizza and cake and ice cream, and my uncles are coming. Uncles are my dad's brothers," he explained to her. "Are you coming, too?"

Hoping Fletch wouldn't be too disappointed, Eli shook his head. "She might already have something else planned."

Eli watched Fletch look at Andie as if he couldn't conceive of anything more important than attending his birthday party.

"I need to check my calendar in the kitchen," Andie gently added, "to make sure I haven't promised I would do something else. Since I'm a nurse for very sick children, different groups ask me to come and talk to them." Andie extended her hand. "Wanna come with me to the kitchen? You can get some fresh water for Stud."

The light went out of Fletch's eyes, but he took Andie's hand. "I don't like hospitals," he confessed in a low voice. "That's where my mommy died."

Eli's heart squeezed. Fletch never talked about his mother's death. He felt Andie's gaze, read the commiseration on her face, and her unique brand of compassion seemed to spill over him.

She turned back to Fletch. "I'm really sorry your mom died. I bet you miss her a lot.

Fletch bit his lip and nodded, then looked down. Eli moved closer and instinctively put his hand on Fletch's shoulder. Fletch whipped around and locked his arms around Eli's legs, taking him by surprise.

"I've still got Dad," Fletch said in a low, uncertain voice.

Fletch's sticky fingers tightly grasped Eli's legs. Eli sensed the fear and desperation in his young son's body and felt a heavy weight in his chest. Would Fletch ever recover from losing his mother? Would Eli ever be able to fill the gap? Filled with doubt, yet determined to help Fletch feel more secure, Eli ruffled

Fletch's hair, then lifted him in his arms. "You're absolutely right. You've got me, and you're stuck with me." He paused, then forced a grin, though his throat was still tight. "Especially since you got sticky lemonade fingers and put them all over me."

Fletch pressed his hands together and glanced shyly at Andie. "She'll let me wash 'em when I get Stud's water."

"Yeah, but will she let me come, too?"

Andie felt both pairs of green eyes trained on her. The scenario was becoming a habit, and she'd have to have been made of stone to remain unaffected by either of them. Just moments before when Eli held her hand, she'd felt breathless and needy. Now, after watching them reach out to each other, her heart felt achy and her eyes were burning. There was a tender awkwardness in Eli's affection for his son that dug deep under her skin. And Fletch was like a little sponge, soaking up every bit of reassurance and encouragement he could get.

With her defenses down, Andie felt more drawn to Eli than ever. "I think I've got enough water for you both. But you look like you might need a shower."

"Is that an offer?"

Andie blinked at the I'm-yours-if-you-want-me undertone in his voice. "For a shower?"

"You said I need one." His eyes glinted with sensual intent. "I might need some help getting all this grease off."

Dr. Frankenstein *flirting* with her? Surely she was mistaken!

Andie cocked her head to one side. "Exactly what kind of help do you think you need?"

"You were doing a good job a few minutes ago." Fletch started to squirm, so Eli put him down. "Of course, you weren't all that thorough."

She stared at him, feeling her stomach take a dip. "Thorough?" she repeated.

"Well, considering your background."

Andie was totally confused. "You mean nursing?" What did nursing have to do with Eli taking a shower? Would someone please tell her?

Eli shook his head. "I was thinking a little farther back than that. Say, sixteenth century."

"Sixteenth," she murmured, shaking her head. Then the light dawned. He was referring to her supposed past life as a courtesan. Feeling her cheeks heat, she rolled her eyes. "I hate to disappoint you, but—"

"Then don't." He stepped closer, and Andie fought a sudden weakness in her knees.

There was a hint of playfulness in his tone, but she couldn't underestimate his appeal. This sexy, incredibly intelligent man not only wanted to romp with her in the shower, he wanted her hands all over his body. An image blasted through her mind so hot it nearly scorched her alive. It was time to put a stop to this. She shook her head, this time adamantly. "I'm not helping you with your shower."

"I'm crushed," Eli said, and she almost believed he was. "But I might get over it if you'll come to Fletch's party." His eyes glinting with mischief, he said soberly, "I'm willing to temporarily deny my needs for my son's happiness."

Still reeling from his come-on, Andie gave him a chastising look. "Very low blow. This is blackmail."

"Of course," he continued as if she hadn't said a word, "I wouldn't want to stifle any charitable urges if you want to do the party *and* the shower."

His approach was almost amusing. "You are really starting to push your luck," she said as sternly as she could manage with her lips twitching.

Eli watched her for a long moment. "Does that mean no?"

Andie groaned and turned toward the house. It darn well should mean no. She should be screaming it and running in the opposite direction. "It means I'm checking my calendar for the birthday party."

She swung through the door with both Masters men right behind her. Before she could even locate the date, Eli's finger marked the white empty square on her calendar. Wordlessly, he met her gaze with a pay-up expression on his face.

Andie turned to Fletch. "Looks like I'm free that day. I can come."

Fletch nodded. "Good. I didn't want you to miss it." That problem solved, he looked at her kitchen faucet. "It's too tall for me."

Andie lifted him to wash his hands and splash his face, then allowed him to fill Stud's water bowl outside. Ending up with a fair amount of water on herself, she wiped her hands on a towel, all the while feeling Eli's gaze on her.

"You don't have to come, if you don't want to," he said after Fletch went out the back door.

"No. I've promised, and—" she hesitated and gave a wry chuckle "—it'll be fun to watch both of you discover the wonders of Chuck E. Cheese's."

"You're an unusual woman," he said quietly.

With Fletch gone, the kitchen was very quiet, and the mood suddenly seemed more intimate. Uncomfortable, Andie shrugged. "Not really." She folded the towel and put it on the counter.

"I appreciate your kindness toward Fletch."

"It's easy to be kind to him. Really." If Eli only knew how easy. The thought troubled her.

"About that shower," Eli began.

Andie jerked up her head. "I thought we'd settled that." She gave a quick, short sigh of frustration. "Eli, I don't know how to say this, but we're neighbors, and I think we should keep things between us..." She groped for a word and couldn't come up with anything that sounded right. "Neighborly," she finally said. "Friendly."

"I was going to tell you that I'm going home to take that shower. I'll take Fletch with me."

Relief rushed through her, followed by a pinch of disappointment she firmly ignored. "Oh," she managed when the silence became awkward. "Well, good." Following him to the door, she remembered her manners. "Thank you for picking me up at the hospital and fixing my car. I'll rest easy knowing it's taken care of. And speaking of rest," she rattled on, "if I'm going to get some sleep, then I need to go to bed."

Eli gave a muffled groan, turned around and lifted the inside of her wrist to his lips. It was such a romantic gesture that she was shocked speechless.

"Thank you, *neighbor,*" he said, using her innocuous term, but wearing an expression that suggested he knew better. "The image of my *friend,* the courtesan, going to bed is just what I need right before I take a shower."

It was almost as if he knew all about her secret fantasies. She had the odd thought he'd take her on the kitchen table if she agreed. Aroused and distressed, she stifled a moan and took back her trembling hand. "I'm not a courtesan, Eli," Andie insisted. "I never have been and never will be. No man has ever even suggested that he saw me that way."

Eli studied her. A flash of primitive masculine intent came and went across his face. "Then I'm glad to know I'm the first."

Eli left another message on his brother Caleb's answering machine and set the remote phone down next to him as he supervised Fletch's bath.

"Did you talk to his tape player again?" Fletch asked, and sank a plastic boat under the water.

"It's called an answering machine, but you've got the right idea," Eli told him, suspecting again that Fletch was headed for gifted classes. He'd caught him reading by himself the other day, and Eli knew for a fact that no one had taught him.

"Why isn't he ever at home?" Fletch asked.

Eli sighed. How could he explain his brother's drive? How could he explain that it was sometimes easier to focus on a problem instead of on the people in your life? "He works in a lab, different than mine. And he works many, many hours.,"

"Does he ever sleep or play?"

"Not much."

Fletch wrinkled his nose. "Sounds boring."

Eli chuckled. "Yeah."

"Do you think he'll come to my party?" Fletch asked, his eyes hopeful.

"I'll do my best to get him here," he told him, thinking he might be forced to arrange for someone to capture Caleb and ship him to Cary by express mail. Eli glanced at his watch. "Time to get out."

"Five more minutes."

Eli shook his head. "You've already said that three times."

"That's only fifteen extra minutes," Fletch wheedled.

Noting the fact that his son had just multiplied five times three and come up with the correct answer, Eli shook his head. "Not tonight. Come on. You've got to get a good night's sleep," he said, flipping the knob on the tub so the water would drain, then putting the still-resistant Fletch on the bathmat. "Mrs. Giordano said you were a little cranky on Thursday and Friday."

Fletch poked out his bottom lip and lifted his arms for Eli to dry his sturdy body.

Eli smothered a grin. He wondered when kids lost "the lip." It usually meant Fletch was in a bad mood, but Eli knew he'd probably miss it, which made him wonder what else he'd missed before Fletch had lived with him.

"I wasn't cranky," Fletch said, interrupting Eli's thoughts.

"Mrs. Giordano seemed to think you were either bored or a little sleepy." He remembered the housekeeper's genuine concern.

"I wasn't sleepy," Fletch told him adamantly.

"Hmm, then maybe you were bored." Eli gave Fletch's head a quick rub with the towel. "Maybe you'd like to do something different every now and then instead of staying home with Mrs. G."

Fletch glanced up at him warily. "What?"

"Mrs. G. says she heard about a great day camp that meets on Tuesdays and Thursdays. That's just two days a—"

Fletch shook his head vehemently. "I don't wanna go to day camp." He stood up and started to walk out of the bathroom.

Eli thought he needed to reach a point where Fletch understood that Eli was trying to do what was best. He caught Fletch's arm and turned him back around. "I want you to think about it. Maybe one of the neighborhood kids will go with you. You'll be starting kindergarten in the fall, so it will help you get used to being in a structured environment."

Fletch frowned. "What's a structured envir—en-vir—"

"Environment," Eli supplied. "It's when there's a teacher in charge and there are planned activities like painting and singing and whatever else kids do at da—" Eli saw Fletch's eyes widen in alarm and caught himself just in time. Fletch went ballistic whenever he mentioned day care. "Like camp or school," he said.

"It sounds like day care," Fletch said, gazing at Eli as if he were the enemy.

"Well, it's not. And I want you to think about just trying it," Eli coaxed.

Fletch's small chin jutted stubbornly. "I don't wanna."

Exasperated, Eli decided he was going to have to review that book about dealing with a strong-willed child. "Well, I might have to take you, anyway. You're not even giving it a chance."

Fletch stomped his foot. "I won't go! You promised. You promised. You promised!"

Torn by the tears he saw forming in Fletch's green eyes, Eli shook his head. "I promised we would wait a while. It's been a while."

Fletch sobbed and shook his head. "I won't go. I'll run away!"

Shocked by Fletch's declaration, Eli felt a cold slice of fear run through his blood. "Fletcher Masters," he said sternly, "I don't ever want to hear that from you again. You're too young to even think about running away."

Tears ran down Fletch's cheeks. "Don't make me go," he pleaded, then hiccuped and threw himself into Eli's arms. "I'll be better. Please don't make me go."

His heart splintering at Fletch's violent reaction, Eli wondered what was the basis for this near-hysteria. Confused, he wrapped his arms around his sobbing son and shook his head. "Fletch, you don't understand. Sending you to day camp isn't punishment. Day camp is supposed to be fun."

"I don't wann—" Fletch began again in a wobbly voice.

Eli held him close. "I hear you. You don't want to go. I won't make you go to the day camp in June." At the same time that Eli relented, he wondered if he should be holding firm. God, how he hated the guesswork in being a parent. He rarely had to "guess" in the lab. He hoped like hell Fletch would grow out of this stage soon.

Sighing, he hauled Fletch up in his arms and headed down the hall. "You need to get into your pajamas and then into bed."

"Oh, Da-ad."

"Don't Da-ad me," he said, and quickly helped Fletch get dressed. When Fletch was tucked beneath the covers, Eli gazed at his son, troubled by his earlier threat to run away. "It would make me very, very sad if you ran away, Fletch."

Fletch looked ashamed. "Well, I probably wouldn't ever run away," he admitted. "And if I did, I probably wouldn't run real far."

Eli nodded thoughtfully. "Where do you think you would go?"

He could practically see the wheels turn as Fletch considered the possibilities. He pictured Fletch dodging cars on a busy highway, or worse, lost on a street where some twisted abductor would take advantage of him. Eli's stomach turned at the images.

"I'd run to Andie's," Fletch finally said. "She likes me."

Relief surged through him. He laughed and shook his head. The world seemed to return to its proper orbit. He kissed his son on the cheek and Fletch kissed him back.

"Why are you laughing?" Fletch asked with a quizzical expression on his face just before he yawned.

Eli smothered a grin and gently chucked Fletch's chin for emphasis. "If you run away to Andie's, then I'm running with you."

Eli prowled restlessly around his downstairs study after providing Fletch with a drink of water, allowing a trip to the bathroom and turning on a night-light. Mrs. Giordano spent most Sunday nights with her daughter in Rocky Mount. Eli usually appreciated the quiet, but not tonight. Tonight he was stuck with himself, and Eli wasn't much enjoying his own company.

Too many things filled his mind. He tasted the isolation of being a single father without all the answers. Fletch's continued resistance to going to day camp disturbed him. Eli wished he could remember what it was like to be five and scared and unable to fully express yourself.

Plowing his hand through his hair, he prowled some more. In trying to provide a sense of family for Fletch, Eli realized he'd neglected his relationship with his own brothers during the past few years. After his parents' death six years ago, he and his brothers had grown apart. Why had he let that happen? he wondered. He didn't like the answers that raced swiftly to his mind.

As the oldest, he should have been the one to keep in touch and get everyone together, although, heaven help him, he'd been known to grab Thanksgiving dinner at a burger joint. His gut twisting with regret, Eli swore under his breath. He'd been too busy screwing up his own life, getting Gail, his ex-wife, pregnant, failing at marriage, then burying himself in his work when he couldn't be the kind of father to Fletch that he wanted to be.

His thoughts filled him with dissatisfaction, and Eli was damn sick of not being satisfied with himself.

Drumming his fingers on the windowsill, he pushed aside the heavy drapery, and glanced toward Andie's driveway with narrowed eyes. Her car was gone, so she was with her kids at the hospital. She cared for sick children while the rest of the world slept. That impressed him. Despite all her warmth and easy friendliness, in her own way, she was a night warrior.

She was an intriguing combination, and he wasn't easily intrigued. She could protest her similarities to a courtesan till the end of time, but Eli had seen a flicker of womanly want and knowledge in her eyes. Maybe that was why he'd asked her to join him in the shower.

She'd thought he was kidding. He hadn't been.

He touched his jaw where Andie had earlier that day. Her hand had been gentle, and her lips had been moist. His blood had run hot, and his body had been aroused. Something, some crazy something, whispered that he would find satisfaction in her. In the sound of her laughter, in a little teasing conversation, in the warmth and eagerness of her body. It was all too easy to imagine how her skin would feel, how her mouth and breasts would taste. Easy to imagine seeing her eyes darken with pleasure and hearing her sigh. It was all too easy to imagine pressing her silken thighs apart and thrusting inside her, inch by incredible inch.

His body betrayed the force of his need, and his arousal throbbed insistently against the front of his jeans. Eli swore at the masculine ache. There would be no satisfaction tonight. Dropping the drapery, he faced the comfortless room and long, comfortless night.

The cynical part of his brain warned him off her. He could do nothing right when it came to the fairer sex. He was a scientist. He didn't believe in luck. Except with women, and his luck with women was rotten.

But his body still throbbed and that persistent whisper that he would find satisfaction in Andie started up again. In the back of his mind, a song played. He'd never identified with Mick Jagger more. Eli felt the driving beat and heard the grind of an electric guitar. He flicked out the light. Under his breath, he muttered about not getting any satisfaction.

Chapter Five

Andie was just about to push Eli's doorbell when the heavy door opened. A brawny man, a few years younger than Eli, with blond hair that just touched his shoulders and trademark Masters green eyes, stared down at her. At her height, it felt as if he stared *way* down at her.

"You're one of the brothers," she concluded aloud, then added, "or uncles. I'm—"

"The next-door neighbor, Andie Reynolds." He gave her a friendly once-over, clasped her hand and shook it. "I'm Ash, Eli's youngest brother. I'm the average one," he told her as if it were his greatest achievement. "Come in."

She could have begged to differ on the rather obvious issue of his height, but Andie just nodded and followed him into the house. "It's nice to meet you."

Inside, she heard the war whoops of ten little Indians, one of whom was distinguished by pigtails and a purple tutu. The children chased each other from room to room.

"Slow down," she heard Eli call to no avail. He glanced up as Andie rounded the corner. His gaze met hers, and Andie felt the nitroglycerin shake-up in her stomach again.

"Thank God you're here," he said, moving toward her. "Do you mind driving a few of these little banshees in your car? I borrowed a van from a guy at work, but I hadn't expected *all* the kids to show." His brow furrowed in confusion. "Especially after a couple of the fathers asked me how I selected the participants in my studies."

Andie groaned. She could imagine who had asked the questions. Some of the neighbors still didn't understand Eli's research. "It's Chuck E. Cheese's," she explained. "The kids love it. They wouldn't miss it."

Ash came up beside her. "The in place for kids?"

"Something like that."

"Fletch, I said slow down," Eli yelled. This time, twenty feet slowed to a fast trot. "Ninety minutes," he muttered. "I can do anything for ninety minutes."

Andie bit back a grin. "Did you hold on to that wine?"

Eli arched a dark eyebrow, and his eyes glittered with sensual threat. "I'm going to need a lot more than wine tonight." He jerked his head in the direction of the den. "You want to get Caleb into your car, Ash."

His brother nodded. "Consider it done."

"He seems nice," Andie said when Ash had left.

Eli nodded and told the kids to line up at the door. "Yeah. He's a good guy. He's the normal one."

Before she could ask what he meant by that, Ash reappeared with another man in tow. Wire-rimmed glasses framed his eyes, his dark brown hair was pulled back into a ponytail and, based on the concentrated way he was staring at a scrap of paper and murmuring, he was clearly somewhere other than this house.

Eli gave a long-suffering sigh. "I'll probably have to do this again, later. Caleb," he said, then raised his voice slightly. "Caleb."

Caleb jerked his head up and stared at Eli.

"This is my neighbor, Andie Reynolds."

Andie felt the man's piercing, assessing gaze.

"Andie, this is my middle brother, Caleb. He works in a lab where he's researching a drug for Alzheimer's. I think it's fair to say that Caleb is married to his job," Eli added dryly.

Caleb extended his hand formally. It reminded her just a bit of when she'd first met Eli. But where Eli emanated an intense masculine energy and intelligence, Caleb reflected an impatient preoccupation with more important matters. "Hello," he said quietly.

"Hi," Andie returned. "I'm glad to meet—"

"Excuse me just a moment," Caleb said with the barest hint of apology, and pulled a pencil from behind his ear to scribble something on the piece of paper.

At a loss, she glanced at Eli, who was watching Caleb with concerned eyes. He gazed at Andie and urged her toward the front door. "Don't take it personally. At least he said hello and shook your hand. Caleb isn't comfortable outside the lab. I hope it's just a stage. I went through one like it a few years ago. He's almost totally absorbed by his work. It's a miracle he showed up today. I must have left a dozen messages on his answering machine." He gave a wry grin and shook his head. "There I go again. Telling you my life story when you don't want to hear it."

Andie opened her mouth to protest, but Eli turned to the kids. "Okay, I need four of you to ride with Miss Reynolds."

Jennifer immediately stepped forward. "She's not Miss Reynolds. She's Andie."

Eli sighed, then hooked his hand around Andie's waist and whispered, "Whatever happened to respecting your elders?"

She laughed, unable to put her finger on just one thing that caused the ripples of pleasure racing through her. The sensation of his mouth at her ear was delicious, his dismay comical, and Andie got a crazy kick out of the fact that he'd confided his revealing comment to her. "I think it went out when the new math came in."

"Save me," Eli muttered, squeezing her waist, then he slipped away to a stop a sword finger fight that was getting out of hand. Within minutes, Andie and Eli managed to divide the children into two groups and get them securely strapped into their seats.

Despite the children's excited chatter on the way to the restaurant, Andie found her mind wandering to Eli's comments about his brother, Caleb. *I hope it's just a stage. I went through one like it a few years ago.* Although she could imagine Eli being absorbed by his work, it was hard for her to picture him so submerged in it that he never came out.

She wondered if he'd gone through that kind of stage because of his divorce. He must have been incredibly lonely and unhappy. Her heart twisted at the thought. She remembered her own dark period last summer after her breakup with Paul. She'd logged in extra hours at work, but the hospital imposed stiff restrictions on overtime. She'd tried to mend her wounds in private by staying at home, but Samantha hadn't let her.

Andie sensed there'd been no best friend to pull Eli back into the land of the living. His ex-wife's death had obviously turned his and Fletch's world upside down. Deep inside her, the part she'd kept well protected since last year ached at the thought of Eli's aloneness. He shouldn't be alone. Sure, he was strong, confident, obscenely intelligent. But Andie saw holes in his life, holes a woman could fill.

Part of her longed to close her eyes to the dangers and allow herself to be drawn into Eli's life, to let down her guard and add a little comfort and warmth, to take him up on that shower, to find out if, despite all her doubts, there was a courtesan inside her. She'd always wanted to make love with a man and get so excited that she went a little wild. And maybe have him get so excited he went a little wild, too.

One of the kids shrieked, jolting Andie back to reality. Blinking, she took a quick breath and felt her cheeks heat. What was wrong with her? Distressed, she bit her lip. She was a nutcase.

When was she going to learn? This overblown nurturing instinct was going to destroy her if she didn't rein it in. She cared too much. She didn't need to lose her heart to a complex single father with an adorable, but vulnerable son. She didn't need to lose her heart to anyone right now.

An hour later, Andie leaned against the side of a pinball machine and smiled at Fletch's persistence with his very absentminded uncle, Caleb. She'd noticed that Fletch hovered on the fringe of the group and sometimes just went off alone. She hated to think of him as a little lone wolf.

"Pizza in five minutes," Eli said and stood beside her. "What are you watching?"

Andie nodded her head in Fletch's direction. "Your son is charming your brother back into the real world."

Eli watched Fletch offer Caleb a copper token in exchange for the scrap of paper in Caleb's hand. Clearly reluctant, his brother shook his head. Fletch offered two tokens and pointed to an electronic game. Caleb hesitated. Fletch pushed his advantage, snatched the paper and stuffed it in Caleb's shirt pocket. His mouth quirking in a slight grin, Caleb took Fletch's hand and allowed the birthday boy to drag him to the game.

"Well, I'll be damned," Eli murmured.

"Fletch is very persuasive."

"He had better luck with Caleb than I did," Eli admitted, still staring at his son and brother.

"You didn't bribe him with tokens," Andie pointed out.

Eli slid his gaze back to her and assessed her as he shifted closer. "Would tokens work with you?"

Andie's heart jolted at the look in his eyes. She was about to give him an absolute unequivocal *no* when Ash joined them.

He gave Eli a sympathetic pat on the back. "I think Fletcher got the Masters 'G' gene."

Eli nodded. "I suspected."

"Is he reading?"

"Yes, and multiplying."

Ash winced. "You've got your hands full."

Confused, Andie looked from Ash to Eli. "The 'G' gene?"

Eli looked uncomfortable. "My mother was . . . academically . . ."

Ash snorted. "Mom was a genius. So are Eli and Caleb. I'd lay odds Fletch is, too." He grinned with great pleasure and answered her unvoiced question. "I'm not." The loudspeaker announced the Masterses' pizza and table were ready. "Time to round up the kids. I'll grab those in the moon walk."

Eli tossed her a wary glance. "You look a little stunned."

Andie followed the group to the table and lifted her shoulders. "Well, he seemed so pleased that he wasn't . . ."

Eli exhaled in disgust. "He has always rubbed it in that he isn't an egghead."

She heard a trace of resentment in Eli's voice that she didn't understand. "Do you think it's a defense mechanism?"

Disbelief skimmed across his face. "Ash?" Eli laughed. "He watched Caleb and me struggle to fit in throughout our entire childhood. I've never seen a kid so relieved as Ash was when his first report card had average grades. There were plenty of times Caleb and I envied him."

Andie shook her head. "But it's wonderful to be intellectually gifted. You can do so much. . . ." She broke off when she saw his eyes darken and his jaw tighten. Immediately, she knew she'd spoken without understanding and she regretted her insensitivity.

"Sometimes it's good. Sometimes it just marks you as different." Glancing at Fletch, Eli pulled out a chair for her. "Have a seat."

Polite again, she thought, unfailingly so. But she was stuck wondering what his deeper thoughts and feelings were, and knowing he wasn't going to share them. He'd closed a door, and she was filled with an odd sense of loss.

The pizza was devoured amid great chaos. The adults spent more time refilling drinks, mopping up spills and serving seconds than actually eating anything themselves. While Eli took pictures, Andie lit the candles on Fletch's cake and led everyone in a rousing chorus of "Happy Birthday." The way Fletch solemnly gazed at the group singing to him caught at her heart. She gave him a quick squeeze. "Make a wish before you blow them out."

Fletch looked at her, wide-eyed. "A wish?"

Andie smiled. "Anything you want."

"Can I make a wish for my mommy?"

Her heart tightened. "Oh, honey." She felt the burn of tears. Other little boys would be wishing for fire trucks or bicycles, but Fletch had suffered a tremendous loss. It was all she could do not to pull him into her arms and try to make his hurt go away.

"Andie?" Eli prompted, glancing from her to Fletch with concern.

She nodded, feeling a tug of compassion for both of them. Eli wanted so badly for Fletch to be happy, especially today. "It's okay," she told him. "We're working on the wish." Then she turned back to Fletch.

"You can make a wish for your mommy if you want to," she said gently. "You can wish that she's happy and well where she is. And you're a really special boy to even think of it. But since it's your birthday, I bet your mommy would want you to make the wish for you."

He took a deep breath. "Think so?"

"Yeah, I think so."

He thought a moment, then took another deep breath and blew out all the candles. The kids cheered, and Andie watched Fletch smile, his dimple making a rare appearance. He leaned close to her and whispered loudly in her ear. "I wished for a puppy."

After everyone returned home and the parents picked up the children, the big house seemed as quiet as a tomb. Surprisingly, Fletch had given in to a nap. Eli sat in the den with Andie and his brothers. It wasn't one of those brotherly bonding moments. An uncomfortable silence hung in the air. Caleb was scribbling on another piece of paper, and Ash was reading the sports section of the newspaper. Eli narrowed his eyes and took a second look. Or was it the stock report?

He rubbed his hands together and glanced at Andie.

The single bit of warmth in the room stood as if she were making her escape. "Thanks for including me. It was a memorable experience," she said with a smile full of gentle amusement.

He stood, too, reluctant for her to leave. "Why don't you stay for dinner?"

She waved her hand in the direction of Caleb and Ash, and moved toward the hall. "Your brothers are here. I don't want to intrude on your family time."

Eli didn't have a clue what family time was. It sounded similar to small talk. "We often include visitors during family time," Eli said, feeling like the blind leading the blind as he joined her in the hall.

Eyebrows furrowing in confusion, she tilted her head to one side thoughtfully. "But I thought you said it's been years since the three of you were together."

"Right." He met her gaze for a long moment, then sighed. "Andie, what did your family do during your family time?"

She shrugged. "Nothing out of the ordinary. We played board games. Sometimes we sang or someone would read. That was usually me." Her mouth tilted in a grin full of reminiscence. "I had three brothers, so when they got a little older, they begged me to bake cookies and we would watch football or basketball games on television."

Eli considered her suggestions and eliminated each one. The only one that held any appeal was the cookies. "Can you remember anything else?"

She blinked and just looked at him for a long moment. Then her eyes widened incredulously. "Eli!" She dropped her voice to a whisper. "Don't tell me you and your brothers have nothing in common."

He crossed his arms over his chest and pondered her statement. "We know a lot about cars, but Caleb hates working on them." Eli didn't think Andie would understand his oddball family. Her frame of reference was totally different. "When we were growing up, our mother encouraged us to develop our individual interests."

"But surely you must have played together some."

"I don't remember playing much, at least in the sense that you would define it."

Andie muffled a groan. "Okay." She pushed her hair behind her ear and pursed her lips as if she were determined to solve this problem. He wondered if she wore that same expression, totally feminine, yet completely unbending, at work. "What about games and books and sports?"

He was so distracted by her effect on him that he almost forgot to answer. He glanced away to clear his head. "The last time Caleb and I played chess, he was eight and I was eleven. He got mad become he was losing. Caleb is incredibly competitive. Middle children often are," he felt compelled to explain, and grimaced in remembrance. "He put the chess pieces in the oven. The set had been an anniversary gift to my mom from my dad. She cried. My dad yelled. No more chess."

She nodded her head in understanding. "Music?"

Eli shook his head. "Shower voices only." Major understatement, he thought, considering his entire family was tone-deaf. "Reading's out, unless we ask Ash to read the sports page. I suppose Caleb could mumble a few chemistry formulas," he added half-seriously.

She closed her eyes. "Let's save that one. What about movies or favorite television shows?"

"My mother believed television was a mental vacuum. Every once in a while, Dad would sneak and let us watch professional wrestling."

"Wrestling?" she echoed in disbelief.

"Nature Boy Rick Flair, Hulk Hogan," he quoted, the names as indelibly imprinted on his brain as his academic knowledge. "Ricky Steamboat, André the Giant—"

She held up a hand for him to stop, then rubbed her forehead. "This is too much," she murmured. "Did your brothers like wrestling? Do you still watch it?"

"We all liked it, but I haven't watched it in years. It was fun until I went away to college. I think it was the forbidden element."

She looked him over for a long considering moment, then her gaze shifted downward and her eyelashes shielded her eyes. Shaking her head, she smiled as if she'd remembered a private joke.

The secret smile took him off guard, and Eli thought about a different forbidden element. He'd like to see her wearing a smile and nothing else. He wished he could crawl inside her mind. Inside her body.

"Okay," she said. "You get started on whatever you were planning to give them for dinner, and I'll be back in about thirty minutes."

She was already moving toward the front door. Eli snagged her hand. "Where are you going?"

"It's a surprise," she said in a dry tone.

"Why are you doing this?"

She stopped, and a fleeting shadow of vulnerability crossed her face. She shrugged and looked away. "Because I was born to," she murmured darkly and pushed open the door.

Eli stared after her, wondering what she was talking about.

Two hours later, Andie viewed Eli's den with a mixture of emotions. Three grown men scarfed down meat-eaters' pizza, guzzled beer and laughed, guffawed and slapped their knees as they watched a video filmfest of the Three Stooges. Fletch sat on his father's knee and alternately followed the movie and fiddled with the steam-cleaned carburetor Caleb had given him as a birthday gift.

Some things never changed.

Andie recalled a similar scene years ago, minus the steam-cleaned carburetor, when she'd been left in charge of her brothers. The weather had been horrible, so they couldn't go outside. Out of desperation, she'd switched on the TV and found Larry, Curly and Moe. Within moments, her brothers were glued to the screen, laughing and pointing at the Stooges. Although she'd been thankful for the Stooges, she'd never shared her brothers' enthusiasm for the trio.

Through no fault of their own, the Stooges became associated with that seemingly endless period of time when she'd taken care of her brothers and missed out on being a teenager. When she left home for college, she'd made a promise to herself that she would never watch another Stooges movie. It had been one small way of disassociating herself from her caretaker role and forging a new identity. Impatience licked through her. So where was her new identity tonight? Saturday night, and she was watching men watch a movie. *For crying out loud.*

Stiffening her spine, she took one last look at the Masters men, her gaze lingering on Eli. Despite her frustration with herself, part of her was pleased that she'd been able to help him. Part of her wanted to take the seat beside him just to be close to him. Part of her wanted to park her brain in neutral and just kiss him, long, and slow, and deep.

Part of her, she told herself grimly, was obviously insane.

With that admonition in mind, she ignored the ache that was becoming more insistent, the heat that threatened to melt her resolve and an insatiable feminine curiosity. Instead she slipped down the hall and out the door.

Walking home to a dark, silent and nearly empty house, Andie squelched the urge to return to Eli's mausoleum. Too restless to go to bed early, she pulled on her long T-shirt and decided to tackle the fascinating task of laundry. Mary Chapin Carpenter belted it out on her CD player, and Stud shifted positions often enough for her to trip over him twice.

She was folding towels when she heard an insistent tap at her back door. Noting the late hour, she ruefully glanced at her state of dress. Although her T-shirt nearly reached her knees, she took a blue bath towel with her to look out the window.

Dr. Frankenstein in the flesh.

Fighting a strange uneasiness, Andie opened the door. Eli walked in, a bottle of wine in one hand, two glasses in the other. "You left," he said, his gaze intense and questioning.

Her stomach took a dip. She hugged the blue towel to her chest and backed away. "I'd already seen those movies," she said. Twenty times at least, she thought.

He stepped closer. "You should have told me."

"I didn't want to interrupt." Dismayed by a sudden jittery feeling, she tried for a slight smile. "You seemed absorbed.

"I kept wondering when you were going to come back." He set the bottle on the table and cocked his head to one side, regarding her curiously. "How did you know we'd like the Stooges?"

Andie relaxed just a little. "Oh, well, that's easy. I had three younger brothers, and along the way, I learned a few common denominators for the male gender. Food, especially pizza and homemade brownies, can distract a guy from the time he's learning to chew until the time he loses his teeth," she told him. "And all men love the Three Stooges. It must be in the Y chromosome."

Eli raised his eyebrows in amusement. "You think it's genetic." His grin was slow. "What an interesting hypothesis. We got the pizza and the Stooges. What do I have to do to get the homemade brownies?"

Andie wondered how he managed to remind her of Fletch negotiating for a treat at the same time that he exuded enough sex appeal to turn her kneecaps to maple syrup. A warning signal went off inside her. "I don't bake on demand anymore, so I guess you have to be around when the mood strikes me."

"I'll remember that," Eli said, and glanced around the kitchen. "Your wine corkscrew?"

"Second drawer on the left." She pointed to it before she realized she'd just agreed to share a glass of wine with him when she should have been shoving him out the door.

With steady hands, he opened the bottle and poured the wine into the glasses. "You mentioned food and the Stooges as common denominators for men. Any other ones you can think of?"

Sex. Bold, erotic, the word and image shot through her like lightning. Feeling her cheeks heat, she accepted the wine he offered and took a quick sip before she set the glass on the counter. "I'm sure there are more."

In the background, she heard Mary Chapin Carpenter singing an instruction to "Shut up and kiss me." Andie resisted the urge to echo those words. "Eli, it's very nice of you to bring this over, but it's late and I'm not really dressed for—" When he stepped closer to her, her voice suddenly failed.

"Dressed for?" he prompted, his gaze wrapping around her like satin on naked skin.

Andie swallowed hard. "Dressed for company. I was going to—bed." The last word came out in a whisper, and Andie forced her mind away from a quicksilver assault of heated images.

"I came over because I didn't get a chance to thank you."

"For what?" she asked in a small voice.

"For coming to Fletch's party, and for renting the videos." He shoved his glass on the counter behind her and threaded his hand through his hair. She could sense his frustration. His tension echoed inside her like a steel coil. "For being sweet."

Something in his eyes shifted, and Andie got a glimpse of that contained energy spilling over. "Aw, hell," he muttered, sliding his hand to the back of her neck.

Before she could think, let alone speak, his mouth took hers. Her heart skipped over itself. She should pull back, her inner voice insisted. But his subtle musky masculine scent distracted her. His mouth was warm and gentle, seeking, not conquering, and something inside her softened.

His tongue teased the seam of her lips, coaxing her to open and accept, to give and take. His body was hard and warm, his chest a strong protective wall that brushed against her breast. Acutely sensitive, she felt her nipples tighten and sucked in a quick breath.

"God, you're sweet," he muttered, pulling her closer and massaging the back of her neck. He pushed the towel she'd held against her to the floor.

"Open up," he urged softly. "You feel so good." He took her mouth again, more urgently. Shifting his mouth first one way, then another, he explored and implored. His obvious arousal hit her where she was most vulnerable, at the deep, dark center of where she doubted her ability to turn him on.

She felt a twisting ache between her thighs. Her breasts swollen, she arched against him and stroked her tongue over his. He gave a rough groan of approval that vibrated through her mouth and nerve endings. She opened wider, wanting more of the taste of wine on his tongue, more of the heady flavor of his passion. More, just more.

Responding to her stifled moan, he slipped his hand beneath her T-shirt and skimmed his palm upward to cup her bottom, gently rotating his pelvis in the notch of her thighs. His tongue slipped in and out in a devastating rhythm. The sensual movement of his masculinity seeking and seducing, his mouth filling and taking, was too much.

Trembling and hot, she gasped when his fingers rubbed the aching swollen part of her through her panties. Alarm shot through her. *What was she doing?* She pulled her head away, and their mouths made a sensuous sucking sound at the disconnection. Struggling for breath, she was conscious of his hand still between her legs, his breath on her face. Andie moaned. "Eli—" She was holding on to his shoulders for dear life, so she couldn't push him away. "Eli, please—"

"I want to," he growled, and lowered his head toward her again.

Chapter Six

Andie ducked her head. "No," she said, shaking her head, "we need to—" She swallowed. "We've got to stop."

Eli's blood pounded through his veins with a fury. "Stop," he repeated, trying to make the word compute. There was too much of her he hadn't touched, too much he hadn't tasted. He wanted to touch her more. He wanted to kiss her again. He wanted inside her. His body clamored for satisfaction, and he knew she could give it to him, knew it deep in his gut. She was like a flower, and he wanted to bury himself in her fragrance.

Stop.

He was breathing as if he'd just run a mile. He reluctantly moved his hand from her thigh.

She risked a glance at him and he saw dismay and arousal warring in her warm brown eyes. Her mouth, swollen from his kisses, drew his gaze like a magnet. He rubbed his thumb over the sensuous puffy curve of her lips and closed his eyes at the need kicking through him. "Are you sure?" he asked her.

Her uneven sigh drifted over his throat. Eli clenched his jaw at the sensation and watched her remove her hands from his shoulders. "I guess things got a little out of hand." She looked away. "I don't know what got into me. I meant to pull away, and then I didn't want to, and then—"

"It was inevitable," Eli cut in, loathing the guilt he heard in her voice.

Andie blinked. "It was?"

"Yes," he said a shade impatiently because the ache he had for her wasn't going anywhere. "I thought about making—" he hesitated and edited the first words that came to mind "—kissing you the first time I met you."

Her eyes widened. "You did?"

"Yes," he repeated in a voice that sounded curt to his own ears. He placed a wineglass in her hand. She looked as if she could use it. Eli thought he would benefit more from a cold shower. Her surprise irritated him. "You haven't thought about it at all."

Her cheeks bloomed with color and she pushed her tousled hair behind her ear. Her gaze skittered away from his. "I—uh—" She cleared her throat and played with the stem of her glass. "I can't say I haven't thought about it," she admitted in a voice so low he barely heard it.

It was the kind of voice he needed to be closer to hear. It was the kind of voice appropriate for the bedroom. Eli stifled an oath. He wondered if she had a clue what she was doing to him. He took a generous swallow of wine and watched her from beneath hooded eyes.

His silence seemed to make her nervous. "Okay, I'll admit I've been curious about you," she confessed. "I've wondered what it would be like to—to—"

"Kiss me," Eli supplied when she couldn't get the words out. Her reluctant confession made him want to take her in his arms and hug the reticence out of her.

"Yes," she said. "It's a normal curiosity, and—"

"I agree. Normal and healthy." And he had a normal, healthy curiosity about every inch of her body and mind.

She glanced at him warily. "Yes, and now that we've satisfied our curiosity, we won't need to satisfy it anymore."

Eli laughed.

"It's true," she told him, setting her chin. "We don't need to repeat this."

Eli shook his head. Torn between amusement and a heavy dose of regret because he apparently wasn't going to satisfy the rest of his curiosity about Andie tonight, he wrapped his hands around both of her shoulders so she wouldn't bolt. Then he teased himself with a brief kiss on her forehead. Reluctantly releasing her, he brushed his finger over her nose. "You've forgotten you're dealing with a scientist, Andie. It takes hundreds of repeat trials to prove a hypothesis." He dropped his finger to her lips. "Hundreds."

The following Friday night, Eli was in a vile mood. There'd been not one single repeat trial of that kiss with Andie. Working four nights out of the past five, she had successfully avoided him.

Since Andie slept during the day, Fletch had missed her and was full of his own crankiness. His housekeeper, Mrs. Giordano, wasn't feeling well, so she wouldn't be available for the rest of the weekend. Add to that the fact that he'd forgotten to cancel dinner at Daphne Sinclair's house tonight, and Eli was ready to chew glass.

On the way to Daphne's, Eli glanced in the direction of Andie's house, and saw her car pull into the driveway. Gripping Eli's hand, Fletch spun around and tugged hard enough to cause whiplash. "Andie's home! Let's go see her. I haven't petted Stud and—"

"Hold on," Eli said. "We've got to eat dinner with Ms. Sinclair, and we're running late." He watched Andie get out of her car with a bag of groceries. "Hello," he called.

She turned and paused. "Hi." She looked from Fletch to Eli. "Are you two out for a walk?"

Fletch shook his head. "No. We're going to Mizz Sinclair's for dinner. Are you finished working? I haven't petted Stud in a long, long time."

Eli's lips twitched at the longing in his son's tone. "He's going through withdrawal. It's been at least four days."

Andie shifted the groceries to her hip, drawing Eli's gaze to her bare legs. His gaze flicked over the rest of her, noting the T-shirt and denim shorts with suspenders that curved around the curve of her breast. Cute, but sexy. Although he knew her friendly, nonthreatening manner was sincere, he'd suspected there was more beneath the surface. Much more. After kissing her the other night, he knew. That knowledge and the desire to know everything about her was frustrating the hell out of him.

"You can come over any time, Fletch," she said, and Eli was in a bad enough frame of mind to notice she didn't include him in her invitation. "I bet Stud has missed you, too."

"Dad said I shouldn't wake you up."

Her gaze met Eli's. "I'm usually up by four o'clock."

"We haven't seen much of you, and we didn't want to wear out our welcome."

"Oh, no. It's not that," she quickly demurred, her face shadowed with guilt. "It's just..."

Her discomfort grated on him. He wanted her warmth. "You're having some anxiety about the repeat test trials," he drawled. He watched her blush and knew he'd hit it on the mark. "The slang term for this anxiety is *chicken.*"

She sucked in a surprised, affronted breath. "I am not chicken," she told him.

"If that's so, then you won't mind—"

"Absolutely not. And you're not going to goad me into ki—" Her gaze lit on Fletch, then returned to Eli. "Repeating."

"Cluck, cluck," Eli said.

She narrowed her eyes, which was a feat, considering how wide they were. "You're being difficult."

"I get that way when I'm frustrated," he said and met her gaze head-on so she wouldn't mistake his meaning.

Her cheeks bloomed again. She blinked and opened her mouth to say something, but just shook her head. She turned to Fletch. "You can come see Stud any time tomorrow. Right now, I've got to get inside before my frozen yogurt melts, and both you guys need to get to your dinner date," she said, tossing Eli an arch glance. "Maybe you won't be so frustrated, then."

Eli sighed, knowing he was acting like an ass and he shouldn't be taking out his frustration on her. He nodded. "Point taken." Turning, he took a step away from her, then hesitated half a beat and glanced over his shoulder. "Andie," he said, "we both missed you."

More than Andie's frozen yogurt was melting.

She frowned as she put away her groceries. Her hands were trembling so that she nearly dropped her skim milk. Her heart banged against her rib cage. She brushed her hair back from her face and sank into a kitchen chair, because her knees were still gooey from those last four words. *We both missed you.*

She might have withstood the pressure for repeat test trials, as he so charmingly put it. Especially if he didn't step within three feet of her and she had the sense to run when she saw him coming. She couldn't have dodged Fletch, though, not after she'd seen his vulnerability. But she'd hoped to keep her relationship with the younger Masters strictly separate from her relationship with his sexy dad.

Eli had sent her into a tailspin when he'd kissed her Saturday night. She'd spent the past week trying to create some distance, gain perspective and forget what it felt like for Eli Masters to steal both her breath and sanity.

The memory popped up like toast in a toaster, and Andie tried to remember when she'd felt so deliciously wanton. Idly fanning herself with a folded paper bag, she recalled the sensation of his mouth and hands in vivid detail. Just his kiss had made her more aroused than she'd ever been, which had her wondering what full-fledged lovemaking with him would be like. The thought sent a sudden rush of heat through her. Groaning, she fanned more quickly. When she realized what she was doing, she slapped the bag on the table and stood.

"You're slipping," she muttered to herself. "He's at Daphne's, and he won't give you a second thought." Cramming the lettuce in the crisper, she resolved to focus on cleaning out her refrigerator. That would at least cool off her body.

An hour later, she hung up from a telephone conversation with her mother, who informed her of her plans to take another trip to the Bahamas. Andie smiled at the irony of the situation. Years ago, when she'd wanted to test her wings, she'd been stuck at home with her brothers. Now that she was on her own and had all the freedom a person could want, she tended to stick close to home except for an occasional trip to the shore.

She didn't resent her parents' freedom. With her youngest brother ready to graduate from high school and her father's health finally on track, Andie was delighted that they *could* go. A trip to the islands didn't stir an ounce of envy in Andie. Not unless an adoring, adorable man was included in the package, perhaps with green eyes, sandy brown hair and a kiss that could make her bones disappear.

Right, she told herself cryptically, *and Elvis is alive and well.*

The knock at her front door was a welcome interruption. In a rare display of excitement, Stud barked and ran to the door. "Quiet down," she told him, gently nudging him out of the way. After flicking on the porch light, she glanced out the peephole and got the surprise of her life.

Andie quickly unhooked the dead bolt and opened the door. Hands stuffed in his pockets, his chin nearly touching the ground, Fletch looked like a stray if ever there was one. She felt a tug at her heartstrings. "Hi there, Fletcher," she said, glancing around for Eli.

"Dad's still at Mizz Sinclair's," he told her before she could ask. "I got bored, so I decided to come see you."

He wasn't quite meeting her gaze, she noted, and felt a dip of uneasiness. "Okay, come on in. Did you tell your dad you were coming?"

Immediately gravitating toward Stud, Fletch took his hands out of his pockets and started rubbing the dog. When Fletch didn't answer, Andie repeated the question.

The little boy's chin dipped lower and he shook his head. "No. He might be mad at me. That Mizz Sinclair sure is."

Concerned, Andie walked over and knelt beside him. "Why do you think they're mad at you?"

"Mizz Sinclair has a white cat. And it just lays there. It doesn't meow or anything, so I petted it." His eyebrows drew into a frown. "And it scratched me." He lifted his hand to show her the small mark.

She kissed his hand. "I'm sorry, Fletch. But I don't think your father will be mad at you about—"

Guilt washed over his small features. "Well, I kinda sorta pulled its tail."

Andie winced. "Oops. I bet it meowed then."

"Yeah, and Mizz Sinclair's face got all red. It was after we finished eatin'. The table was pretty. I played with one of the candles till Dad made me stop, but the food was major yukky." He made a face. "All I ate was the rolls. She gave us gross fishy stuff and I told her I would throw up if I had to eat it." He looked up at her earnestly. "Why couldn't she fix hot dogs and hamburgers like you?"

Andie bit her lip at the image of Daphne's seduction scene going awry. "Sometimes adults like different kinds of foods."

He nodded solemnly. "Yeah, my dad says as you get older your taste buds die, so you can eat gross stuff without throwing up."

Stifling a chuckle at his logic, she shook her head. "I think I'd better give your dad a call so he'll know where you are."

Fletch began to fidget. "You're not gonna make me go back over there, are you? Dad told her we were gonna go, but she wanted to show him some pictures of curtains and stuff. Then she told me to color on the kitchen table after I spilled my grape juice on her rug, but..."

Andie grimaced again. She knew that Daphne had decorated her house in white on white. She also knew that a grape juice stain had a tendency to stay forever. Little boys and white just didn't go together. She looked down at Fletch and ruffled his hair. "I'm glad you came to see me. How about if you pet Stud while I call your dad? Then I'll think of something we can do."

Daphne picked up on the fifth ring. Andie wondered if she'd interrupted a passionate kiss and banished the thought from her mind. "I just wanted to let you know that I have a visitor," Andie told Eli after Daphne transferred the phone to him.

"He's at your house." Eli swore. "We've been looking through Daphne's closets trying to find him."

"He's fine," Andie reassured him. "Petting Stud and checking out my CD collection."

"I'll be right over."

"There's no need. We'll be fine. Take your time. If he gets sleepy, I'll put him in my guest bed."

"But—"

"Really," Andie said. "I'm fine with this."

She hung up the phone and an insidious thought crossed her mind; last summer she'd frequently kept her ex-fiancé's little girl while he supposedly worked late. There were no similarities between that situation and this one, she told herself. She'd been engaged to Paul and he had secretly cheated on her. Andie wasn't even dating Eli, and she'd practically arranged his dinner with Daphne. Hadn't she encouraged Eli's involvement with her? Mentally, she accepted the differences, but she was left with a pang of discomfort that reinforced her inclination to remain uninvolved with Eli.

Determined to wipe away the ugly memory and her conflicting feelings, she turned her attention to Fletch. "Have you picked one you want to hear?" she asked, when she saw him looking through her CDs.

"She's got red hair like you," he said, pointing to Bonnie Raitt.

Not the exact shade, she thought, but she was charmed anyway. She smiled. "So she does." Recalling her brothers' need for independence, Andie instructed Fletch how to put the CD in the player and allowed him to do it himself. He was extremely interested in her stereo system, checking out the various controls, lowering and raising the volume.

A fast song came on and Andie held out her arms. "Wanna dance?"

He looked at her doubtfully. "You're too tall," he said, but nodded his head in rhythm to the music.

This kid was just a little too serious for his own good, she thought. She impulsively scooped him up in her arms. "Not anymore. Hang on."

His face flushed with exhilaration, he hooked his legs around her waist as she placed his right hand on her left shoulder and took his other hand in hers. She spun him around in time to the driving beat of the music.

That was how Eli found them. After knocking and getting no answer, he'd pushed open the door to the sound of Bonnie Raitt singing "That's just love sneakin' up on you." When Andie swung his son into a deep dip, Fletch giggled. The sound grabbed at his gut, and for a moment he just stared. He didn't think he'd heard Fletch laugh, truly laugh with childish abandon, since he'd gotten custody.

She dipped again, folding Fletch into a hug. Fletch's hair flew at the movement and that wonderful childish giggle bubbled out again. Andie rubbed her nose against Fletch's, and Eli was struck with an insane stab of envy. He was envious of Andie's natural ability with his son, and heaven help him, he wanted his own dance with her.

The loud, fast song ended, and a slower one began. Eli took it as his cue. Stepping behind Andie, he touched her shoulder, then steadied her waist when she swiveled to look at him.

Andie's eyes widened in surprise. "I didn't hear you."

"The music's a little loud," he pointed out in a dry tone.

Fletch craned his head forward. "Are you mad at me?"

Eli shook his head. How could he be made at anyone right now? Eli thought. His son had laughed. That sound could keep him high for hours. "No, but we'll need to talk about this later." He glanced back to Andie and shifted position to face her. "Any chance I can join in here?"

"Yeah," Fletch said eagerly at the same time Andie shook her head.

"You wouldn't discriminate on the basis of age, would you," Eli asked her as he enveloped both Andie's and Fletch's hands in one of his and put the other on Andie's slim waist.

"Well, no, but—"

"We're a sandwich," Fletch interrupted, leaning back against Eli's chest. "You're the breads and I'm the bologna."

Eli's lips twitched. "You must still be hungry from dinner. I should take you home and get you something to eat."

"I wanna play with Stud some more first." Fletch promptly let go of Andie and tried to slide down. Eli caught him with one hand and eased him to the ground. Without missing a beat, he pulled Andie back into his arms.

She stiffened slightly but didn't pull away. "You could have stayed at Daphne's."

"I was almost on my way out the door when you called," he assured her, savoring the sensation of her hand in his, the warmth of her body close to his. "Your waist is so small," he mused.

Her gaze locked with his for a brief sizzling moment, then her eyelids fluttered down and her eyelashes became a dark, feathery shield. She cleared her throat. "I'm sure Daphne would understand if you explain..."

Eli chuckled. "After that dining experience, Daphne might need therapy."

Andie gave a soft wince. "That's bad? I heard about the grape juice."

Eli nodded soberly. "A grape juice stain has a half-life that rivals plutonium." He lowered his voice. "Did he tell you he nearly set her lace tablecloth on fire with the candles?"

Horrified, Andie groaned, shaking her head. "Maybe you can try flowers."

"Why?" His green eyes were intent and slightly puzzled.

"Well, if you want to see her again, then—"

"And if I don't?"

Her stomach took a dip at the expression on his face. She was acutely aware of the difference between holding Fletch and being held by Eli. Eli didn't let her forget her femininity for a minute. Nor for that matter could she forget his sexuality. She was reminded by the flex of his broad shoulder beneath her hand, his larger hand swallowing hers, the brush of his thighs against her bare legs and, perhaps most of all, the way he watched her. Right now, he was waiting for her response. "I—uh—you don't?"

"I don't want Daphne," he told her in a voice that sent her heart into a frenzy.

I want you. He didn't say it aloud, but his eyes said it loud and clear. Trapped by the blatant need in his gaze, Andie held her breath.

"The administrators for the research center where I work are holding a mandatory cocktail party next week. I want you to come with me."

She blinked. Bolder than brass, no subtlety, he laid it flat out on the table. "That's not exactly asking."

"That's right."

His deep voice rumbled through her like the beginning of an earthquake. "I don't know what to say."

"Say yes." He tugged her closer and lowered his mouth to her ear. "Stop running. Test the hypothesis."

Andie felt a delicious shiver. "What hypothesis?" she whispered breathlessly.

"When Eli and Andie spend time together, they like it," he said, "a lot. When Eli kisses Andie, he gets hot." He tilted his head to look at her. "And Andie does, too."

Excitement roared through her at an alarming rate, Andie couldn't have dodged him if she'd wanted to. "Yes to the cocktail party."

Eli's mouth tilted in a seductive grin. "When Eli and Andie make love—"

Sucking in a quick breath, Andie shook her head. "You're pushing—"

"My luck." His grin faded slightly, and this time he was stepping back, not her. "Don't worry. I don't have much luck when it comes to women."

She struggled with the urge to wipe away his cynicism. It was more than her everyday instinct to heal or nurture. He called to something deep inside her, a womanly part of her that was untouched and untried, but bursting to get out. Andie swallowed hard and tried to come to grips with the powerful feeling.

But the moment passed too quickly. Loosening his hold on her, Eli looked around the room. "Where did he go?" Eli muttered. "Fletch," he called and turned toward the kitchen.

Wondering what had hit her, Andie gave herself a hard mental shake and followed after him.

"Fletch." Eli paused. "Oh, Fletch, not again," he said, his voice shadowed with weary disappointment.

Andie rounded the corner to find Eli staring down in exasperation at Fletch, who had his hands in the guts of her kitchen clock radio. Fletch looked up, his green eyes full of guilt. "It's a really neat clock, Dad," he said in a low voice.

Eli nodded. "Who's going to put it back together?"

"I dunno," Fletch said, defeat tugging at his features.

Eli knew he needed to make his point without squashing Fletch's self-esteem. "I thought we'd settled this. No more taking clocks apart without my permission."

Andie sensed an unhappy and ultimately unnecessary scene on the horizon. She walked over to Fletch and patted him on the back. "It's okay. I was going to replace it anyway."

Eli concluded that part of the reason Fletch had torn apart Andie's clock was, ironically enough, because he was so comfortable in her home. "He hasn't done this since Caleb gave him the distributor," Eli muttered, frowning as he looked down at the clock. He ran his fingers over the wires and assorted metal parts. "Clock radios aren't my speciality, but I might be able to put it back together."

"It's really no big deal," she insisted. "I told you I was going to replace it. I just hadn't gotten around to it."

"He's got to learn to respect others' property." Eli decided he was going to have to get a book on how to raise a gifted kid. He shook his head, turning the shell of the clock radio in his hands. "It looks new," he said, and glanced up at Andie. "When did you get it?"

She blushed, and he wondered at the reason for it. "It's just a clock radio, Eli," she hedged. "It's not as if it's state-of-the-art electronic equipment." Her gaze skittered away and she smiled at Fletch. "Why don't we have some of that frozen yogurt I brought home from the grocery store?"

Out of the corner of his eye, he saw Fletch brighten. Although Eli was usually about as intuitive as a block of wood, he had learned that Andie used diversionary tactics when she was uncomfortable. Studying her, he saw a hint of turmoil clouding her eyes. Before she could slip past him to the refrigerator, he caught her arm. "When did you get it?"

Annoyance flickered across her features. "It was a Christmas gift I received year before last."

Eli nodded, but didn't release her arm. "From one of your brothers?"

"No." The way she drew out that one syllable revealed a wealth of reluctance. "Paul gave it to me."

Eli heard the slightest edge in her voice and felt as if he were pulling teeth. If he were polite and gentlemanly, he might just have let it slide. His feelings for Andie, however, weren't particularly polite. For no logical reason, he felt possessive as hell. "Paul," he prompted, not bothering to hide his demand for clarification.

She met his gaze and the emotions swirling in her
eyes hit him like a punch in the gut. Pain, anger and
shame. The shame was the worst.

"Paul's the man I was going to marry."

Chapter Seven

"When?" Eli asked without missing a beat. He looked at her as if she was a puzzle he was determined to solve.

Her stomach took a tumble. The power of his determination was daunting. He saw more than she wanted him to. She didn't want to discuss Paul with Eli, with anyone for that matter. "Last summer," she finally said and pulled free from his grasp. "Now let me get that yogurt."

Eli sighed and stood. "We can't have yogurt tonight."

Andie swung around from the freezer. "Why—"

"Why not?" demanded Fletch

"Because it would be rewarding you for something you shouldn't have done," Eli said firmly. "We need to talk about some important things tonight, like respecting other people's property and going to another person's house without asking for permission." He glanced at Andie. "Another time?"

Andie nodded, immediately seeing the wisdom in his plan. It was dangerous for Fletch to go off on his own, especially at night, and his curiosity could end up getting him into trouble if he didn't accept some limits. "Of course."

Reluctant to give up the treat, Fletch jutted out his chin. "But I'm hungry."

Eli tugged him to his feet. "Then I'll fix you a peanut butter sandwich after we finish talking."

"Aw, Dad—"

Eli shook his head. "No. Andie said we could come for yogurt another time."

"But—"

"Tell Andie you're sorry for taking apart her clock," Eli instructed his son in a quiet, but no-nonsense voice.

Fletch dipped his head and gazed up at her. "I'm sorry, Andie."

"I know you are. It's okay." Andie's heart went out to him, to both of them. For all Eli's firm resolve, she could tell he didn't like meting out discipline. "You listen to what your dad says," she told him and smoothed his hair back from his forehead.

Eli frowned at the mess on the table. "Can I use the paper bag on the chair?"

"Sure." She watched in surprise as he swept the remains of her clock radio into the bag. "You don't have to fix it."

"I'm getting you a new one."

She rolled her eyes. "It's not necessary. I really don't—"

"I want to." His gaze captured hers with the same intensity he'd exhibited when he'd told her he didn't want Daphne. *I want you.*

A shiver ran down her spine. Distress and feminine anticipation tangled inside her. What could she say? *Don't make me want you. You could ruin me.*

He stepped closer and by the look in his eyes, she knew he wanted to kiss her, would have if Fletch hadn't been there. Instead, he lifted his hand to the curve of her jaw in a brief, yet possessive caress. "Stop running, Andie," he told her in a low, intimate voice.

She held her breath until they left, and lifted a trembling hand to where he'd touched her. Putting her other hand against her throat, she glanced around her kitchen. Everything looked the same. On the outside, it didn't appear that a tornado had raced through her and tumbled everything upside down. *Stop running, Andie.* Her heart squeezed tight. Could she stop? Could she stop and see what would happen? More important, did she dare?

"Are you mad at me?" Fletch asked, drinking his last swallow of milk. His stomach felt better after the peanut butter sandwich, but he was still afraid he was going to get in trouble.

"Not mad," his dad said as he tossed Fletch's paper plate into the trash can. "I'm not pleased about what you did with Andie's clock. What if someone had taken apart your clock? How would you feel?"

Fletch frowned. "I would have already taken apart my clock if I had one."

His dad closed his eyes and sighed. "If you didn't want your clock torn apart and you wanted to use it, how would you feel?"

That was hard for Fletch to imagine because he really liked looking at the inside of clocks better than the outside. He shrugged. "I dunno."

Dad sat next to him and nodded. "Okay. How would you feel if one of the neighborhood kids tore apart your boom box and it wouldn't play music anymore?"

Fletch loved playing tapes on his boom box. "I would be sad if my boom box didn't work," he said, and thought about Andie's clock. He felt ashamed. "Does that mean I made Andie sad?"

"Not this time. But it's wrong to take apart other people's things." Dad looked at him right in the eye.

That look made it hard for Fletch to sit still in the chair. "Even if I want to find out how they work?"

"Even if you want to find out how they work," he said in a firm voice. "You're a smart boy, and—"

"Not as smart as you are," Fletch pointed out.

His dad laughed. "The jury's still out on that one, but you're going to be curious about many things and you're going to have to tell yourself not to take things apart. If you've got questions, come talk to me. If you don't want people to tear up your things, then you can't take apart theirs."

Fletch didn't understand the stuff about the jury, but he and Mrs. G. had talked before about being curious. "Being curious isn't bad."

"Right." Eli messed with Fletch's hair and sort of smiled. "Being curious is actually good."

Fletch started to feel better inside until his dad stopped smiling. "There's one other thing. *Do not ever* go to another person's house without my permission."

"Even if I'm bored?"

"Even if you're bored. Daphne and I looked all over her house for you. When I couldn't find you—" His dad paused and shook his head. "I was scared."

Fletch was shocked. "But you're big. You're the dad. You don't get scared."

"I did when I couldn't find you." His dad pointed his finger at Fletch's chest. "How would you feel if you and I went somewhere and I left without telling you?"

His stomach turned. "I wouldn't like that. But I'm a kid."

"And I'm your dad," he said in a quiet voice. "And you're the most important thing in the world to me. I don't want to lose you."

Fletch got a warm gooey feeling inside him. "You're not gonna lose me," he assured him. "You said I'm stuck with you, so that means you're stuck with me, too."

"Good, but I need you to promise that you won't run off ever again without asking my permission."

Fletch jumped out of his chair and put his arms around his dad. He liked it when Dad squeezed him real tight. "I promise." He could think of only one reason why he'd ever break that promise, and he was determined to never let that happen.

Did she dare? That question preyed on Andie's mind over the next several days. Did she dare? Andie had never been much of a daredevil. She didn't smoke, didn't drink much, ate the right foods most of the time, and though she hated it, she dragged herself to a step aerobics class at the hospital two or three times a week.

After today's torture session, the instructor with the perky voice told everyone to give themselves a hand. Andie buried her face in a hand towel.

"Let's grab a quick shower and go across the street for cheesecake," Samantha whispered.

Andie groaned. "The reason we're exercising is to combat the effects of food like cheesecake."

"Right," Sam said with a nod. "We did combat. Now we get to eat turtle cheesecake."

Andie weakened. Turtle cheesecake was her favorite. Brushing aside thoughts of swollen arteries, bulging thighs and the harsh reality that swimsuit season had arrived, she surrendered. "Okay. In fifteen minutes."

For some reason, when Andie sat down in the small café to eat turtle cheesecake, her mind was drawn to Eli. The similarities between her favorite dessert and Eli plagued her while Samantha chattered on about Brad and how she didn't think he was the twentieth century's Mark Anthony after all.

It was the forbidden element, Andie decided, as she savored each bite. Distracted by her thoughts, she automatically exchanged a few pleasantries with the new surgeon Samantha introduced. After he left their table, Sam leaned forward, her eyes full of anticipation. "So what did you think?"

Andie blinked. "Of what?"

Sam rolled her eyes heavenward. "Not what. Who! What did you think of the new surgeon, Walter?"

Andie shrugged. "He seemed nice. I hear he's very talented."

Sam gave her a long-suffering glance. "I think that cheesecake did something to your brain cells. Walter's single," she said, counting off his attributes on her fingers. "He has *no* children. He drives a Corvette. He said he'd like to meet you. And I think he may be your long-lost French king."

Andie sighed and shook her heard. The only way to reason with her friend when she got this determined was to play along. "Sam, I don't know how to tell you this, but I'm not in the market for a reincarnated French king." She raised a hand when Samantha opened her mouth to protest. "Look at it from my point of view. If I were the favored courtesan to a French king, and that's a very big if, then I was in love with a man destined never to marry me. Why would I want to get involved with another French king type if I knew he might give me a good time in the sack and a few gifts but he would never make a commitment?"

Sam stared at her for a long moment and frowned. "I hadn't thought of that."

Suppressing a sigh of relief, Andie took the last bite of cheesecake and thought again of Eli.

"But we don't really know that Walter won't ever make a commitment. The important thing is that he doesn't have children. He told me he has season tickets to the symphony. I bet if I dropped a hint he'd invite you to Saturday night's performance."

"I can't do it. I've got other plans," Andie told her, hoping her friend wouldn't grill her. She signaled for the waiter.

"What are you doing?" Samantha asked, killing Andie's hopes.

"I'm going to a cocktail party with Eli Masters." She lifted her hand again when she saw Samantha's mouth open. "Don't say it. It's just a cocktail party."

"That's how it started with—"

"No, it didn't. My first date with Paul was a trip to the fair with him and his daughter. When I look back on it, Paul's daughter was more fun than he was." Andie paused. "Besides, Eli kisses better than Paul."

Samantha's openmouthed silence conveyed her complete astonishment more effectively than words. She tossed Andie a considering glance. "And what else does he do better than Paul?"

"I don't know, but I suspect quite a bit," she murmured, remembering how easily he'd aroused her. She glanced up to find her friend regarding her with a worried expression.

"Oh, Andie, you know, your hair hasn't grown back all the way yet," Sam said with a halfhearted smile.

Feeling a wave of turmoil rise inside her again, Andie lifted her fingers to her chin-length hair. She remembered when it had hung halfway down her back. A week after she'd broken up with Paul, she'd cut it off. At the time, she'd insisted her motivation for cutting it was merely that she needed a change. Looking back, she realized it had been an outer symbol of what was going on inside her.

The silence lengthened and Samantha's face turned serious. "Are you sure about this? I just don't want you to get hurt again."

Her heart caught. When she thought about Eli she wasn't sure of anything except that he drew her as no man had before. "I'm not sure, and I don't want to get hurt again, either. But it's not as if I've made any long-term plans that include Eli, and I certainly haven't promised eternity," she told Samantha with grim determination. "It's just a cocktail party."

The rest of the week passed in a blur. With summer vacations, the hospital was running short-staffed, so Andie pulled a few extra hours Wednesday morning after her Tuesday night shift. When she arrived home, she slept like a zombie until dinner time, then gave a presentation for a local community association. The next morning, her youngest brother, Drew, drove up from Wilmington to look at North Carolina State University. She led him on a walking tour and took him to lunch before sending him home.

By late afternoon, she was ready to crash again, but from past experience she knew she'd wake up at 3:00 a.m. and want to do something impossible like go shopping.

The sun was warm, but a gentle breeze and low humidity lured her outdoors. Still wearing her white cotton sundress from her earlier outing, she stretched out on a chaise lounge on her patio and dozed for a while. She awoke to the sound of a loud whisper.

"Do you think she's asleep?"

"Maybe," Eli said in a low voice.

"She looks like she's asleep," Fletch whispered.

With amusement, Andie wondered why a five-year-old's whisper had such an attention-getting capability. "She's not," she told them, opening her eyes. "She's just being lazy." Sitting up, she swung her legs around and smiled in surprise when she saw what Eli and Fletch had brought. Fletch held a bunch of daisies in his fist. Leaning against the big old maple tree, Eli carried a single red rose. Her heart clutched and she shook her head. "What's this?" she asked, standing.

"It was Fletch's idea," Eli said, his gaze traveling over her in warm masculine appreciation. "He wanted to bring you flowers as an apology." He glanced down at his rose and his mouth quirked in a wry grin. "We just had different ideas about what kind we should get you."

Fletch stepped forward and thrust the flowers in her hand. "I'm sorry 'bout what I did to your clock." He shifted from one foot to the other and bounced his fingertips against one another. "We got you a new one, and I put it on the porch. Dad says it's better than your old one."

Andie bit her lip at his frankness. At the same time she was incredibly touched. "That was very nice of you. You didn't have—"

"We wanted to," Eli said, his expression indicating there'd been a major discussion about this.

"Do you like the flowers?" Fletch asked, his face eager.

"Oh, I love daisies," she assured him, reaching down to hug his sturdy little body. The way Fletch snuggled against her plucked at her heart. She blinked at a sudden burning sensation in her eyes. Noticing a few of the stems still had clumps of dirt on the bottom of them, she tossed an inquiring glance at Eli. "They look freshly picked."

Eli cleared his throat. "That's another story."

Fletch gave her another quick squeeze and wiggled free. "Mizz Grandview said I could have 'em, but she made me promise to ask before I pick next time. Where's Stud?"

Andie pointed to a shady spot, and Fletch immediately took off.

Eli pushed away from the tree and walked closer. "We're fortunate Mrs. Grandview has a sense of humor."

Andie nodded and laughed softly. "I think she has a few grandsons who've helped her with pruning at one time or another."

"You've had a busy week," he said, and Andie felt his mercilessly thorough gaze clear to the bone. "You look—"

"Oh, please," she protested. Flustered, she pushed back her hair, suddenly realizing she was probably a mess. "I can imagine how I look."

"Fletch said you looked like Sleeping Beauty."

"Bless him. He can tear apart my clocks any time."

He handed her the rose. "I agree."

Her heart turning over at the look in his eyes, Andie ducked her head and smelled the rose to cover her heated cheeks. "Thank you. I really do love flowers." Feeling uncomfortable, she gestured toward Fletch. "How's he doing about his mother?"

"He doesn't talk about her much. I've tried, but he doesn't want to." He paused. "He still falls asleep crying sometimes."

Andie heard the restrained grief in his voice, and her heart went out to him, to both of them. The urge to touch his shoulder in comfort tied her in knots. Feeling as if she were fighting an instinct older than time, she swallowed hard. "I know it's tough right now, but it will get better eventually."

"I hope so," he said quietly. He glanced back at her, and his intent gaze was one more battle she had to fight. "We're going out for burgers in a few minutes. Come with us."

His directive put her off-balance. If he'd asked, she could have said no. Andie hesitated. "I don't—"

He studied her. "You're not still running, are you?"

For a second, Andie held her breath in indecision. A hovering self-protective urge to back away made her second-guess. Then she realized she was being ridiculous. For Pete's sake, it was just a burger, she told herself in exasperation, and she wasn't in the mood to cook tonight. "No," she finally said. "Thanks for inviting me. Just let me put my flowers in water."

Forty-five minutes later, Eli looked at Fletch's empty seat and half-eaten burger and shook his head. Not exactly the kind of dinner to start a new romance off with a bang, but when the lady wasn't cooperating a man had to modify his plans. Even with twenty-five kids screaming in the restaurant playroom. Eli felt a gut level sense of satisfaction that Andie was sitting across the table from *him*. "Remind me not to let Fletch pick the—" Eli glanced around the fast food restaurant "—dining establishment the next time we eat out."

"You were being a good father, one who believes in a child developing his sense of power by making his own decisions," Andie told him with a mock-serious expression on her face.

"Damn," he said. "And I thought it was because I didn't want him to whine while you were with us."

She laughed, and he wanted to absorb the warm, husky sound. It was as seductive as the touch of a feather on bare skin.

"I've heard whining before," she said, waving at Fletch through the window separating the restaurant from the indoor playground. "He was obviously more interested in the playground than the food." She glanced back at Eli and wrinkled her eyebrows in concern. "Is something wrong with your eyes? You keep rubbing them."

Eli glanced at the hand he'd just pulled away from his eyes. "I guess I'm doing it without thinking. Nonstop computer time is hell on my eyes. I spent the past three days in front of the computer, and I put in a few extra hours at home after Fletch went to bed."

"So that's eight during the day," she began with a lifted eyebrow.

"Or ten," he said with a shrug.

"Then three or four at night. Fourteen hours a day." She winced. "No wonder your eyes are irritated."

Eli bit back a grin. She sounded irritated, too. "I didn't have anything else to do," he said.

"You could watch a movie, especially now that you've discovered the Three Stooges."

"I'd still be watching a screen."

"What about closing your eyes and listening to a CD?"

He shook his head. "I'm too restless."

"You could always sleep. I understand even research scientists need rest."

His lips twitched at the concern in her voice. God, when had anyone given a damn how long he worked? "Can't rest," he told her. "Every time I go to bed, I end up thinking about my next-door neighbor."

He watched excitement flicker through her eyes before she mustered a chiding look. "You're being dif—"

"Andie! Andie!" A little girl darted toward her and flung her arms around her.

"Kendall." Andie's voice was full of surprise. "What are you doing here?"

Kendall pulled back but still held onto Andie's arm. "Bobby Richardson is having his birthday party. I got him some slime 'cause he likes gross stuff." She lifted her hand to Andie's hair. "You cut your hair. It's short now," she said in dismay.

Andie laughed and touched Kendall's long brown ponytail. "And yours has grown. It's beautiful." She glanced at Eli. "Kendall, this is my next-door neighbor, Eli."

Eli nodded at her. "Hello."

Kendall looked at him with shy blue eyes. "Hi." She glanced back at Andie. "I gotta go back to the party. We're getting ready to eat cake." She leaned forward to whisper something in Andie's ear, then darted away.

Andie looked after her with an expression of regret.

"One of your kids?" Eli asked, curious about the sad expression on her face.

She looked at him in confusion. "My kids?" Her eyes widened in comprehension before he could elaborate. "Oh, from the hospital." She shook her head and turned her gaze to Kendall again. "No, that was Paul's little girl. And she looks like she's grown a half a foot. Seeing her reminds me how much I've missed her."

The hint of longing in her voice clawed at his gut. He couldn't put his finger on why. Something that bordered on possessiveness trickled through him, but Eli knew that couldn't be right. He'd never felt possessive about a woman. And there was no reason for him to feel possessive about Andie. He made a steeple out of his hands and rubbed his forefingers together thoughtfully. "Does he call you?"

She looked at Eli, and he watched the war between regret and resolve in her brown eyes. "No. I asked him not to. The breakup was hard for Kendall, too, because I had often taken care of her when Paul—'' she hesitated ''—worked in the evenings. It wouldn't have been fair to play seesaw with Kendall's feelings. Children become attached so easily.'' As if she'd grown uncomfortable with the discussion, Andie shifted her attention to the table and stood. She put their trash on the serving tray. ''Do you think Fletch will want the rest of his burger?''

''No.'' He stood and joined her. ''It sounds like you took care of Kendall even after the breakup,'' he mused.

She shrugged and crumpled a paper wrapper. ''I tried.''

He saw the tension around her mouth and felt a corresponding tightness in his gut. The dark notion that Andie could also be missing her former fiancé burned like indigestion, and that no-way-it-could-be-possessiveness sense infiltrated again.

His mind clicking through the possibilities, he watched her carefully. He was doing what men through the ages had done about women—guess. Eli scowled, and the darkness inside him intensified. Andie took care of people as a matter of course. It seemed like second nature to her. Whom, he wondered, did Andie allow close enough to take care of her?

Chapter Eight

Andie poked a fingernail through her nylons at the same moment a knock sounded at her door. She swore, then glanced at the clock and moaned. "Just a minute," she yelled, knowing it was Eli. The knowledge did little to calm her nerves.

She shouldn't be nervous. There was no reason for it, she told herself. But deep inside, Andie felt a hum of anticipation, a buzz of excitement and a top-of-the-ferris-wheel sensation in her stomach. It had nothing to do with rubbing elbows with Raleigh's elite and everything to do with one man.

The reason she was going to such trouble over her appearance had more to do with the occasion than the man, though, she assured herself, and ignored the mocking hoot from her conscience. She had no illusions about being able to drop a man at fifty paces. She would just like to have him look and keep looking, want and keep wanting. Her stomach twisted at the unfulfilled feminine need and she tried to think about something else.

She took a deep breath and pulled out the only other black stockings in her drawer—a pair of thigh-highs she'd bought, but been too wary to try. She didn't trust the elastic, and the image of what she would look like if the elastic failed was almost enough to have her reaching for her white support hose.

She chewed her lip as she carefully pulled up the nylons. Relief and irony rushed through her when she finished. Her thighs were indeed sufficient to keep the elastic secure.

She heard the front door open. "Andie," Eli called.

Her heart raced at the sound of his voice. She pressed her hand to her chest. "I'll be out in a minute," she managed, and scowled when she glanced in the mirror and saw that she'd mutilated her lipstick. Her hands shaking too much to risk lip liner, she settled for gloss and a quick spritz of perfume that caught in her throat. Coughing, she stepped into heels, grabbed her purse and walked from her bedroom.

Rounding the hall corner, she stumbled over Stud and scraped her finger on a rough place on the door facing. "Well, darn," she muttered, bending to quickly pet the dog, who regarded her with wounded eyes.

Smooth, graceful, sophisticated.

In another life.

Andie hesitantly looked across the room in Eli's direction and drank in the sight of him. His shoulders looked impossibly, wonderfully wide in the dark suit jacket. The crisp white shirt emphasized his naturally tanned complexion. His tie was a bright splash of crimson color that could use the slightest adjustment, she thought. Her hands itched to take care of it.

Unnerved and compelled by the tension coiling inside her, she finally met his gaze. His expression was intent, and the look in his green eyes stopped her survey along with her heart.

Eli looked and kept looking. There wasn't anything leisurely about it. He had too much energy for that. No, he watched her with a knee-melting, resolve-busting thoroughness that had her breath backing up into her lungs. His gaze traced the square neckline of her black cocktail dress and lingered at her breasts. Her nipples tingled. She felt them jut against the lining of her dress.

He traced the curve of her waist and lower until her mind raced to the next step and she could almost swear he'd wrapped his hands around her hips. He studied her thighs with possessive intent, then contemplated the rest of her legs and feet. She didn't know exactly what he was contemplating, but the mere suggestion had her curling her toes inside her shoes. She sucked in a quick little breath and bit her lip.

Eli's head turned at the soft sound, and he walked toward her. "I don't want to take you to this party."

Uncertainty trickled through her. She swallowed over the lump in her throat. "You don't?"

"No. I—" he lifted his hand to fiddle with one of her dangling earrings "—I want to look at you without any distractions."

Her stomach flipped. "You do?"

"Yeah," he said, wrapping his finger around one of her curls. "Your hair's different."

"I rolled it," she said inanely, standing as still as a statue.

AN IMPORTANT MESSAGE FROM THE EDITORS OF SILHOUETTE®

Dear Reader,

Because you've chosen to read one of our fine romance novels, we'd like to say "thank you"! And, as a **special** way to thank you, we've selected <u>four more</u> of the <u>books</u> you love so well, **and** a Porcelain Trinket Box to send you absolutely _**FREE!**_

Please enjoy them with our compliments...

Nora Gavin Senior Editor,
Silhouette Special Edition

P.S. And because we value our customers, we've attached something extra inside ...

EDITOR'S
FREE
GIFT
SEAL
THANK YOU

PEEL OFF SEAL AND PLACE INSIDE

HOW TO VALIDATE
YOUR
EDITOR'S FREE GIFT
"THANK YOU"

1. Peel off gift seal from front cover. Place it in space provided at right. This automatically entitles you to receive four free books and a beautiful Porcelain Trinket Box.

2. Send back this card and you'll get brand-new Silhouette Special Edition® novels. These books have a cover price of $3.75 each, but they are yours to keep absolutely free.

3. There's no catch. You're under no obligation to buy anything. We charge nothing—ZERO—for your first shipment. And you don't have to make any minimum number of purchases—not even one!

4. The fact is thousands of readers enjoy receiving books by mail from the Silhouette Reader Service™ months before they're available in stores. They like the convenience of home delivery and they love our discount prices!

5. We hope that after receiving your free books you'll want to remain a subscriber. But the choice is yours—to continue or cancel, anytime at all! So why not take us up on our invitation, with no risk of any kind. You'll be glad you did!

6. Don't forget to detach your FREE BOOKMARK. And remember...just for validating your Editor's Free Gift Offer, we'll send you FIVE MORE gifts, *ABSOLUTELY FREE!*

YOURS FREE!

*This beautiful porcelain box is topped with a lovely bouquet of porcelain flowers, perfect for holding rings, pins or other precious trinkets — and is yours **absolutely free** when you accept our no risk offer!*

SILHOUETTE®

*WITH OUR
COMPLIMENTS*

THE EDITORS

THE SILHOUETTE READER SERVICE™: HERE'S HOW IT WORKS

Accepting free books places you under no obligation to buy anything. You may keep the books and gift and return the shipping statement marked "cancel". If you do not cancel, about a month later we will send you 6 additional novels, and bill you just $3.12 each plus 25¢ delivery and applicable sales tax, if any.* That's the complete price, and—compared to cover prices of $3.75 each—quite a bargain! You may cancel at any time, but if you choose to continue, every month we'll send you 6 more books, which you may either purchase at the discount price...or return at our expense and cancel your subscription.

*Terms and prices subject to change without notice. Sales tax applicable in N.Y.

If offer card is missing write to: Silhouette Reader Service, 3010 Walden Ave., P.O. Box 1867, Buffalo, NY 14269-1867

BUSINESS REPLY MAIL
FIRST CLASS MAIL   PERMIT NO. 717   BUFFALO NY

POSTAGE WILL BE PAID BY ADDRESSEE

SILHOUETTE READER SERVICE
3010 WALDEN AVE
PO BOX 1867
BUFFALO NY 14240-9952

NO POSTAGE
NECESSARY
IF MAILED
IN THE
UNITED STATES

"I like it." He cocked his head to one side consideringly. "I like it straight, too."

He dropped his hand to the golden puffed heart pendant resting against her chest and slid it between his fingers. "Pretty. Another gift?"

Despite the warmth of his hand near her breasts, Andie felt a breathless amusement at the slight edge in his voice. "I bought it to celebrate my first nursing job."

He nodded, and as if he couldn't keep from touching her, he abandoned the gold heart to cup her chin. She felt a swift visceral twist in her stomach at the way he studied her mouth. "Eli, didn't you say this cocktail party was mandatory?"

He sighed, but didn't move his hand or his gaze. "Yeah. Dr. Berylman said something about them holding it in my honor."

If he kissed her, it would be all over, Andie thought, her heart pounding against her rib cage. He could take her against the wall. And Eli looked as if that was just one of many blatantly sexual thoughts consuming his mind. It must have been the one drop of self-preservation she still possessed that helped her find her mental faculties and her voice. "We need to go," she told him, tilting her chin away from him and taking a step back.

Eli immediately reached for her, but Andie lifted her hand to block him. "We really need to go," she said as firmly as she could manage when his after-shave suggested he'd be better than turtle cheesecake.

He hesitated, then muttered something under his breath and crammed his fists into his pockets. "How long do you have to stay at a cocktail party?"

"Stay," she repeated, confused. "You mean how long does etiquette require you to stay at a cocktail party?"

He nodded. "Fifteen minutes should be adequate. Right?"

She looked at him in disbelief. "For a party where you're the guest of honor?" She shook her head. "I don't think so. You'd better plan on an hour or two."

"Why don't they just put me in hell?" he muttered under his breath.

He looked like a cornered tiger. Struck by a wave of commiseration, she stepped closer and adjusted his tie. "It won't be that bad. They'll probably fawn all over you and stuff you with hors d'oeuvres and—"

Eli caught one of her hands in his. "I don't want food."

His gaze flickered with a checked passion that caused a corresponding burn in her. Feeling the thunder of his heart beneath her hand, she cleared her throat and backed away. "Maybe you'll change your mind when you get there."

Her gaze swerved from his, flitting around until she saw the new clock radio on the counter. There was a rose on top of the clock. Her heart squeezed and she picked up the flower. "Eli, it's beautiful. You shouldn't have." She meant it. Roses and relationships and romance went together, and Andie wasn't sure she was ready to take on the three R's with Eli. "And the new radio sounds wonderful. But you really didn't have to get it for me."

There was a long pause before she heard him make a sound somewhere between a growl and a cough. Andie turned around and glanced at him curiously. He was rubbing his forehead. "Eli?"

He sighed and stared to the left of her. "Yeah, I should have. My son wrecked your clock and you needed a new one. But I didn't get it because I should have. I got it because I wanted to—" Breaking off, he swore in masculine frustration. "Andie, next time you decide to wear a dress that doesn't have a back, I'd appreciate a warning."

She had forgotten about the sheer insert in the back of the dress as soon as she'd put it on. "Well, it has one," she said. "It's just covered in—"

"Something as substantial as hydrogen."

"Nylon with little golden threads," she corrected, unable to tell if he liked it or not. "It's just my back."

Eli's jaw was so set it could have been chiseled from stone. He stepped closer. "Where's your cover-up?"

Indignation threatened inside her like a storm warning. "There is none," she told him. "And if there were, I wouldn't wear it in eighty-degree weather in June. Besides, it's not as if I'm baring my—" When Eli's gaze drifted down to her pendant, Andie suddenly changed her mind about bringing up the subject of her breasts. "Well, I'm not baring anything I shouldn't. Aren't you being a little stuffy?"

Eli blinked and his green eyes glinted dangerously. "Stuffy," he repeated, grinding his teeth. "You think I'm being stuffy when I'm trying to keep my colleagues' teeth marks out of your back."

The image was so ludicrous she exhaled in disgust. "Oh, now you're exaggerating." She stiffened her spine and looked up at him. "I'm sorry if you don't like this dress, but I do."

Eli's gaze meshed silently with hers for a long, heated moment, then he stepped closer and lifted his hand to cup her chin. "I didn't say I didn't like it. As

a matter of fact, I like it so much I want to remove it,"
he said in a low intimate voice that turned her to butter as he dipped his head toward hers. "I'd just as
soon stay here and find out what's underneath."

His mouth brushed hers and excitement raced
through her. Skimming back and forth with just
enough pressure to make her want more, it was the
most tantalizing kiss she'd ever experienced. "Stay?"
he asked against her lips.

Heaven help her, she was tempted. She knew, however, that Eli should make this appearance for the sake
of his career. And she still wasn't sure she should get
more deeply involved with him. Andie muffled a
moan. Her body and heart warred with her better
judgment. She thought about giving him what he
wanted, giving herself what she wanted, but she still
feared for her heart—the little organ wasn't quite
healed from a bad bruise.

"No, we need to go," she said, thinking he would
never know how much they needed to go. Avoiding his
gaze, she forced her feet to move in the direction of her
side door and walked outside. The hot, humid night
offered little respite from her simmering, turbulent
emotions.

Within seconds, Eli joined her and opened the car's
passenger door for her. Resting his hand on the door,
he looked down at her as she slid in. "I don't think
you understand the scientific mind. Every man in my
lab will look at your dress and dedicate himself to
solving the logistical question of what kind of bra
you're wearing."

Bemused, Andie stared at him. She shook her head.
"The salesclerk told me I didn't really—" She quickly

shut her mouth before she spouted the rest of the salesclerk's wisdom.

"Didn't really what?"

Uncomfortable, Andie glanced away. "Well, she said I wouldn't need—" Feeling her cheeks flood with heat, she broke off again. Torn between embarrassment and irritation, she wondered what it was about the way he asked a question that compelled her to answer. "Must we discuss this?"

"Okay," he relented in a low voice. "As long as you understand that every man in my lab includes me."

Her heart pounded in an unfamiliar, heady rhythm. She looked at him and fought the excitement and the faintest trickle of secret guilt. It hadn't been her goal to drive Eli crazy, but she had to admit the idea was decadent and exhilarating.

He narrowed his eyes in comprehension. As if he could read her like a book, his gaze dropped to her breasts. "You're not wearing one at all," he said and swore under his breath. "Next, you'll be putting bamboo sticks under my fingernails," he muttered, and slammed her car door closed.

They drove to the cocktail party in silence. All that internal masculine energy Eli kept restrained seemed ready to burst forth any minute. He exuded so much of it Andie wondered how the car contained it all; she had never been so aware of being a mere mortal woman of average intelligence and energy. She felt distinctly out of her league.

They entered the elegantly appointed and spacious home of Dr. Berylman, the director of the research center, and they were immediately surrounded. Nearly tripping over his tongue with praise, the director patted Eli on the back and introduced him to a studious-looking group of men. Heads turned, people whispered and nodded. Andie noticed several others jockeying for position to meet Eli. Within five minutes, Andie learned something about Eli.

He was obviously the king of this jungle.

He was also having to work at maintaining a polite facade of interest. With all the shifting and introductions, Andie soon got separated from Eli. She took advantage of the opportunity to get something cool to drink.

A thin dark-haired young woman stood beside her and nodded. "The Chablis is nice," she said.

Andie shook her head and patted her evening purse. "My beeper's in here. I'm on call at the hospital tonight, so I have to stick with ginger ale. Andie Reynolds," she said, extending her hand.

"Dr. Rachel Cudahey," the woman said, shaking Andie's hand. "I notice you arrived with Dr. Masters. I work with him in the lab."

It took a moment for that to compute. "Oh, Eli," Andie said, amused at her momentary inability to connect Dr. Masters with Eli.

Rachel regarded her curiously. "You know him well?"

Not as well as she'd like to. She tripped over the unchecked thought. "We're neighbors," she told Rachel.

"Hey, Rachel, looks like our golden boy is setting them on their ears tonight," a man said in a dry voice as he approached.

Irritation flickered across Rachel's features. "Dr. Sampson, meet Andie Reynolds, Dr. Masters's guest for the evening. She's his neighbor."

In his early thirties with a receding hairline, Dr. Sampson looked abashed for all of one moment. "Pardon me, and please call me Bill." He stared at Andie. "I didn't expect Dr. Masters to bring someone with him, particularly such an attractive woman."

Rachel rolled her eyes. "Forgive him. He has the social manners of a cow."

Undaunted, Bill went on. "Rachel's as curious as I am. She's just too uptight to admit it." He leaned forward in a confiding manner. "So tell me what do you and the great Masters talk about?"

Taken aback, Andie's mind went blank. She hesitated. "Well . . ."

Bill lifted an eyebrow and gave her a considering look. "Or maybe you don't do much talking."

Rachel tossed Bill a withering glance. "You're such an idiot. Andie is a doctor at the hospital."

"She is?"

"No, I'm not. I'm a nurse," Andie told them.

While the uncomfortable silence hung for a moment, she let that information sink in. She realized his co-workers were bursting with curiosity about Eli. Otherwise she could have been offended. "Eli and I have discussed his son, his brothers, my dog, my work, automobile maintenance and the Three Stooges," she added on a wry note. "That's not a complete list, but since I've answered your question, I'd like you to answer one of mine."

"Of course," Rachel said. "Brothers? I didn't know he had brothers."

"Younger," Andie told her. "Caleb and Ash."

Bill chuckled. "The Three Stooges," he said absently, confirming Andie's theory about the widespread appeal of the Stooges among men.

"So, what kind of woman did you expect Eli to bring tonight?"

"None," Rachel said.

"A brain-surgeon type," Bill said at the same time.

"He doesn't even notice women at the lab," Rachel argued, and Andie thought she detected a bit of feminine pique.

"I didn't expect a looker, more of a cerebral type. Definitely someone in Mensa and..."

Bill was still talking, but Andie's mind hung on two words, *looker* and *Mensa*. She didn't know whether to be flattered or offended. She'd never been called a looker, and she'd never been overly concerned about her average intelligence. Until now.

Feeling a hand on her back, in the middle of the nylon cutout, she turned around to face a tall blond man.

He smiled. "Hello there, I'm Dr. Tim Wollking. I'm sure we haven't met."

"Andie Reynolds," she said, stepping slightly away. Unfortunately Dr. Wollking's hand followed.

"Lovely dress," he murmured, gazing at her black chemise as if he'd like to take it apart. Eli's comment floated back to her.

"Thank—"

"Andie." She heard Eli's voice and felt his hand on her arm. The strangest relief ran through her.

"Rachel, Bill." Eli nodded, then fixed his gaze on the man whose hand had rested on Andie's back. Eli wasn't prone to violence, but he'd nearly snapped his wineglass when he'd seen Wollking moving in on Andie. "Dr. Wollking. You've met my—" he paused, stifling a primitive urge to say my woman "—date."

Wollking nodded, but still eyed the back of Andie's dress.

Bill cleared his throat nervously. It seemed to Eli that Bill was always nervous. "Yes, Dr. Masters, she mentioned that she's your neighbor."

"Yes." *My neighbor, my date, my lover,* if he had anything to do with it. Feeling Andie's curious gaze on him, Eli reined himself under control. "Dr. Berylman missed meeting her. You'll have to excuse us. Enjoy your evening. Good to see you, Rachel," he managed to say, thinking his limited supply of social small talk was nearly depleted. He led Andie away.

"Interesting people," she murmured. "Are all of them in your lab?"

"Wollking's at the same center, but not in my lab. He's very competitive."

"Didn't you say that about Caleb?"

"Caleb's different." He waved to an approaching colleague, but kept moving. "He wouldn't stab you in the back. He'd just run himself into the ground to win a race with a different research group."

"And Wollking would," she mused. "He seemed a little—"

"Lecherous," Eli supplied grimly as he turned the corner away from the bulk of the party guests. "I saw his hand on your back. He was trying to look down the front of your dress."

"Is this where you say I told you so?" Andie asked.

Eli drew in a deep breath and stopped in the hallway. He looked at her, and despite her testiness, he felt the same strange combination of relief and excitement he always felt when he was with her. He shook his head, wondering why. "Saying I told you so would be redundant."

She held his gaze for a moment as if she couldn't decide whether to remain irritated with him or not, then she glanced away. "You know Bill and Rachel are dying of curiosity about you."

Eli did a mental double take. "You must be mistaken. They know my qualifications, degrees and—"

Andie shook her head. "But what do they know about you personally?"

Eli drew back. "Nothing. I make a point of separating my professional life from my personal life."

Andie nodded slowly with a considering expression on her face. "What do you know about Bill?"

Eli called up the stats in his memory. "He graduated at the top of his class in chemistry. He's published several articles in assorted professional journals, won an award for a paper he wrote when he was working on his doctorate."

Andie shrugged. "And personally?"

Eli thought of the one way he could characterize Bill. "He's nervous."

"Around you. This sounds like a wonderful work environment."

Determined not to take offense, he watched her. "You're being sarcastic."

She crossed her arms over her chest. "Yes. Is the reason you don't develop some sort of relationship with one another because the competition is so fierce?"

Eli thought about that. "No. But researchers do their share of moving around."

"Don't you think the group might work together more cohesively if you knew one another a little better?"

"You're suggesting some sort of bonding activity," he said, unable to hide his distaste. "Perhaps a communication retreat."

"No." Andie sighed. "Nothing that formal or time-consuming. Just a backyard barbe—"

He groaned. "Save me."

Andie's chin lifted. "Say what you want, Dr. Masters, but your two colleagues were pumping me for every bit of information I would give. They don't really know you at all. Bill pictured you with a brain surgeon, Mensa type of woman. Not a looker, he said." Andie shook her head as if she still couldn't comprehend it. "He doesn't get out much, does he?"

Eli was trying to sift through her various comments. He chuckled. "It's good to know Bill has such good taste."

She rolled her eyes. "That's not the point. The point is if they want to know, why don't they ask you?"

Eli shrugged. "I don't know. Maybe they're intimidated. It doesn't matter if it doesn't affect their work." He found her concern both heartwarming and exasperating. "You don't understand research labs. We operate from a scientific point of view. You operate from a more nurturing..." Eli's words faded as he saw from Andie's facial expression that he'd offended her.

Her eyes flashed and she let out her breath in a little huff. "What you're saying is that since I'm not in Mensa, my poor little brain couldn't begin to comprehend your complex world." She pointed to her chest. "Surely I couldn't offer any helpful advice...."

Andie was just starting to wind up when Eli heard the voices of approaching guests. He swore under his breath. Refusing to go back into that crowd, he glanced around and spotted a door. He jerked it open and pulled her into a large closet.

She gave a muffled squeak of surprise. "What—"

Eli covered her mouth with his hand. "Shh." Through the cracks around the door, light from the hall filtered into the small cubicle. He looked down into Andie's wide-eyed gaze of astonishment and kept his hand over her mouth even when the guests had passed. Lord, he'd never been this frustrated in his life, sexually, mentally, emotionally. Her self-deprecating little speech had nearly driven him nuts.

Taking a deep breath to get a grip, he shook his head. "You think you're not a looker," he said in disbelief.

Her eyes widened.

He backed her toward the wall. "You actually think I don't consider you a damn intelligent woman."

She made a muffled sound that vibrated against his hand.

"Miss Reynolds, you have underestimated yourself." He chuckled grimly and lifted his other hand to her hip. "I believe it's time I showed you just how much you've underestimated yourself. Time I showed you exactly what I think of you."

Chapter Nine

Andie stared into Eli's eyes and nearly fainted with shock. He removed his hand from her mouth and she sucked in a quick, shallow breath. "You're going to show me in a closet!"

Unfazed by the shrill note in her voice, he kept his gaze on her with singular intent. "If necessary." He dropped his lips to her neck, making her heart race.

A wicked, wicked thrill raced through her. "Oh, Eli, we—we—" His mouth swallowed her protest. His tongue slid deliciously past her lips and every cell in her body responded.

Eli tugged the skirt of her dress upward and skimmed his hand down to the top of her thigh. He stopped when he connected with bare flesh. Dragging his mouth from hers, he heaved a broken breath. His green eyes latched onto hers with laserlike intensity. "I can feel your skin," he said in husky amazement and gently squeezed her bare thigh. "*What* are you wearing?"

His touch was an intimate hug. Andie bit her lip. "Thigh-high stockings," she managed breathlessly. "They stay up with—"

Eli groaned. "God help me, I'm imagining what you look like in your stockings, heels and nothing else."

Another wild, decadent thrill shot through her, weakening her knees. "Eli, we can't do this," she whispered as she clung to him. "We're in your director's home," she said, grasping for some shred of sanity even as he nuzzled her neck again. "This can't be happening. This kind of thing doesn't happen to me. Men don't act crazy around me." When he nudged her dress past one shoulder, she moaned. He was so warm, so solid, so aroused. "I'm the sister type, the girl next door, faithful friend—"

Eli gave a growl of frustration, and gently but firmly shoved her dress down her arms baring her breasts. He sucked in a deep breath and his eyes filled with desire. "Oh, Andie, you might be a faithful friend, and you might live next door, but you are definitely not my sister." He lifted his hands to cup her breasts. "You're so beautiful."

Her breath stopped. She couldn't speak, wasn't sure she could think, could only feel. His thumbs brushed her nipples and she closed her eyes in pleasure.

His mouth covered hers again and she was lost in the slide of his tongue on hers, the caress of his large warm hands on her breasts. He made her feel sexy. It was a heady, addicting sensation.

"Softer than a rose petal," he murmured against her mouth as he stroked her nipples. "I've got to taste you." Before she could take a breath, he lowered his head and took her into his mouth.

Andie cried out at the sweet, raw sensation that tightened from her breasts to her thighs. Craving the way he made her feel, she lifted her hands to his head and slipped her fingers through his hair. He aligned her intimately to him, branding her with the knowledge of his hardened masculinity.

He lifted his head, kissing her fingers as her hands cradled his face. His eyes nearly black with desire, he deliberately nudged his arousal between her thighs. "This is how you affect me, faithful friend."

Instinctively, she clamped her thighs closed around him. "Ohhhh, Eli, you're so—"

He thrust again, and she moaned. He gave her a swift, sensual French kiss. "So what?" he prodded, and slid his hand inside her panties.

"So good," she whispered. "So hard." One of his fingers found her most sensitive spot. "Oh, God."

"You're wet," he said with rough, masculine approval. He slid his finger inside her. "And you're tight." Her moan mingled with his groan. "Touch me," he told her and brought her hand to his erection.

Compelled by the appealing masculine need in his voice, she fumbled past his zipper and briefs and wrapped her fingers around his swollen shaft. He blew out his breath in a quick stream, then took her mouth again and stroked her with teasing, taunting strokes.

Inside her she could feel the beat of her heart, could practically hear it. Insistent and fast, the high-pitched sound didn't distract. It only added to her sense of urgency. Andie felt herself spiraling toward a dangerously steep crest and something inside her snapped.

"You're still dressed," she said, tugging at his tie, pulling at his shirt.

"Andie," he murmured in a soothing voice, but his fingers still taunted her.

Wanting more, needing more, she ran her hands over his flat abdomen and pressed her open mouth to his throat. Eli made a rough yearning sound that tore at her. She glanced down at the sight of his jutting masculinity and a wicked, shocking image nearly had her kneeling before him.

She began to tremble. "Eli, I need—I need—" She still heard the high-pitched sound of her heart.

"I know," he said, nuzzling her. "I do, too." His chest swelled against hers. His hand stilled. "For God's sake, where is that sound coming from?"

It's my heart, she almost said, but frowned. She pressed her hand to her chest. The rhythm of her heart wasn't the same as the sound she heard. Confused, she stumbled backward. "What—"

Eli steadied her.

Still unbearably aroused, she lifted her hand to her head and tried to focus, but his scent made her dizzy. She closed her eyes, listened, and gradually the realization dawned. She took a shallow unsteady breath. "It's my beeper." Muffling a sound that was half-sob and half-moan, she looked down for where she'd dropped her purse. "I'm on call."

"Call," Eli repeated.

At the same time that Andie spotted her purse and bent down to retrieve it, voices sounded in the hall. Her gaze locked with Eli's as the voices came closer.

"Cut off the beeper," he told her quietly and adjusted his clothing.

Apprehension racing through her, Andie fumbled with her bag and tried to pull up her dress at the same time. She nearly wailed when she couldn't find the switch to stop it.

He stretched out his hand. "Let me."

Andie found the damn switch and felt a trickle of relief. "Thank good—"

Eli lifted his finger to his lips and stepped in front of her. Footsteps stopped outside the closet door. Her heart rose to her throat. The voices could be clearly heard. With a sense of unreality, Andie listened and she looked at shelves and shelves of sheets, towels and blankets.

"Which one is the bathroom?"

"I can't remember. Did she say it was on the left or the right?"

The doorknob turned, Andie held her breath and squished her eyes closed. An old habit from childhood; if she couldn't see them, then they couldn't see her.

The door cracked open.

She bit her lip.

"Looks like a closet."

The door closed. Andie sagged with relief. She ruffled a hand through her hair and made sure the top of her dress was in place. "We have got to get out of here!" she whispered emphatically. "Now." She stepped around Eli.

His hand reached out to stop her.

A thread of hysteria ran through her. Andie shook her head. "Eli, I can't stay in here one minute longer."

"Andie—"

"I would die if anyone found out what we were—" she swallowed hard, her face flaming with the knowledge of just how far they'd gone "—doing in here."

"Andie," he began again.

"I've got to go."

Eli put his hands on her arms. "Less than one minute," he corrected. Andie watched him pull the skirt of her dress down over her hips, past her bare thighs, back into place. At that point, she realized that if Eli hadn't stopped her, she would have walked out in front of the cream of Raleigh's academia with the top of her thigh-highs and her skimpy lace panties in full view.

She met his gaze. The gentle affection in his eyes warmed her. She took a deep breath and tried for a little smile. "Thanks," she murmured, and smoothed his hair with her fingers.

He caught her hand and kissed it. "Any time, Andie," he murmured, then opened the door and checked the doorway. Offering his arm, he looked at her and shook his head. "The only good thing I can say about your beeper is that it's getting me away from this party. If it goes off again, don't be surprised if I give it to Fletch."

Within minutes, they made their excuses, thanked the host, and were riding home. In the silent darkness of the car, Andie was still trying to come to grips with her wanton behavior.

"You shouldn't beat yourself up about it," Eli said.

She sighed and looked out the window. "Eli, I have never ever done anything like that in my life."

He chuckled and loosened his tie. "Then it was about time."

She gaped at him. "I'm not the kind to—"

"You didn't find it exciting," he cut in in a neutral tone.

That brought her up short. She couldn't lie. She'd never been that aroused in her life. "I—uh—it was exciting," she admitted in a low voice.

"That's putting it mildly," he muttered, shifting gears. "Did I push you to do something you didn't want—"

"Oh, no," Andie said, shaking her head. "I wanted—to. I wanted you."

"And I wanted you. I still want you." He reached for her hand. "What's behind the faithful friend story?"

She curled her fingers around his, relishing the warmth and strength of his hand. "You know, different women tend to have different images with men." When he remained silent, she was thankful for the darkness inside the car. "For example, Madonna's a sex symbol. Daphne's—"

"A barracuda," he supplied dryly.

She swallowed her amusement. "I was going to say a femme fatale." She sighed. "And then there's the woman who's the girl next door, the one you call when you need a friend, the one you can depend on, but you just don't think of her in a sexual way."

Eli was quiet for a long moment. "Why do you keep saying *you?*"

"It wasn't personal," she said. "It was a generic comment about my history with men."

Eli nodded. "You've been involved with idiots." He kept her hand in his as he downshifted and exited the freeway.

She laughed softly. "You sound like Samantha."

Eli didn't laugh. Through the lights of the oncoming traffic, Andie saw Eli's face tight, his eyes narrowed. "You should know that I haven't had many serious relationships with women," Eli said. "Between my education and research there hasn't been time. Fletch's mother, Gail, and I met at a party. We saw each other a few times. When she got pregnant, I convinced her we should get married."

He pulled to a stop and still held her hand. "It was a mistake. She said I was book-smart and people-stupid." He gave a short, bitter laugh. "She said she hoped Fletch didn't turn out like me."

Andie sucked in a sharp breath. Even hearing Gail's remarks secondhand, the words hurt. She shook her head. "That was incredibly cruel to both you and Fletch."

"Yes. Cruel, but true." When she protested, he gently squeezed her hand and shook his head. "I didn't understand Gail, and she didn't really understand me." His mouth twisted grimly. "I have little patience and minimal tolerance for social conventions. I've been told I'm rude and insensitive, and before I got custody of Fletch, I'd gotten to the point where I didn't give a damn about much."

She remembered Eli had told her that he once went through a stage like Caleb, when he lived in the lab. He wasn't painting a pretty picture, and if Andie went by his words, she would run in the opposite direction. If he wasn't holding her hand, she would think he was trying to warn her off. Instead she was totally confused. "Why are you telling me this?"

"Because I want you to know what you've gotten into." He pulled into her driveway and stopped the car, then turned to her. "And you *have* gotten into something with me. Things are different for me now. There's Fletch and there's you."

Andie met his gaze, helpless to look away, yet unable to pull her thoughts together. Her heart was beating too hard.

"I have two regrets about what happened in that closet tonight. One, that we didn't finish what we started. Two, that what we did embarrassed you."

She glanced away. "It wasn't so much what we did as where we did it," she said quickly. "Or maybe it wasn't even where we were as much as the idea of how horrible I would have felt if someone had seen." She was afraid of leaving something out. "It probably wouldn't have been the end of the world if someone had seen. I just—"

Eli put his hands on her shoulders to halt her breathless explanation. "Next time, we won't be in a closet," he promised, then he kissed her.

After a busy emergency shift at the hospital and a lot of soul-searching, Andie wasn't so sure *next time* was a good idea after all. Eli wasn't really pleased when she conveyed her doubts to him. He'd been going through some old lab boxes in his garage when he'd spotted her taking Stud for a walk on the sidewalk. Wearing a T-shirt and worn jeans with old protective glasses hanging around his neck, he was in his element.

"What do you mean we might need to slow down?" he demanded, standing over her with a proprietary attitude.

Andie twisted Stud's leash. "I just don't think we need to rush into anything."

"Rushing," he said, clearly unhappy with her choice of words. "Rushing is getting together the first night you meet, the first week. We're into the second month."

"I'm talking more about emotional time," Andie told him in a quiet voice. She self-consciously waved at the man across the street, who was staring at them as he trimmed his hedges. "A relationship doesn't necessarily develop on schedule."

"Fletch," he called toward the garage, then trained his wary gaze on her. "Emotional time." He muttered the words skeptically. "Is this one of those women things?"

Andie could tell her explanation wasn't washing with Eli. She tried again. "Not really. Usually relationships are affected by people's histories and—"

"Fletch! Come here!" Eli called again, then turned back to her. "Excuse me," he muttered, looking as if he was struggling for patience. "You know my history and I know as much of yours as you've told me. You know I married someone I shouldn't have. I know you were engaged to an idiot. I want you. You want me. What else is there?"

If only it were that simple. Andie gave a distracted wave in response to Mrs. Grandview's greeting and sighed. "It's not that easy. Even *you* said there's more involved here. There's Fletch."

"Fletch is fine," Eli told her. "We've discussed it, and we both like you better than Daphne. Fletch is fine," he repeated emphatically.

At that moment, a loud boom sounded from the garage.

Eli's face went rigid with alarm. Swearing, he ran toward his house. "Fletch!"

Her heart racing a mile a minute, Andie followed him. Distantly she heard the excited voices of her neighbors as they gathered at Eli's gate.

"Dr. Frankenstein strikes again," one man said.

"Maybe we should back off," another muttered. "Next thing you know there'll be a mushroom-shaped cloud coming from that house."

Her feet automatically skimmed over the ground. She was so intent to see Fletch that she nearly ran into Eli's broad back.

"Fletch," Eli said, as he ran his hands over his son. "Are you okay? Is anything hurt?" Andie's heart constricted at the way Eli checked Fletch's face and counted the little boy's fingers. "Good Lord, what happened?"

Backed into the corner, Fletch looked as if he were all wide green eyes and pale skin. He bounced his fingertips together and shook his head. "I just—I just—" He gulped. "I just put some of your Play-Doh in the sink."

"Play-Doh," Eli echoed, his brow wrinkling in confusion. "I don't have any Play-Doh out here."

Eli nodded vigorously and pointed toward the sink where a puff of smoke still hovered. "Yes, you do. It's gray and it was in one of your little bottles. It had an *N* and an *a* on it."

Comprehension dawned on Eli's face. "Oh, my God." Glancing at Andie, he wiped his hand over his forehead. "Sodium," he told her, his face pale. "Mixing pure sodium and water is explosive. . . ." He turned to Fletch and brought him close.

"It was a really loud 'splosion. Are you mad at me?" Fletch asked anxiously.

"No," Eli said, shaking his head. "No. I'm just waiting for my heart rate to approach normal." He eased slightly away from Fletch and looked down at him. "You could have been hurt, son. We're going to have to talk about playing with chemicals. And I'm putting my lab materials under lock and key."

Eli glanced at Andie and she saw the distress still drawing his features tight. "Is there anything I can do?"

"Not now. Not unless I have a coronary," he added with a forced, rough chuckle. He met her gaze, turmoil darkening his eyes to forest green.

With no defense against the dichotomy of Eli's strength and vulnerability, she reached out and touched his arm. "Are you sure you two are going to be okay?" she asked.

He slipped his hand through hers in a move that bonded her to him. She felt it past her skin and nerve endings, deeper than her blood, clear to her bones. Could one brief touch change her?

Reluctantly releasing her hand, he drew a breath. "Yeah, we'll be okay." Still holding her with his gaze, he took Fletch by the hand. "You and I will finish our discussion later," he said in a low but firm voice, then led Fletch into the house.

Her hand at her throat, Andie stared after them. She had to resist the urge to gather Fletch in her arms to relieve his fear and her own. *Explosive.* She shuddered when she considered what could have happened.

"It's dangerous having them in the neighborhood," one of the men standing just inside the gate said.

Protective instincts nearly bursting from her, Andie wheeled around and walked toward them. Ed Kenworth, the father of twins, was shaking his head.

"It's not dangerous," she said. "This was an accident. You've had your share of accidents with Timmy and Jonathan."

"My kids get into normal accidents."

"Getting washed halfway down the river in a canoeing accident is normal?"

Ben Hammond crossed his arms over his chest. "Daphne doesn't like him, either."

Andie thought about pulling out Daphne's long black hair the next time she saw her. "Which child," she asked, "does Daphne really like?"

Ed looked uncomfortable. "Well, he's not like all the other kids."

Andie resisted the urge to chew him out. Instead she took a calming breath. "You're right. He's a gifted little boy who recently lost his mother and has been uprooted to a new neighborhood where he doesn't know anyone. The question is, are you helping or hurting him with your attitude?"

Chastened, Ed ducked his head. "Hell, Andie, I'm not trying to hurt him. That explosion nearly gave me a heart attack."

"Me, too," she admitted. "And probably everyone else. But we all reacted the same way when Jennifer walked into that beehive last summer."

"Yeah." Ed nodded and looked toward the garage. "If he's gonna keep this stuff in the garage, he'd better either lock it up or attach a shelf to the ceiling. And if his kid's half as curious as Timmy or Jonathan, he might need to do both."

"Damn chemicals are like having a gun in the house," Ben said. "Mary is always nagging me to keep my hunting rifles locked up. I'll give little Fletch the benefit of the doubt, here, but you better tell Eli there's no way Mary'll let the kids come over here if he doesn't do something about that lab."

"Eli already said he's locking them up," Andie insisted. "I'm sure you can imagine how alarmed he was."

Ed nodded, his face etched with a trace of sympathy. "Yeah, well nobody ever said raising kids was easy on your nerves." He eyed her curiously. "Something brewing between you and Masters?"

At a loss, Andie shrugged. "They're my next-door neighbors. Fletch plays with Stud a lot, and Eli fixed my car once." *I care about them. Probably too much.* Her throat tightened at the unspoken words.

Ben nodded. "Well, tell Eli we're glad everybody's okay." They shuffled out the gate. Andie stared after them, torn between an overwhelming instinct to return to Eli and the sensible thought to go home. She took Stud for a short walk and led him home, then followed her nagging instinct back to Eli's garage.

Eli had never felt more grim in his life. Lost in his self-disgust, he sat on a bench and sifted through the contents of his lab boxes. He dreaded finding the other potentially dangerous combinations that lurked in the benign-looking cardboard.

"How's Fletch?" Andie asked from behind him.

At the sound of her warm soft voice, his gut tightened. He looked up at her. "He's fine. Taking a nap right now, so I decided to get through these chemicals." A bitter taste filled his mouth as the thought hit him again that Fletch could have been injured. He turned his attention back to the box, the reality hanging through his mind. "God, he could have been hurt."

"And you're blaming yourself."

Eli rejected her comfort. He was blaming himself, and he damn well should. As far as he was concerned the situation was straightforward. "I'm the adult. I'm the parent. I'm the one responsible."

He heard her move closer. "But you couldn't have dreamed he would put water and sodium together."

"Maybe," he conceded, narrowing his eyes as he continued sifting through the box. "But it's my job to prevent accidents, to keep him safe. And it sure as hell looks like I'm doing a lousy job of it."

"You are not," she insisted. "You expect yourself to be a perfect parent, and parenting is not an exact science."

Eli frowned. She hit him at a vulnerable spot. He was far more comfortable with science than with parenting. With Fletch, the stakes were too high to experiment. Frustration trickled through him. "Why do you know so much about this when you haven't had kids?"

"I practically raised my three brothers. You wouldn't believe the stuff they got into. They did everything from setting the house on fire to getting lost in the woods overnight to borrowing candy from the candy store without paying for it. Surprisingly enough, they survived their childhood. I did, too." She tugged him around to face her and knelt between his knees. "You and Fletch will, too."

Her face was so earnest, her eyes so warm. "I'd like to believe you."

She lifted her hand to his jaw, and he wanted to absorb her into his ravaged conscience.

"Then do," she said. "The road's going to be bumpy. You might need some of those shock—things—"

Eli cracked a grin at the way she waved her other hand as she searched for the right word. "Absorbers," he supplied, then stopped depriving himself and drew her closer. "How come you're so damn sweet to a mediocre parent like me?"

Andie's soft laughter vibrated against his throat as she slipped her arms around the back of his neck. "What an ego. There's nothing mediocre about you, and you know it."

He inhaled her scent and rubbed his lips against her hair. "Then why do you need to slow down? Why do you need more time?"

He felt her long sigh. "I think it's more me than you."

"Running?"

"No, just standing still and thinking."

Eli groaned. "Chicken."

She pulled back slightly, her eyebrows puckered in irritation. "I really don't like that term."

"Then prove me wrong."

For a long moment, she wanted to. Her brown eyes said it all. *Take me, let me take you.* That glance made him ache. Then she took a short breath and seduction turned to vulnerability just before she looked away. "I don't—"

"Yeah, yeah," Eli said before she could push him away. "You need *emotional* time." He nuzzled her neck. "It doesn't have to be all or nothing, Andie."

"No?" she said doubtfully, and looked up at him from hooded eyes.

"No." He kissed her because he needed to and he hoped like hell she did, too. She was warm and responsive, filling up his empty places, at the same time digging his well of need for her deeper. His heart pumped against his rib cage, and he wanted to pull her against him, onto him. He slipped his tongue past her lips, and her taste was so full of promise he wanted to howl.

He pulled away with a groan, and her dazed, sensual expression was one more scrape across his deprived soul. "It doesn't have to be all or nothing," he assured her, then forced a rough chuckle. "It just feels like it does."

Chapter Ten

Her mother used to call it the blues.

Andie called it the pits.

She wished she could blame it on the weather, but the sun was persistently, annoyingly bright. Her current patients were progressing well, so it wasn't that. Eli wasn't pushing. In fact, he'd given her the space she requested.

So, Andie wondered, why did she feel like sighing? She could practically hear the heartrending sound of violins in the back of her mind. Why did she feel down? She brooded over the feeling as she finished her shift and walked through the hospital hallway.

"Earth to Andie," Sam said, stepping in front of her. "Must have been one heck of a shift."

Andie stopped and gave her friend a sheepish smile. "Sorry. I guess I'm a little tired. How's everything with Brad?"

"I dumped him," she said cheerfully. "He probably won't realize it until he gets through this rotation." She cocked her head to one side thoughtfully as she joined Andie on her path toward the exit. "I'm a little worried about my sister, though. She's got three kids. Her husband has left her. And she's running as wild as a March hare."

"Your younger sister?"

Sam nodded and made a face. "Guess who's been baby-sitting lately?"

Andie bit back a grin. "Your opportunity to experience all those repressed maternal urges."

"Not funny." She looked at Andie. "You really do look kinda down. Something wrong?"

Andie groaned. "Not really. I just have this irrational urge to rent a slew of sad videos and cry."

"Yuck. Are you sure it's not related to monthly hormonal variations?"

"Yeah." Andie pushed open the door. "Maybe I haven't eaten enough chocolate lately."

"Could be. To my way of thinking, you should be celebrating. This time last year you'd just dumped Paul and shaved your head."

Andie stopped in her tracks. She looked at Sam. Sam looked at her. Andie grimaced as the realization hit her. "My wedding—"

"Your wedding—" Sam said at the same time. She nodded. "When was it exactly?"

The date was branded on her brain. "This weekend a year ago."

Sam frowned. "I'm working this weekend."

"So am I. It's no big deal," she said, determined to believe it and irritated with herself that she'd been moping over Paul.

"Are you off Thursday?"

"Yes . . ."

"Okay. That settles it." Sam had a determined gleam in her eye. "Ladies' night out at the Carolina Club."

Andie's stomach turned. She shook her head. "Not the Carolina Club. It's a serious pickup joint, which in my book equals a serious pain."

Sam disagreed. "You need a serious distraction, and there'll be plenty of distractions to choose from."

Andie didn't want that kind of distraction. Just the thought of it had the same effect on her nerves as the sound of fingernails scraping down a blackboard. "Couldn't a bunch of us just get together and have dinner at a wonderful restaurant? We could go to that new steak place. Aside from hamburger, it's been ages since I've had red meat."

Clearly determined, Sam shook her head and laughed in a way that did not reassure Andie. "Darlin', there's all kinds of fresh meat at the Carolina Club."

On Thursday night, Andie shrugged into the white jacket that covered her white shift and grimaced into the mirror. She wasn't sure the Carolina Club was what she needed tonight, but Samantha had been right when she'd said Andie needed a distraction. Since she'd realized what was eating at her, Andie had been able to identify more specifically the basis for her feelings. Intellectually, she could tell herself this little emotional dip was normal, it would pass soon, and it was no big deal.

But her memories scraped over her like thorns from a rosebush. It wasn't that she wished she'd married

Paul. It was the feeling of failure that plagued her. No matter how much she told herself she wasn't at fault, she still had her secret agonizing doubts. Maybe Paul wouldn't have strayed if she'd been prettier or if she'd been sexier.

She hated those doubts. They undermined her confidence and made her feel less appealing as a woman. Less . . .

The doorbell rang, interrupting her reverie. Wondering if Samantha had changed her mind about meeting at the Club, Andie grabbed her keys off the kitchen counter and opened the door to Eli.

"Hi."

His warm gaze made her chest tighten. "Hi," she managed.

He gave her a doubt-dissolving once-over full of masculine appreciation. "Unless someone has vastly improved the design of nursing uniforms, you must not be working tonight."

"I'm not."

She didn't expound, and a heavy, questioning silence hung between them. Eli broke it. "I was going to invite you to join Fletch and me for dinner, but since you're already committed . . ."

"I'm going out. It's not a date, though," she clarified. For some reason, she didn't want him to think she was going out with a man. She didn't want to play stupid games with Eli. He deserved better. "Ladies' night out. A group of us get together for special occasions every now and then."

Eli nodded. "A group of women from the hospital," he concluded.

"Some," she said, flicking on her porch light and stepping through the doorway. "Everybody knows

Samantha. I guess she's both the instigator and the common denominator."

Eli stepped aside while she locked the door behind her. She turned back around to find him mere inches from her.

"Men are going to hit on you tonight," he told her, his voice carefully neutral.

"I think that was Sam's plan," she said dryly.

Something hot and reckless flickered through his eyes. "Then let me be the first." He dipped his head closer to hers and brushed his mouth over her lips. A brief kindling, claiming kiss that took her breath and jacked her heart into overdrive. Then he pulled away, shoving his hands into his pockets as if he could barely keep from touching her.

Andie just stared at him, rocked by her body's immediate response to him. She sucked in a quick breath and swallowed hard.

"What's the special occasion you're celebrating tonight?" he asked, his gaze returning to her mouth.

Andie glanced away so she could think. *The reason she was celebrating tonight.* Her emotions jerked from one end of the spectrum to another, plunging her into the mire of yesterday's broken promises and disappointments. Avoiding Eli's gaze, she shook her head. "I'm chasing some memories."

"Why is there a *gh* in night?" Fletch asked as Eli sat beside him and read a bedtime story.

The question gave Eli a moment's pause. "It's silent. Sometimes there are letters in words that aren't pronounced."

Fletch frowned. "Then why put 'em there?"

Eli chuckled. "Good question. We'll have to ask Mr. Webster."

"Who's Mr. Webster?"

"He's the one who put together that big fat dictionary in my library." He arched his eyebrow and looked at Fletch. "Would you like to read, or do you want me to finish?"

Fletch snuggled further under the covers and hugged his stuffed llama to his chest. "You."

In the quiet of the evening, with his mind drifting back to Andie, Eli finished the story about a little boy named Freddie and his adventure at summer camp. He was so distracted he almost missed the opportunity to see if Fletch was still resistant to the idea of a structured environment. "I hear Jennifer's going to summer camp in two weeks."

Fletch's eyes widened. "She's gonna sleep there?"

"No, she's just going for a few hours a day. She'll do things like go swimming and draw pictures and play games and probably eat Popsicles."

Fletch was silent for a long moment. "I like Popsicles," he said quietly.

Eli smothered a smile and nodded.

"I want to learn how to swim, too."

"That's good. Maybe you can learn next summer." He leaned down to kiss his son and rose from the bed. "Get some sleep."

Moving in silence, Eli flicked off the table lamp, turned on the Flintstones night-light and walked toward the door.

"Does she get to wear her tutu?" Fletch asked.

This time Eli did smile. "I can't imagine Jennifer going anywhere without her tutu, although she might have to take it off if she doesn't want to get it wet in the pool." He waited a few seconds, practically hearing the gears of his son's quick brain turn. "I love you. Good—"

"Well, what if I maybe—sorta—might, just might," he emphasized, "want to go to day camp with Jennifer?"

Eli's heart twisted at the strained sound of his son's voice. Even though he knew Fletch was bored out of his mind, there was no way Eli would push him, not when Fletch was so obviously torn. Eli went back to the bed and crouched down beside it. "You don't have to decide tonight, Fletch." He tucked the covers around his son and ruffled his hair. "Why don't you just sleep on it?"

Fletch gave a heavy sigh of relief and nodded. "Okay." He lifted his arms in the universal request for a hug. "I love you, Dad."

Eli's chest expanded as he held his son. It amazed him how much power Fletch held. He thought of the awards and recognition he'd received, but none of it came close to the swelling of pride and emotion that filled his gut at Fletch's affection.

After a few minutes, he left Fletch's room and wandered down to his study. Adjusting the heavy drapes, he glanced out the window at Andie's house and his sense of well-being turned to restlessness.

Chasing memories, she'd said. It had something to do with the man she'd been engaged to. The knowledge was a splinter inside him, bringing back his own memories. He and Gail hadn't argued, but they hadn't talked much, either. He remembered the day Gail had asked him to leave, and the bone-deep failure he'd felt.

He'd been unable to read Gail. Conversely, he *could* read Andie's emotions. The ability gave him a rush. It also made him possessive and impatient. He'd never been consumed by such an incredible urge to absorb a woman, to join his body and mind and whatever else that was inside him with a woman—Andie.

Primitive and unyielding, the drive dominated his waking thoughts. He frowned, thinking again of Gail. He didn't want the same thing to happen with Andie.

Resolve hardened inside him. He might be able to read Andie, but he didn't understand her. Understanding required proximity.

Andie slammed the car door closed and crossed her arms over her chest as she walked toward her door. Grateful for Samantha's effort to cheer her up, she'd smiled, she'd laughed and she'd had a reasonably good time. Unfortunately, the laughter and the conversation hadn't filled up the emptiness inside her. The emptiness was odd, and she greatly resented it. She wanted—no, needed—to be self-sufficient. Add in her distraction with Eli and Andie was totally disgusted with herself. He might as well have kissed her one minute ago instead of hours before. Her mind was still scrambled.

She glanced at his dark house and figured he was asleep. *Must be nice.* Fumbling for her key, she unlocked the door and shoved it open. She dumped her purse on the kitchen table, stepped out of her shoes and scooped them up in one hand. After shrugging off her jacket, she'd already walked partway down the hall before she noticed the light in the den.

Although unable to recall leaving that light on, she shrugged and headed back to turn it off. She stopped when she saw Eli sitting in one of her wing-back recliners and reading a journal. For a moment she wondered how he'd gotten in, then she remembered giving him a key in case she locked herself out.

From behind his wire-rimmed glasses, he glanced up. "Did you have a good time?" he asked as if it were the most natural thing in the world for him to be in her house after midnight.

"I guess," she managed. Her stomach tightened at his intent gaze. "I—uh—what are you doing here?"

Removing his glasses and setting aside the journal, he rose from the chair and walked toward her. "Waiting for you." He took her shoes, then took her hand and led her back toward the recliner.

Andie was too off-balance to protest. If she'd been surprised before, she was stunned now. And more moved than she'd ever be able to explain. He sat down and pulled her onto his lap. Her throat tightened. "Why?" she asked in a husky voice.

"You were upset earlier. I didn't want you to be alone."

Staring at him, she felt her defenses crumble. She shook her head. "I don't know what to say. No one's ever waited for me before." Particularly a man.

With the ease of a man who knew he was in for the long haul, he shifted his hips so that she sank against him, then wrapped his hand possessively around her hip. "Before you left, you said you were chasing memories. I'm not sure what you're running from, but if you're going to run," he told her, his voice low and sure, "run to me."

Her heart filled her chest, and she tried to breathe. She struggled with the urge to run. Now more than ever, it was clear why she'd tried to keep her distance from Eli. Her instinct had been right on target. He had the power to touch a part of herself she kept hidden from everyone. It was enough to frighten the dickens out of her, but he was giving her every reason to trust him.

"If you're chasing memories, Andie, I want to be the man to help you chase them."

His quiet assertion was more effective than a dozen grand gestures. His gaze was so steady. Everything about him said, "Count on me." Floundering on her own, she looked away. "It's hard to explain—what's been going on the past few days. I'm not sure it really makes sense."

"Do you want to talk about it?"

Talk about Paul? Dig up the details of her failed engagement? Her stomach turned. She was sick of exhuming the past. "Not really," she confessed, and allowed him to draw her against his chest.

Eli paused. "Okay," he finally said, a wealth of reluctance in that one word.

Silently, he stroked her hair from her face. His strength and his warmth quelled the doubts that had been plaguing her for the past few days. Surrounded by his scent, enveloped in his arms, supported between his hard thighs, she felt both protected and acutely sensitive to his sexual appeal. "How long have you been here?"

"About two hours. I made sure Mrs. Giordano knew I would be gone so she would keep an ear out for Fletch." He nuzzled her neck and inhaled deeply. "Your perfume drives me crazy."

"Apricots must make you crazy," she said.

"Andie makes me crazy," he corrected her.

Her heart quickened. Lord, he knew how to get to her. Sighing, she sifted her hand through the sandy hair at his nape, and the thought, the wish, the need that had been running through her since she'd first seen him in her den pulled at her again. "Please kiss me," she whispered before she could stop herself.

She didn't have to say it twice, and he didn't give her an opportunity to call it back. His lips descended on hers in a warm caress. His tongue slipped inside to dally with hers. His gentleness, a product of his formidable self-control, made her feel both cherished and seduced. The combination was heady, and her hunger for him grew to a sweet feminine ache.

"I haven't been able to stop thinking about you," he muttered against her lips, then dropped his open mouth to her throat.

Andie sucked in a quick breath and arched her neck. "Ohhh, Eli, I don't know about this."

"Maybe you'll like this better," he muttered, skimming his mouth down to her chest. He nudged the sleeve of her dress off her shoulder and kissed the upper curve of her breast.

Her mouth went dry. His beard scraped slightly over her tender skin, and she felt her nipples strain against her bra. Before she could tell him to stop or beg him to go on, he drew her lace-covered nipple into his mouth.

Her womb twisted, and her sweet feminine ache turned into a roaring need. "Oh, my God." She wasn't sure they should go on, but she didn't want him to stop. "I—I—"

Eli ran his tongue around the beaded tip and pulled back slightly. "You want?" he asked, watching her with green eyes glinting with desire.

The sight of his mouth so close to her breast was too erotic for words. Andie closed her eyes. "I'm not sure this is such a good idea."

"Don't close your eyes," Eli urged and squeezed her hip. "Look at me."

Struggling with arousal and uncertainty, Andie did as he said.

"You try so hard not to see everything you do to me." He cupped her jaw and rubbed his thumb over her bottom lip, a tenderly sensual gesture that made her weak. "Why?"

She swallowed. "It's hard to believe, and I'm not sure how to handle it. When you touch me . . ." He continued his tender massage and she sighed.

"When I touch you," he prompted.

Andie bit back a moan. "I feel out of control."

He lifted her hand to his chest in a gesture that felt incredibly intimate. "What do you feel now?"

"Your heart beating."

"You're an experienced nurse. Would you say it's beating at the average rate for a physically fit thirty-something man when he's sitting down?"

"No," she admitted. "It's fast."

"Because I want you."

His blunt announcement made her puny defenses fold. "Oh."

He shook his head in wonder. "Every time I learn something about you I want to know more. And I don't feel particularly reasonable about it. If I had my way, you'd save every minute of your time to be with me because, lady, you're a cool drink of water and I've been in the desert too damn long. You're the most special woman I've ever known. I want tonight. I want more." He gave a wry chuckle. "But I can tell by your face that I'm scaring you. God knows I don't want to do that. So, the question is, are you going to let me show you how much I want you?"

Stunned by his declaration, Andie sat there trying to register all that he'd said. No man, not even her fiancé, had been so direct about his feelings for her. What struck her most was that he'd bared himself, yet wasn't requiring the same from her.

Honest, straightforward, no games. Her head spun, but the culminating moment hung between them. It was a moment when she had the power, when she could play it safe and close the door or take a double dare and open it. With his face mere inches from hers, his gaze holding hers, her indecision faded. She shouldn't allow her past to decide her present. She couldn't run from Eli anymore. She didn't want to. "Yes," she whispered.

His eyes darkening to forest green, he leaned nearer until she closed her eyes and he kissed her as if he would never stop. The deep kiss went on for long soul-stirring moments. His hand squeezed her waist, and distantly she felt the hem of her dress pushed up to her hips. He flicked the peak of her nipple with his thumb.

A million sensations coursed through her as she clung to him.

"Tell me what you like," he murmured, gently biting her earlobe.

Her heart pounding in her head, Andie swallowed. "Everything."

He chuckled and the sound sent a shimmy of vibrations through her blood. "That covers a lot of ground, Andie. I'm not sure we have time for all of it tonight."

Heaven help her, she hoped they found the time. Her zipper made a soft hissing sound when he pulled it down. He kissed her again, an open-mouth promise of what was to come. By the time they came up for air, her dress was on the floor beside the chair. Her bra straps hung limply on her arms, her breasts swelled against the lacy cups.

He drew his finger across her cleavage. "So pretty."

When she saw the way Eli looked at her at this very moment, Andie believed pretty was a possibility. When he unsnapped the clasp and her bra fell to her waist, he hiked her up so that he could take her breast into his mouth again. He moved from one breast to the other, sucking her sensitive nipples until she felt a rippling tension between her legs.

He pulled away and eased her back onto his thighs. His eyes hooded with arousal, he drew in a deep breath. "I'm overdressed. Your turn. Unbutton my shirt," he told her.

With unsteady fingers, she released the buttons and pushed his shirt aside. A shadow of uncertainty came over her. She hesitated. What if she didn't please him?

"Do you want to touch me?"

"Yes. I was waiting for—"

He shook his head. "You don't have to wait for anything. I'm yours for the taking."

Her heart contracted. She sank her fingers into the soft hair covering his hard chest. He sat still and quiet as she played her hands over the muscular planes of his chest and shoulders. When she skimmed her fingernail lightly over his flat brown nipple, he jerked. His reaction gave her more than an incredible sense of power. It made her hot. Her gaze flicked up to meet his and she slowly lowered her head to slide her tongue around his nipple.

She felt his body tense beneath her and did it again. He slid his hands through her hair. "You like this, don't you?"

"Like what?"

"Being in control."

Andie hadn't thought much about it, but she supposed she'd been fairly passive in her intimate relationships. She'd never felt secure enough to be any other way. If truth were told, her longest sexual experience had lasted about fifteen minutes. Old doubts crept in. She wondered if she'd misread his pleasure. "I don't want all the control. I just want to share it."

She tried to pull away, but he scooped her in his arms and dragged her back against him. "What's going on here?"

Andie bit her lip. Suddenly she felt too bare. "I— uh, I wasn't sure if you liked—"

"I want everything," he told her, his voice an intimate caress. "Every touch. Every kiss. Every word. I want inside." He swore softly. "When you put your mouth on me, I started reciting chemical equations in my mind to keep from exploding."

"Chemical equations?" she echoed. Her confidence swiftly soared, releasing a wave of sexual energy in her veins and a thud of arousal in her femininity. She backed slightly away. "I just wasn't sure—"

Her explanation fizzled when he took her hand and eased it slowly but deliberately to the hot, swollen ridge in his jeans. "I like it. I meant it when I said I'm yours for the taking." He moved his hand away and looked as if he expected her to remove hers, too.

She didn't and was shocked and secretly pleased at her boldness. His invitation was irresistible. He was irresistible. His blatant desire made her ache in all the right places. Unfastening his jeans, she watched his

Adam's apple bob in his throat. "This isn't going to be over in five minutes, is it?"

"It could be," he said in a low, strained voice, "if we don't share a little of that control." He took her curious hands and pulled her against him, distracting her with a kiss. He slipped his hand beneath her panties to cup her bottom. "These pretty little panties are going to be history soon." He moved his fingers around to her moist femininity and gently stroked her. "You've got the sweetest . . ." He kissed her again.

Something deep inside her ripped open, and want and need flew out of control. Andie moaned at the sensations rocking through her. She'd suspected that making love with Eli would turn her heart upside down, but she'd never dreamed how much he could make her want. With each stroke, the coil inside her tightened. Aching with the need to be closer than close, she slid her hand inside the opening of his jeans, past his briefs, to his full arousal.

He stiffened, but didn't pull away. "Andie, I'm gonna end up making love to you in this chair if we don't get to your bed."

Despite his protest, he continued his ardent caresses and she continued her upward spiral. His tongue thrust into her mouth, and she felt the fine sheen of his perspiration mingle with hers. She could feel the battle for restraint raging inside him, but she didn't want his restraint. She rubbed her thumb over the moistened head of his full arousal.

He tore his mouth from hers and exhaled in a long hiss. "Andie," he said in a warning voice.

"I don't care where," she whispered, urgency driving her, sudden and intense frustration bringing tears to her eyes. She'd denied the truth too long. "I just want you." She heard her voice tremble and couldn't do a damn thing about it. "Now." She arched into his hand. "Please say you have something," she said breathlessly.

He swore and fumbled in his pocket. Clearly loath to pull away from her, he shifted her slightly and stopped his excruciating caress long enough to retrieve a plastic packet and open it.

Boldness and need had her taking it from his hand. With his help, they pushed his jeans and briefs past his hips. Her hands trembled, but she managed to slide the protection on his jutting masculinity.

His aroused gaze holding hers, he got rid of her last silken barrier and supported her over his hard shaft. Slowly, deliberately, he lowered her onto him. She held her breath while she adjusted to his fullness and watched him shudder with pleasure. "You are so tight, so sweet," he whispered, rocking his pelvis so he thrust deeper inside her. "I want—" he shuddered again "—as close as I can get."

His words wrapped around her heart and took a piece of her soul. Could he know what he was doing to her? Could he know that she'd never be the same? Emotion surging through her, she flowed against him and he pumped inside her. She could tell by the sheer tension emanating from his whole body that he was riding the edge. His face drawn tight with arousal, he shook his head and lowered his hand between them. "Oh, no, sweetheart," he assured her, finding her most sensitive spot with unerring accuracy. "I'm not going anywhere without you."

He moved his fingers in heart-stopping strokes and murmured dark words of sensual praise that turned her to liquid in his hands. She spiked, then jerked, suspended with Eli inside and out. Holding on to his shoulders, clinging to his gaze, she cried out and they tumbled over the edge together.

A full moment passed before Eli could see straight. His mind-blowing climax had commandeered every nerve ending in his body. His chest heaved with the effort to breathe, and the woman responsible for his pleasure was struggling for her own breath.

His pounding heart turned over and he sifted his hand through her hair. Still intimately joined with him, she lay like a wilted flower on his chest. He liked their position. He liked the sensation of her clinging to him. He liked the idea of her doing it for the rest of the night.

He liked the idea of her doing it for a hell of a lot longer. She was his now, and though he'd known one time, even one night with her wouldn't be enough, he hadn't known he might want forever.

All his life, he'd sensed something was missing. From a human genetics standpoint, it was as if part of his DNA had malfunctioned. Although he'd been productive, he'd always felt a gap, a lack. With Andie the gap was closed, the lack was filled. What she did went deeper than his heart. It was as if she provided the missing cells that made everything come together.

Eli stared at her and a primitive possessiveness raced through him. She might not know it yet, but she belonged to him. And the fact that she was gloriously wasted after they'd made love filled him with masculine pride. Reluctantly, he shifted her beside him and pushed his jeans the rest of the way to the floor.

When he turned back to her, she extended her arms so trustingly that it turned him inside out. "I'll always have a fondness for this chair," he said, "but I think it's time for bed."

"I'm not sure I can walk," she confessed.

"You don't have to," he told her and lifted her naked body in his arms.

Her heavy eyelids fluttered in surprise. "You keep surprising me. Are you staying?"

He laughed at the question. No chance in hell of him leaving. "Yes," he said, walking toward the hall. "This way?"

She nodded. "I need to thank you."

Eli looked at her in disbelief.

"Not for that, but—" She stopped and her voice grew husky. "Well, I guess for that, too. But the reason I wanted to thank you was for being here when I came home. It meant a lot to me."

He stepped through her doorway. "Should I say you're welcome?"

She tugged his head down and pressed her lips to his. "I think you already have."

In the soft darkness of her room, his heart raced and he took her mouth in a long, intimate joining. When they pulled apart, she took a deep breath. "Before I forget, there was one thing I wanted to ask you."

He gently set her on the bed and followed her down. "Anything."

"How long have you carried that condom around in your pocket? You must have been pretty sure of me."

Hearing the faintest bit of feminine pique in her voice, Eli chose his words with care. "I was sure I wanted you. I've been carrying the condom since the night of the party."

"Oh," she said, her indignation melting. Her brown eyes softened.

His body hardened with arousal. Eli kissed her neck and skimmed his hand down her bare side. He smiled at her delicate shiver. She would be his again. The knowledge filled him with pleasure and anticipation. "I had one condom, so a more pressing question, before I forget, is do you have any more?"

Chapter Eleven

Andie woke to his kiss.

"I need to go," Eli told her in a morning-husky voice. "I should be home when Fletch wakes up."

"Okay," she murmured, forcing her eyes open. Dressed in his jeans and partially buttoned shirt, he looked appealingly rumpled as he leaned over the bed and watched her with a bone-melting gaze. After last night, she would never be able to look at him the same way. He had taken her body and given his, repeatedly, and sometime in the night, he'd touched her heart. The shadow of his beard, rough and masculine, made something inside her twist and turn. How many times had he rubbed his cheek against her cheek, against her breast and belly? She reached up to touch his jaw.

He captured her hand and pressed it to his mouth. "I'll see you tonight."

She nodded, then stopped and shook her head. Her mind was sludge. "I'm working the next four nights. Saturday afternoon?"

"Okay," he said, but he continued to stand there looking at her. A full moment passed. "I don't want to go."

She could see it on his face, the war between doing what he should and what he wanted to. "It's not that long," she told him and waved her free hand half-heartedly. "Shoo."

He frowned at her. "You could show a little more reluctance."

Andie laughed. "I need recovery time. This incredibly sexy research scientist invaded my home, kept me awake all night and did shocking things to my body."

Leaning closer, he allowed his hand to stray beneath the covers. "Like this."

"Yes, but—Eli!" she said, when his palm found her breast. Sexual adrenaline bolted through her.

"Shocking things all night," he prompted, clearly waiting for her to expound.

"Yes. It was wonderful. On a scale of one to ten, you were fifteen. Is your head big enough now?"

He bent his face down to hers and brushed his open mouth back and forth against hers, just barely touching her lips. She lifted her head to increase the erotic pressure, but he backed away, promising, but not delivering. Arousal burned inside her. "You're teasing," she said accusingly.

He nodded with a wicked glint in his eyes. "Sharing the control is what you called it." He stood and, as if he were relishing the prospect, he said, "Your turn next."

Andie scowled and threw a pillow at him.

Dr. Frankenstein just laughed.

* * *

Eli's brother Ash paid an unexpected visit on Saturday, so Eli and Andie couldn't manage more than a few private moments together. Although she missed him, she shrugged it off and looked forward to their date on Thursday night. Unfortunately, Eli had arrived at a strategic time-intensive phase in his research. He began pulling long hours at the lab, and she didn't see him for several days. He sent her roses when he had to cancel the date on Thursday. He called her on the telephone and told her he missed her.

When Mrs. Giordano had to leave town to attend her cousin's funeral, Eli called her again.

"I hate to ask this of you," he said. "But I don't know where else to turn."

"It's no problem. I'm off for the next two days," she told him, agreeing to take care of Fletch. "Fletch and I will keep each other company."

"Lucky Fletch."

Andie smiled. "How's your research?"

Eli sighed. "Slow going. It's taking longer than I expected to get through this."

Her heart sank. "How soon until you're back on regular schedule?"

"I don't know. A week, maybe two. I try not to think about the time and focus on getting the job done."

Two weeks felt like an eternity, but she didn't tell him that. "That's probably for the best." She was beginning to wonder if he even remembered the night they'd shared. "I hope you're taking care of yourself."

"Yeah, as much as—" He broke off at the sound of voices on his end of the line. "I'm sorry. I've got to go. Another meeting."

"Okay, I miss you." She wanted to say more, but the time wasn't right. Lately, it seemed the time was never right.

"Me too," he said in a distracted tone. "Talk to you later."

Andie hung up and tried not to let the phone call eat at her. Eli had not sounded like a man head over heels in love with her. He was in the middle of a worka-thon, she argued with herself. Still, an insidious doubt was planted.

Throwing herself into the task of caring for Fletch, she took the little boy to a children's movie the first day, the park on the second day.

She watched him play on the jungle gym as he chattered away. "I'm going to summer camp with Jennifer, next week," he told her. "I'm gonna get Popsicles, and I get to learn to swim."

She smiled. "You're going to have fun."

"Yeah. Dad says I need to spend some time in a structured 'vironment. He read it in a book about gifted kids. Did you know I'm gifted?"

"I did." She watched him hang upside down like a monkey, his sun-lightened hair sticking out from his head.

"I'm not real sure what gifted means. Dad says it means I've got an extraspecial mind. Mrs. G. says it means I'm curious." He skinned the cat to the ground. "Timmy Kenworth's mom says it means I need extra super—supervi—"

"Supervision?" she guessed.

He nodded. "And Timmy says it just means I'm a pain." He scowled. "I think Timmy's a pain. I told him he can't even spell the word right, and he got real mad."

Andie's lips twitched. "I think I like your dad's definition the best."

"Yeah." He rubbed his nose. "I wish he wasn't gone in the lab all the time. He's acting like Uncle Caleb, and Uncle Caleb never has any fun."

A trace of uneasiness swept through her, but she talked herself out of it. "I think your Uncle Caleb works this hard all the time. Your dad is just working this hard on a temporary basis."

"That means just for a little while, right?"

Andie nodded and brushed the dirt from his chin. "Right."

He took her hand and stood silently thoughtful for a moment. "My mom isn't gone away for just a little while, is she?"

Andie's heart twisted. She pressed her lips together. "No, sweetheart." She bent down to look at him. "But it's okay to miss her and love her. And it's okay to talk about her."

He took a deep breath. "She was really good at taking pictures." He swallowed audibly. "I really miss her at night. She used to rub my cheek sometimes."

Andie struggled with a burning sensation in her eyes. "I bet that felt good. When I was little, my mother sang songs."

Fletch nodded solemnly. "Dad does that, too, but he's not very good. Did your mom sing something about not getting any satisfaction?"

The image was too much. Andie burst into laughter. "No," she finally said when she regained control. "She sang 'Three Little Fishies.'"

The sound of children's voices broke Fletch's concentration. He turned to look at them with a pensive expression. "Why are they here?"

Andie saw a van sporting the logo of a local day care. "It looks like a group of kids from a day-care center. This is probably a field trip."

He clutched her hand tighter. "Do you think they have a virus?"

His question caught her off guard. "Well, I don't know. Probably not. But people get viruses all the time. A cold is a virus," she told him.

He watched them for a moment longer.

"You can play with them if you want."

Fletch shook his head. "Nope. I want to go home."

Concerned, she studied him. "Are you tired of playing?"

"I just want to go home. Did you know my dad told me I get a puppy when he finds the cromzome?"

"Chromosome. No," she said as they left.

As the day wore on, Andie found herself falling as hard for the younger Masters as she had for the older one. That night when she put him to bed, she taught him "Three Little Fishies."

"Boop, boop, didam, dadam, whaduma choo!"

Fletch delivered that last syllable with such vigor that he spit. "You really oughta teach my dad this one. It's a lot better than that satisfaction song."

"I'll remember that," she said with a smile. "I like your llama."

He stoked the stuffed animal. "My mom brought him back from one of her trips."

"That makes him extraspecial." She adjusted his covers. "What do you think about before you go to sleep?"

He sighed and wiggled his head from side to side on the pillow. "If I think about my mom, it makes me feel kinda sad, so I think about clocks and numbers."

Her throat tightened. "Would you like me to rub your cheek?" she asked softly.

Fletch nodded and closed his eyes. "And sing the fishy song again."

Andie stroked his child-soft cheek and sang the fishy song until she was nearly hoarse. She sang it until she was sure he was asleep. Then she left the room and cried.

Before Andie knew it, she was into another rotation at the hospital. Temporarily assigned to day shift, she arranged to join Samantha for lunch in the crowded cafeteria with persistently uninspiring food.

"You look tired," Andie told her friend as they took a recently vacated corner table.

Samantha gave a wry smile. "Thanks. I've been spending a lot of time with my sister's children."

Andie shook her head in concern and poured dressing on her green salad. "Is she still having problems?"

Sam nodded. "She's really mixed up, and I hate to see the kids suffer." She took a bite of her turkey sandwich.

"Have you suggested counseling?"

Sam nodded again. "She says she doesn't need it."

"Why don't you let me take them one night so you can have a break?" Andie grinned. "You could go out and torture the male population of Raleigh."

Sam sighed. "They're cute, but kids can be hell on your social life."

"So lend them to me." She hated to see Sam so worn-out.

"I don't know, Andie. They're pretty wild. The eldest might be a saint, but the two little ones—" She shook her head in dismay. "Conan and Conanina." Stalling, Sam lifted the bread off her sandwich, looked at it, then put it back. "I wouldn't want to strain our friendship."

She might have been amused at Sam's evaluation of her nieces and nephew if she hadn't been so appalled by her unwillingness to let her help. Astonishment surged through Andie. "I don't believe you. You know I've got tons of experience with kids. It's no hardship for me to pitch in for one night. What kind of friend do you think I am, anyway?"

Wincing, Sam held up her hand. "Okay, okay. I'm sorry. This situation has me a little off-kilter. You're a great friend. The very best. You can take the hellions Friday or Saturday night. At your own risk," she added and took another bite of her sandwich.

Mollified, Andie settled back in her seat. "Good."

Sam eyed her thoughtfully. "What's new with Dr. Frankenstein?"

Discomfort shimmered through her. It had been so long since she and Eli had shared that unforgettable night that she was beginning to wonder if she'd imagined it. "He's got a tough schedule right now. I haven't spent much time with him."

"That's the problem with Viking explorers. They've got to go off on those voyages every now and then."

Andie laughed shortly. "That's an interesting way of looking at it."

Sam raised her eyebrows. "Thought you two were headed for something hot and heavy."

Andie hesitated, not sure what to say. "We were," she finally admitted. "But it's difficult to maintain hot and heavy when you don't see each other. I kept Fletch last week—"

"You kept Fletch?"

"Yes, the housekeeper had to go to a funeral, so Eli asked me. I didn't mind," she said defensively. "Fletch is a great kid."

"I'm sure he is. I'm just not so sure his father's motives are great."

"Sam," she chided. "Everyone has busy times at work."

"Yeah," she said skeptically. "And there are no similarities between Eli and—" she paused meaningfully "—a certain man in your past."

Andie shook her head. "Absolutely not," she said in her most implacable voice. She hoped her righteous indignation hid the cracks in her confidence. "They're not from the same species."

She successfully closed the discussion, but later that night all Andie's doubts ganged up on her. Wide-awake at the lonely hour of midnight, she sat at her kitchen table and drank a glass of water. Stud thumped his tail at her bare feet.

"Thanks," she said, petting him. "I like you, too."

Eli hadn't meant what he'd said.

He didn't want her anymore.

She'd messed up again.

She'd made a huge mistake when she'd let Eli into her heart, and it had been a major error in judgment to make love with him. Andie wasn't a modern woman when it came to sex. She simply couldn't be casual about it. There were too many ramifications, physically and emotionally. It was her belief that sex was reserved for a man and woman who wanted to share more than one night. So far, one night was all she and Eli had shared. Andie's feelings for Eli put her tepid affection for Paul to shame. The realization didn't cheer her. She should have known better.

Hurting, she bowed her head and covered her face. Crippling uncertainty crowded out that wonderful high she'd been on since making love with Eli. She'd let down her guard and hoped for more. Now, she felt like crying. Andie firmed her mouth and refused to give in to the urge.

If she had to pick herself up and dust herself off, then she would do it. She'd certainly had to before. This time, at least, her pain could be private. She and Eli had never made a commitment. She'd been careful not to want one, she told herself. Still, she found herself biting her lip at the bitter edge of loss stabbing through her flimsy self-protective wall. She had hoped for more than she'd admitted to herself.

Taking a deep breath, Andie pushed past it. There were other ways to spend her time, to gain the space she needed. Replacing Eli's image, she filled her mind with plans. She could visit her parents in Wilmington and go to the beach. She could look into a graduate school program. She might even sign up for one of those medical volunteer trips to a foreign country. They were always looking for pediatric nurses.

Rising, she finished her glass of water and put it in the sink. Her gaze fell on the clock radio Eli had gotten her. On the kitchen counter beside it stood the glass vase of roses. They were withering. Her heart twisted. Down deep, all her plans felt like second best.

What she wanted was to be with Eli and Fletch. To be a part of them and for them to be a part of her. To be important to them. But Andie had learned the hard way that sometimes she had to take action before her feelings changed.

They'd done it.

They'd found the chromosome.

Nothing like a little brute force, Eli thought cryptically, as he recalled how he and his lab partners had attacked the data with unrelenting persistence. Afterward, they'd briefly exchanged congratulations and patted each other on the back. The next step was to find the gene.

Eli leaned back from his computer and yawned. Rubbing his irritated eyes, he didn't know whether to lie down and sleep for a week or go for a steak dinner. He felt victorious at the same time he felt deprived. At the thought of deprivation, an image of Andie flashed through his mind. He automatically reached for the phone. The first thing he wanted to do was call her.

He pushed the first three digits, then glanced at his watch, then stopped. Two o'clock in the morning. Muttering an oath, he hung up the receiver. If she wasn't at work, he supposed she wouldn't appreciate him waking her to tell her about how they'd found the chromosome that contained the gene causing seizure problems. Especially since finding the chromosome was just the first step. It could take years to find the gene.

He rubbed his hand over his bearded face and sighed. So busy he hadn't shaved in ten days, he felt like the creature from the black lagoon. Reluctantly, he decided to wait until he appeared a little more human before he tried to see Andie. Sleep, shave, haircut, then a romantic dinner. If Fletch was okay with it, Eli might even try to take Andie away for the weekend in a few days.

He wanted to see her again. It was more than want. They could take away his sleep and deprive him of food, but Eli was finding he needed continual contact with the people who mattered to him most to keep him from going nuts. Those people were Andie and Fletch.

He glanced around the lab to see Bill Sampson, his lab coat rumpled and stained, staring into his coffee cup. Rachel, almost as rumpled, rested her head on the table. He chuckled. They all looked like hell, and well they should. His respect for Bill and Rachel had mounted during the past week. They'd worked every bit as hard as he had.

Andie's advice came to mind. Eli couldn't rustle up a barbecue, but he supposed there should be some restaurant open this time of night. He stood and shrugged. "Anyone for beer and pizza?" he offered.

Bill and Rachel looked at him in surprise.

After several hours of sleep, Eli called Andie the next afternoon, only to get her answering machine. She called back when he took Fletch out for a burger and listened to his son's account of summer camp. They played telephone tag until he tracked her down late Friday evening.

"I've missed you," he began.

There was silence on the other end of the line, then she said, "I've missed you, too."

Her voice was a balm to his soul. Everything inside him shifted into place. "I thought we could go out tomorrow. In the afternoon if you're working. This time, we'll go somewhere nice. Alone," he added meaningfully.

Another pause followed his words. "I'm keeping Samantha's nieces and nephew tomorrow night to give her a little break. Sam's been spending a lot of time with them because her sister's having a rough time."

He rubbed his brow in confusion. "I thought you worked nights."

"I've been temporarily assigned to day shift. One of the nurses is on maternity leave, so I guess it's my turn to see how the other half lives." She took a breath. "Did your research turn out well?"

"Yeah." He chuckled. "We had a pizza at three o'clock in the morning to celebrate. Now that we've found the right chromosome . . ." Eli explained a few of the ins and outs of the process. Near the end of the conversation, he told her he'd like to see her tonight. She reluctantly begged off, telling him she had to get up early in the morning.

He hung up the phone, pleased that he'd finally spoken with her, yet oddly distracted. She'd *sounded* regretful that they couldn't get together. On the other hand, he wondered why he'd had the sensation that Andie was a thousand miles away instead of right next door.

On Sunday, he played with Fletch and the new dachshund puppy, appropriately named Brownie, in the backyard. Fletch talked more about summer camp and Eli was delighted that he'd enjoyed it so much. It was a hot, lazy afternoon. Fletch thought a sprinkler sounded like a good idea. Eli thought cool, crisp sheets, the whir of a ceiling fan and making love to the woman who made everything come together for him sounded like a good idea. He found himself glancing at Andie's house repeatedly. Her car wasn't in the driveway.

"She's at the beach," Fletch told him, giggling when the puppy licked his neck.

Surprised, Eli swung his head around. "The beach?"

"Yep." He gave the slippery dog a squeeze toy. "Her mom and dad live in Wimulton."

"Wilmington," Eli automatically corrected.

Fletch nodded. "Yep. I asked her if I could go, but she said I should stay with you. She won't be back till Tuesday."

Eli stifled an oath. Why had she told Fletch and not him?

He was past disappointment, past longing, roaring into full-fledged need. He wanted Andie's brand of feminine conversation, wanted to steep himself in her scent, wanted to just look at her. Determination hardened inside him. Come hell or high water, Tuesday evening, he would be knocking on her door.

Tuesday, Andie still wasn't home. Another man might have naively assumed it was just bad timing that he hadn't connected with her. Still another might have gotten the message and cut his losses.

Eli knew something was wrong, and he damn well wasn't cutting his losses. Rosebud in hand, he strode into the busy hospital cafeteria on Wednesday. It took a couple of minutes before he spotted her.

She sat at a table for two next to the window, and her smile could melt the fury of a Tasmanian devil. Unfortunately, she was smiling at the man sitting across from her. The same man who held her hand in his.

Eli ground his teeth together. Then he crossed the room.

"It's no big deal," Andie said. "I should have been paying better attention."

Dr. Warren Koch frowned. "You're sure you don't want me to look at it and see if you need stitches?"

His concern was cute. She stifled a laugh. "No. I don't think I need one of the nation's top neurosurgeons stitching up the equivalent of a bad paper cut."

A shadow fell over the table, and Andie glanced up. Her eyes widened and her heart took a dip. "Eli," she said in surprise.

"Andie," he returned with a stiff nod.

His eyes glittered with anger, his gaze moved from her eyes to her hand, which Warren Koch held. If Eli were the crazy aggressive physical type, she'd have feared for Dr. Koch's gifted hand. She assured herself that Eli was an evolved man. Nothing would happen. Still he'd never reminded her more of a Viking explorer than at this moment. Muttering a little "Oops," she removed her hand from Warren's. "Dr. Warren Koch, this is Dr. Eli Masters. He's a scientist at the research center." She gave Eli an encouraging smile. "Dr. Koch's in neurology."

"Hello," Eli managed and shook Warren's hand. Andie sensed it had been a stretch for Eli to do that much. Holding her gaze, he pulled a chair over to the table and sat down next to her. He slid his thigh next to her leg, then leaned closer, letting his shoulder brush hers. Andie stared at him.

"Nice to meet you." Warren nodded. "You're doing some impressive work over there. How do you know An—"

Ignoring Warren, Eli covered her mouth with his. With no time to brace herself, Andie's heart clutched in her chest. His lips were warm and passionate, his kiss thorough. Want and need spilled through her, seeping past her refortified defenses. Just when she thought she would drown, he pulled away.

His electric green gaze still locked onto hers, he said to Warren, "I had the good fortune of moving next door to Andie." he took her hand. "I've been stuck in the lab, so I couldn't see her."

Pushing his chair back, Warren gave a discreet cough. "Well, uh—" He cleared his throat again. "Excuse me while I make my rounds."

Struggling to breathe, Andie blinked and jerked her gaze from Eli's. She opened her mouth to say something to Warren, but he was already three tables away.

She sighed and pressed her hand to her forehead. She didn't dare look at him. The room was still whirling. He put a rose in her field of vision, his strong hand encircling the delicate stem.

"For you," he said.

Swallowing over the lump in her throat, Andie accepted it. "Thank you." Feeling the eyes of her co-workers on her, she was struck with a wave of self-consciousness. Her cheeks were probably the color of her ripened Big Boy tomatoes. "I didn't expect to see you today."

"He was holding your hand," he said in a carefully neutral voice that conveyed a world of masculine anger.

Looking at the ceiling, she lifted her bandaged palm for his inspection and stifled a sigh. "He was concerned about my scrape."

Eli enveloped her hand in his. "Are you okay?"

She finally looked at him. "Yes."

"You've been avoiding me."

Fighting an overwhelming sense of turmoil, she let out a long breath. "Yes."

He raked his hand through his hair. "If this has something to do with us not seeing each other for the past couple of weeks—"

"Three weeks," she corrected.

He arched an eyebrow and gave her a considering look. "Except for the lab, my life might as well have stopped."

Andie shrugged. "My life didn't." Unprepared for a full-scale emotional discussion with Eli, she arranged her plate on the tray, fully intending to leave. "And I've got to get back to work now."

When she stood, he did, too. "We need to talk."

Andie looked at him and got the odd impression that he would like to sling her over his shoulder. He gazed at her with an intensity that wouldn't be denied. Her stomach knotted. "Not now," she told him.

"Tonight." His voice was as flexible as granite.

She refused to shiver, quiver or give any other weak, feminine response. Who did he think he was bursting into her workplace and laying claim to her as if she were his? Then she saw it in his eyes.

He had damn well decided she was his.

Chapter Twelve

Andie almost didn't answer the knock at her back door. The prospect of matching wits with a man whose IQ probably belonged in *The Guinness Book of World Records* didn't make her day. She was still trying to recover from that public kiss in the hospital cafeteria.

She toyed with the idea of begging off. And just what could she use as an excuse, she asked herself cryptically? A killer paper cut?

Swearing, she walked to the door, fighting the notion that she was facing her doom. She was in control. This was her home, her body, her life. Taking a deep breath, she pulled open the door.

No romantic rose tonight.

He looked at her impatiently, emanating the darkest of moods. Dressed in dark shirt and jeans, he didn't attempt small talk, and beyond his shoulder, she saw a flash of lightning in the sky. Even the weather was in sync with him tonight.

"We need to go to my house. Mrs. Giordano asked for the night off. She's due. She's put in a lot of extra time with Fletch."

Andie hesitated, but the change in plans was reasonable.

"Better grab your key," he told her. "It's getting ready to rain."

Her home, her body, her life. Two out of three wasn't bad, she told herself as she reached for her key. But when she pulled the door closed behind her, Eli took her arm and the thunder rolled.

He guided her silently through the gate to his home, up the cracked sidewalk, through the front door, and Andie remembered the first time she'd made this same trip, the first time she'd felt the impact of his green-eyed gaze. Lightning flashed again, and she shivered.

He closed the door behind them and led her to the den. "Have a seat," he said, gesturing toward the sofa. "Would you like some wine?"

"Yes, thank you." When he left, she meandered around the dark paneled room trying to dispel the gloomy mood by turning on another lamp and pushing the heavy drapes apart. It was useless. Even the sofa and two chairs were upholstered in dark burgundy. She wondered, and not for the first time, if Eli had bought the furniture with the house. She felt him return and her nerve endings stood at attention. He offered the wine and nodded, then shoved his hands in his pockets as he watched her.

"What's going on?"

Andie took a quick breath. "It's nice to see you, too."

"We spent the night making love, and the next time I saw you, a neurosurgeon's hitting on you."

"There *was* a gap in time."

"Not for me," he said, his jaw tightening.

"Well, the rest of the world kept turning, Eli. And I'm part of the rest of the world. You can't make love and not see someone for three weeks and expect to pick up everything exactly where you left it."

He hesitated, then took a step closer to her. "Why not? Do you have a problem with my job?"

Andie's heart tightened. "Not really. I think it was more a case of bad timing."

He frowned. "How?"

To gain some time and space, Andie turned around to place her wineglass on the end table. Sighing, she wondered how she could possibly answer Eli's question when everything was as clear as mud to her, too. "It's hard to explain," she said. "We got very—close that night. When we didn't see each other for weeks, I started wondering—" She bit her lip. "Started feeling—"

His hands encircled her shoulders. "What?"

His low voice so close to her ear made her head spin. She closed her eyes against it. "I started wondering if we'd made a mistake," she whispered.

He squeezed her shoulders, then turned her around. "A mistake," he repeated in disbelief and shook his head. "I'm not getting this, Andie."

"I don't understand it either." She felt impatient with him, with herself for not being able to articulate her feelings better. "I was disappointed when we didn't get together on Sunday, but that was okay. The canceled dinner date bothered me a little more. Then you didn't call for over a week, and when you did you asked me to take care of Fletch. The next time I heard from you was last week."

Eli narrowed his eyes. "If you had a problem with taking care of Fletch, then you should have told me."

Andie shook her head vehemently. "I adore Fletch. He's a great kid. I tried to explain all this to Sam, and she brought up—" She stopped dead in the water.

He watched her. "Brought up what?"

Her heart sank. She swallowed the bitter taste of a bad memory. "I really don't want to talk about that."

"Tough."

"Okay, Paul."

Like lightning, his expression shifted to hot anger, then he seemed to regain his control. "I think it's time we had a little talk about Paul," he said quietly.

"I don't want to."

"Believe me, I don't think I could stomach the intimate details of your entire engagement. All I want is the breakup."

She felt her cheeks heat. "The breakup was the worst part."

"It usually is."

The ruthless tone of his voice left her with a chill. Feeling as if a net had been thrown over her, she squared her shoulders and backed away from his touch. He was forcing her to reveal the most humiliating experience in her life. A surge of anger rolled through her. She would give him his answer, then leave.

Taking a breath, she stared at the ugly red vase on the entertainment center, determined to keep the story short and simple. "Toward the end of our engagement, I took care of Paul's daughter when he had to work late. It was no problem. She played at my house, then Paul would pick her up. One afternoon, she went to a friend's birthday party. As I was dropping her off, she remembered she'd left the present at home. I told her to go on, then went to the house and found Paul in bed with another woman."

In retrospect, Andie felt a measure of pity for the woman. She shook her head. "I was so stunned I couldn't come up with a thing to say. Paul said he could explain it all. It was just an unplanned fling. After that, it was as if my heart and mind slammed the door on him. I didn't hear anything more. His mouth was moving, but I couldn't hear his voice. I just took off the engagement ring, dropped it on the floor and left."

She couldn't hear his voice, but to this day, she could still hear the ping, ping, ping of fourteen-karat gold bouncing on the hardwood floor. Shaking herself, she pressed her lips together. "There it is," she said, desperately wanting to leave. "Short, but definitely not sweet."

"I didn't want sweet," Eli said. "I just wanted the truth. And you believe I'm like Paul."

Adamant, Andie shook her head and stared at him. "No. I don't."

He arched an eyebrow in disbelief. "The situation looks the same to me. I have custody of a young child, and you've taken care of him while I worked overtime."

"It's not the same. For one thing, we haven't made any promises to each other. We're not engaged."

"How do you know I haven't thought about it?"

Andie's heart stuttered. "You're crazy," she managed in a husky whisper.

"Perhaps," he said dryly. He cupped her chin. "Tell me, Andie, do I look like him?"

Shocked, she gasped. "No."

"Do I act like him?" he asked, his voice deepening.

Confused by his persistence, she jerked away from him. "Why are you doing this? Why are you trying to make it look like you're just like him? Except for being a single parent, you're not," she insisted. "You don't look like him, and you don't act like him. You don't act like you want me just so I can take care of Fletch." Her heart dipped and her voice softened. "You act like you really want me for me."

"Because I do," he told her in a rough voice. His face dead serious, he pulled her against his chest. "I told you before, and nothing has changed." He took her mouth in a melting, mind-blowing kiss.

When he stopped, her head was spinning. She clung to his shoulders and squeezed her eyes closed. "I don't know, Eli. Before today I had decided I needed some space, to gain some perspective and get control of my life."

She heard his softly uttered oath of frustration just before he hauled her up in his arms and walked to the sofa. "We started having problems because there was too much space between us."

She couldn't deny that.

He sat down and held her on his lap. Sinking into his strong thighs, Andie experienced a sharp pang of déjà vu.

"I don't want anything between us," he said. His gaze dropped down to the ribbon holding the top edges of her shirt together. "There's a term we use in the lab when we allow a collaborating lab team access to our data. It's a very rare occurrence. Do you know what unlimited access is?" he asked, tugging gently on her shirt ribbon as he met her gaze straight on. "It means no boundaries, no secrets, complete and total sharing."

Her chest grew tight. She could see the sand blowing across the boundary lines she'd drawn in his absence. The ease with which he obliterated her safe distance rocked her world.

He stopped playing with the ribbon and gave it a swift decisive jerk, pulling it loose. "I want unlimited access to your mind and body." His hot gaze fell over her. He didn't hide his intentions. He didn't hide his need. "Every minute of your waking time that you don't spend at work, I want you to spend with me."

Her heart banged against her rib cage. She opened her mouth to tell him he was presumptuous, that he was asking for the impossible, but he continued.

He bent down to kiss her where he had pushed her blouse apart. "I want every minute of your nonwaking time, too. I want to spend the night in your bed, and I want you spending the night in mine." His mouth took a tender journey over the slope of her breast, heating her skin, building a fire inside her.

She was having trouble breathing. "You're being unreasonable," she managed.

"Tell me what to do about it. I don't feel reasonable about you," he growled. "I've admired the way you get along with Fletch. Hell, I've even envied it. But I don't want you for Fletch, Andie. I want you for me."

That last statement burst her fortress of glass into a thousand pieces. She was struck by the inherent strength in his arms and the aching, masculine vulnerability in his eyes.

"You're right. I'm not reasonable, Andie. So tell me what to do about it."

Her heart was a fist in her chest. He was overwhelmed by his feelings *for her*. She almost couldn't believe it, but there it was, staring her in the face, clear as the desperate need written in his eyes and echoed through the edge in his voice. Gulping, she lifted her hands to either side of his stubborn jaw. "You're not making this easy for me," she told him in an unsteady voice.

"I could say the same of you." He tilted his head so he could press his mouth to her palm. "Maybe we could change that."

Heaven help her, he was dangerous. He made her want. He made her hope. "I absolutely cannot be with you every waking minute," she told him as sternly as she could manage when she was melting into him.

"Every other minute," he said.

"And every night is imposs—"

He covered her mouth with his hand. "Don't make me compromise on everything. If you can't promise to let me keep you locked in my bedroom for the next month," he said with a hint of intimate humor, "then promise tonight."

She closed her eyes at the emotions unfurling inside her. "Oh, Eli, you're doing it again."

"Not yet," he murmured with a sexy laugh. His hands slid beneath her shirt and tugged it loose. "But we will be soon."

She sighed, accepting the inevitable. "Okay, let me get this straight. What have I agreed to? Tonight."

He unfastened her jeans. "And Friday night. And—"

"You're confusing me."

"Thank God," he muttered and kissed her, long and deep.

When they broke apart, she was ready to slip completely under him and his spell. His green eyes were full of arousal and something deeper than affection. "I have another request, Andie," he said. "Be gentle with me."

A lump formed in her throat. It could have been just a teasing request or even a sensual joke between them. Beyond the teasing sensuality, Andie saw that he was asking for more than physical consideration. He was concerned about what she could do to his heart.

She blinked back the burning sensation in her eyes. "I will," she promised and she meant it.

That was all Eli needed. He scooped up the wine, carried her upstairs and dumped her on his bed. "You look good there," he said, filled with satisfaction at the sight of her tousled hair on his pillow and her huge eyes focused on him.

She looked at him blankly. "Good where?"

"On my bed."

He felt her gaze as he unbuttoned his shirt. "Do you want some of that wine now?" Pouring the Chablis into the glass, he offered it to her. "You didn't touch it downstairs."

She raised herself on one elbow. "I figured I would need every one of my brain cells for that discussion," she said, making him grin. She took a sip, then offered the glass to him.

The simple gesture was eminently sexy to Eli. Instead of taking the glass with his hand, he lowered his mouth to it. Her eyelids swept down as she tilted the glass for him to drink.

He pressed his mouth to hers, dipping his tongue past her wine-moistened lips. Her taste was sweet and heady, making arousal pulse through him. He would have to fight the urge to gorge himself on her. Stifling a groan, he pulled away and stared at her. Her lips were wet, her eyes dazed, dark and sultry.

Swallowing, he took the glass from her weaving hand. "Can you take off your blouse?" he asked, wanting to see her bare.

"Yes," she murmured low and husky. Her gaze trained on him, she pushed it down her arms. As if she could read his mind, though, she didn't stop there. She unhooked her bra and tossed it aside, then undulated out of her shorts and underwear. Her nipples were like raspberries on cream, her skin ivory satin in the moonlight. She rubbed her thighs together delicately, betraying her own arousal.

She was the sweetest, sexiest invitation he'd ever received.

Eli sucked in a quick breath and took another drink of wine. Unable to tear his gaze from her, he set the glass on the nightstand, then grabbed his stash of protection from the drawer and tossed the packets beside the wineglass. In one swift movement, he shucked his jeans and briefs.

Joining her on the bed, he ran his hand over the delicate bones of her rib cage. "I told you before that the world stopped for me when I went into the lab, but right now I'm feeling every single one of those twenty-three days without you, Andie."

He slid his hand up to her breast, and she arched prettily into his palm. "Twenty-three days is a lot to make up for," he told her, closing his eyes briefly when her bare thigh rubbed against his hardened masculinity. "For you and me."

She sighed and wrapped her fingers around his biceps, as if the muscle fascinated her. Her eyebrows furrowed together. "The next time you're in the lab for a marathon session of gene mapping, do you think you could call me every now and then?"

Eli swallowed a mouthful of regret. He didn't like it that he'd hurt her. "I thought about calling several times, but it was usually two o'clock in the morning." Although she was as open to him as she could be, he sensed his neglect still affected her. "I'm sorry."

Her gaze not quite meeting his, she took a deep breath and skimmed her hand down his arm. "I wondered if you forgot about me," she confessed.

His heart tightened in his chest. How could she possibly think that, he wondered, when she was in him, as deep as his blood? "I swear I didn't," he told her, cupping her chin so that she met his gaze. "Not then. Not ever."

She bit her lip and the uncertainty still hung between them, straining their closeness.

"I need you to believe me."

He felt her eyes search his. When her lips tilted in a tentative smile, it was like the stars flickering on a cloudy night. "Then I guess I'll have to."

The notion that she could have even a trace of a lingering doubt made him crazy. He couldn't allow it between them. He would have to convince her, because his need for her wasn't a temporary thing. Unable to fathom a time when he wouldn't desire her, he wanted to bind her to him in every physical, emotional and legal way. She would flip if he told her right now, though.

Right now, he would have to push the doubt away.

Looking at her from head to toe, he ran his finger down her rib cage, past her waist and hips, to her thigh.

She shivered.

He smiled and reached for the forgotten wineglass on the nightstand. Sweet, little Andie didn't have a clue what he had planned for her. "Do you trust me?"

Her eyes dark but earnest, she whispered, "Yes."

He lifted the glass, took a quick sip, then deliberately spilled the wine on her chest. It ran like a shiny, bubbly river between her breasts and down her sides, pooling in her belly button and dampening the wispy tuft of hair at her thighs.

Andie gasped. "Eli!"

He shoved the glass back on the nightstand. "Cold?"

"Ye-e-es." She stared at him in wide-eyed shock.

"It won't last. I promise," he murmured, then lowered his mouth to her, sipping the wine from her skin. He skimmed his tongue between her breasts and across her erect nipples.

Eli heard her muted whimper. "What are you doing?" she asked breathlessly.

He laughed against her stomach. "Oh, honey, I'm just getting started. And I'm gonna make your toes curl." He slipped his tongue into her belly button and felt her stiffen beneath him.

"They're curled," she practically moaned.

Lowering his head to her damp femininity, he felt her hand in his hair.

"Oh, no!" she gasped. "Absolutely not. Absolutely, positively—"

He glanced up and met her aroused but uncertain gaze. "Are you still cold?"

She hesitated, then swallowed. "No."

"Do you trust me?"

She hesitated again. "Yes, but..."

"Hold on."

He nuzzled her femininity and she closed her eyes. Moving slow and easy, he kissed her intimately. Andie started to swear in whispers. It was the sexiest sound he'd ever heard.

Wrapping his hand around her thighs, he lost himself in the taste and texture of her, pushing her beyond her self-consciousness to acceptance of her arousal, acceptance of her incredible sensuality. Her whispers turned to erotic moans that might as well have been a physical caress. Her body grew tense as a bow. He grew hard with sexual need, yet more desperate to convince, to shatter doubt, to make her his.

He felt her begin to shake and knew she was close. He flicked his tongue against her tender bead once, twice. She jerked and came undone.

"Eli," she cried, nearly sobbing.

Hearing the panic in her voice, he swiftly covered her body with his to still her shudders. He covered her mouth to capture her cry. She wrapped her arms around him and held on so tightly he thought his heart would break. "Go again?" he murmured, lowering his hand between them.

She reached for his hand and shook her head. "Not again." Her eyes were dazed and her voice trembled. "Not without you."

"But it would be so easy," he coaxed, wanting to feel her come apart again.

"Then come with me," she whispered and gave him a French kiss that took him around the world. Her inhibitions must have burned to cinders; she kissed him and skimmed her hands down his stomach, to his aching masculinity.

Eli groaned and reluctantly pulled his mouth away. "Just a—"

She tilted her hips and took him between her thighs.

"Holy—" He felt his forehead dampen with perspiration. Her sweet, hot femininity was so close. Just a shift of his hips and he'd be inside. Swearing, he stretched out his hand and groped for a packet. "When did you get so damn hard to resist?"

She undulated against him, bringing him that much closer. He pulled on the protection. Then, with a rough growl, he thrust inside her. They moaned together. Holding his gaze, she moved in deliberately provocative feminine counterpoint to his thrusts. Feeling his muscles tense, he stared at her, wondering what he had loosed inside her. No more restrained, tentative Andie. She was taking and giving.

Lowering her hands between them, she cupped her hands around him and stroked as he pumped. His arousal spiked. He gritted his teeth. "What are you doing?"

She closed her eyes as if she was having trouble concentrating. "Sharing," she whispered, and he lost it.

Fast and furious, he exploded. Through the haze of his climax, he felt her little shudder and knew she was with him.

When he began to breathe again, he rolled off her and entwined his fingers through hers. Trembling with aftershocks, Andie curled into his side. Her uneven breath puffed against his chest. "Eli," she said in a strained voice.

He looked into her bottomless eyes and felt his heart take a double dip. "Yeah."

"I don't think I can do this every night."

Eli chuckled and hugged her to him. "I'm not sure I can, either, but I'd damn well like to try."

Chapter Thirteen

Andie spent the next week in bliss. Her co-workers noticed the change and remarked on it. Every time Andie came around wearing a huge grin on her face, Samantha rolled her eyes and started playing an imaginary violin. Although Eli's ability to close down communication for more than three weeks still haunted her at secret moments, Andie felt herself instinctively turn to him on a regular basis. It was so natural it might have scared her if she'd had time to think about it.

Everything would have been perfect if she hadn't caught a miserable case of summer flu. "I'll be fine," she told Eli when he telephoned. Stretched out on her sofa like an overcooked noddle, she turned her head to sneeze away from the receiver. "Excuse me," she murmured and wiped her nose with a tissue.

"You sound horrible," he said.

Andie gave a wry smile. "Thank you. I look even worse."

"Have you seen the doctor?" he asked, ignoring her self-deprecating humor.

"No need to. This is one of those things that just has to run its course. I'm sure it's viral." She sniffed. "I should be better in a few days." She prayed she would be. The only thing worse than a summer cold was a summer flu. At the moment, Andie was sure the only thing worse than a summer flu was heart surgery.

"Do you have a fever?"

Andie hesitated. The concern in his voice warmed her, but she didn't want him to worry. "It's no big deal. Just a little above normal."

"What are you eating?"

She grimaced. "Not much. I'm not very hungry."

"I'll ask Mrs. G. to make some chicken soup," he said firmly. "Tell me your symptoms and I'll pick up a couple of over-the-counter medications for you at the drug store. While we're at it, what are your favorite soft drinks and juices? I can—"

Andie shook her head from side to side, which only served to make it hurt more. She winced. "This is really unnecessary. I'll just sleep through it and—"

"I insist," he said, quietly but oh so firmly.

Andie sighed.

"Symptoms," he prompted.

She answered him as if he were a medical doctor supervising her case. "Headache, fever, upper respiratory congestion, scratchy throat, general yuckiness."

"Poor baby."

She rolled her eyes and coughed. "You asked."

"Beverages."

She shrugged. "The regular, cola and ginger ale." He was being so serious she wondered if he was writing all this down. A wicked thought crossed her mind. "And I find I'm partial to Chablis." She grinned at the long silence that followed.

"You are a bad girl, Andie," he said in a rough-and-ready voice.

"Not me," she immediately said, but a forbidden thrill raced through her. She'd never been called a bad girl in her life. She wondered if she should thank him.

"Yes, you are. You brought up an incredibly pleasurable, intimate memory when I can't do a damn thing about it."

"Oops," she said, trying, but not succeeding, to inject a note of regret in her voice. "In that case, just forget I mentioned it."

"Do you know what the statistical probability of that is?"

"A little low, huh?"

"Nil." She heard him take a long-suffering breath. "Just remember sweetheart, payback's hell."

Fletch followed his dad around the kitchen. "What's wrong with Andie?"

Eli shrugged and poured soup from the big pot on the stove into a little container on the counter. "It sounds like she has a bad cold. Nothing major, probably viral."

Fletch felt a little bit worried. "What's viral?"

"Oh, a virus. Like the flu." Dad patted him on the head. "That means it's not bacterial like an ear infection."

Alarmed, Fletch bounced his fingers together. "A virus. Is she gonna have to go to the hospital?"

"Oh, no. She'll be better in a few days."

Fletch frowned. *A virus.* "But how do you know she'll get better so fast?"

Dad glanced down at him. "Because that's what usually happens when people get a cold. They feel bad for a while, then they get better." He pointed to the soup and grocery bag. "I'm taking her soup and drinks to help her feel better."

Fletch thought about that for a minute. He wasn't sure he understood about viruses. His mom had died because she'd caught a virus. His stomach hurt when he thought about it because she'd caught it from him. He'd caught his virus at day care. But he hadn't caught one at summer camp a few weeks ago. Andie had told him colds were viruses. He scratched his head. "Can you catch her virus?"

Dad paused. "I guess I could. I don't get sick very often, so I probably won't." He bent down. "But you know Andie's done some nice things for us, and we both like her, don't we?"

Fletch nodded. He liked Andie a whole lot.

"She lives alone so we need to help take care of her when she's sick. She would help take care of us, wouldn't she?"

Fletch nodded again. His throat felt like peanut butter was stuck in it. "Do you want me to go with you?"

"You can if you want to."

Scared, Fletch held his breath. "Do I have to?"

Dad tilted his head to one side and squeezed Fletch's shoulder. He wasn't frowning, but he wasn't smiling either. "You don't have to. Do you want me to tell her something for you?"

Fletch let out his breath in relief and shook his head. "Nah. I think I'll just go play with Brownie."

His dad looked at him some more, then nodded and stood. "Okay. Don't go outside without Mrs. G. She's in the den, and I'll be back in a little while."

Bouncing his fingers together, Fletch watched his dad leave. His chest felt heavy and his stomach hurt like it did when he disobeyed. He wondered if he was bad because he wasn't going to help take care of Andie. He was just too afraid.

Eli stood over Andie as she sipped the soup. He'd tried to talk her into going to bed, but she'd resisted the idea, so he brought her a pillow and blanket and set up a tray beside her. Her nose was pink and she looked so miserable that he wanted to hold her, but she said she was a germ factory and wouldn't let him touch her. "Want me to adjust your thermostat?"

She shrugged. "Just leave it, please. I'm cold right now, but in a few minutes I'll be kicking off the covers."

"You should stay at my house for the next few days so Mrs. G. and I can look after you," he told her.

Andie gave him a long-suffering glance and shook her head. "If I stayed at your house, I'd probably share this with Fletch and Mrs. G. It's not as if it's a serious illness."

Irritation tugged at him. "Are you always this difficult when you're sick?"

"Not difficult, just practical," she corrected and sneezed into her tissue. She looked up at him with a soft gaze. "The soup is delicious. Please tell Mrs.

Giordano how much I appreciate it. Did I tell you you're wonderful to bring it?''

Slightly mollified, he shook his head and sat in one of the wing chairs. ''No,'' he grumbled. ''I think Fletch is worried about you. He asked if you would have to go to the hospital.''

Her face shadowed with concern. ''You told him I wouldn't.''

''Yes.'' Eli had several concerns on his mind. He rubbed the back of his neck and sighed. ''I've told you I want you for me, Andie. But Fletch is very attached to you, growing more attached every day. There will come a time when we have to make plans.''

She paused midstroke with her spoon. ''Plans?''

''Long-term,'' he clarified.

He saw her throat work in a swallow. Her gaze flitted away, and he fought a spurt of impatience. More and more with each passing day, he found he wanted their relationship chiseled in stone. There was no need for him to wonder anymore. She was the woman for him. He knew she loved him. His only problem was that she wasn't moving at the same speed he was.

She set the spoon aside. ''Not now. It's too soon.''

''But you understand why I have to consider Fletch. He's been through a lot.''

She nodded, meeting his gaze. ''I don't think I would care about you as much if you didn't think about Fletch's welfare. Please trust that I'll do everything in my power to make sure he isn't hurt by what does or doesn't happen between you and me.''

She still regarded their future with an *if*. His impatience spiked, but he tamped it down with an attempt at levity. ''If I were a French king and you were my courtesan, I could order you to marry me.''

She relaxed her tense posture and her lips tilted into a grin. "You weren't a French king, though. Remember? You were a Viking explorer."

Standing, he crossed his arms over his chest and gazed at her. He was generally a reasonable man, practical, logical. He believed in gender equality. Any other belief was nonsense. So why did Andie make him feel like a loaded cannon of testosterone? "If I were a Viking explorer and I wanted you for my bride, what do you think I would do?"

She sneezed again. "I envision something like you grunting, throwing me over your shoulder and carting me off. It's a relief to know men don't behave that way in this modern age."

Eli yearned for the good ol' days.

If he continued in this vein it wasn't going to help his case, he realized with a sigh. Turning to the matter of her medication, he pulled the assorted remedies the pharmacist had recommended from the bag at the other end of the couch.

"Take this for fever," he instructed, putting two pills on her tray. "You probably want to sleep," he said, adding another pill, "so we'll save the non-drowsy formula for tomorrow. The lady at the cash register recommended this brand of tissues so your nose won't get chapped." He handed her the box, then took the cellophane off the box of wild-cherry throat lozenges. "In case you get a sore throat," he added and looked up to find her smiling at him. She didn't say anything, she just smiled. Waiting expectantly, he grew uncomfortable with the silence. "What?"

"You're making me adore you."

Eli's heart swelled in his chest. He grinned wryly. "What is it? The throat lozenges? The antihistamine? Tell me what it is so I can do it again."

Andie laughed, but Eli was shocked to see tears in her eyes. He reached for her, but she shook her head and held up her hands to ward him off. "Germs," she said, pressing her fingers to the corners of her eyes. "Do you have any idea how long it has been since someone looked after me like this?" She looked up at the ceiling as if she were remembering. "I must have been ten or eleven with a horrible case of strep throat. My mother hadn't gotten a job yet and she coddled me for three days. Soon after that, my father injured his back, so my mother went to work, and I took care of my brothers until I left home."

"Until you left home to take care of more people," Eli said, thinking Andie's statement made several things click together in his mind.

She shrugged and blew her nose. "Destiny." She looked up at him again. "I don't want to offend your masculine sensibilities, but this is so sweet. I don't know how to thank you."

Slightly uncomfortable with her praise, he raised an eyebrow. "I guess that depends on how grateful you are."

She hesitated half a beat, then caught on. "Is this going to involve whips and chains or twin cheerleaders?"

Eli barked out a laugh. "Neither. With your courtesan background, you should be able to come up with something inventive."

"Inventive," she repeated with a scowl. "The reason a favored courtesan is favored is because she knows her *master's* secrets," she said, slyly emphasizing Eli's last name.

He wondered how a woman who'd sneezed ten times in the past thirty minutes and had a pink nose and bloodshot eyes, managed to turn him inside out. "So the courtesan wants to know the master's secrets."

"Yes." Her voice was hushed.

He'd heard the same quality in her voice before when she'd been bare beneath him. The atmosphere in the room shifted to sexual curiosity and electric anticipation. Feeling his body heat, he moved closer to her and lowered his voice. "I'm partial to satin on beds and skin. And I've always been curious about feathers."

Her eyes widened and he brushed his mouth across her forehead before she could protest. "Get well soon, Andie."

Although Eli hovered over Andie when she was sick, he didn't bring up marriage again. She should have been relieved. Instead his comments about Fletch haunted her during those long hours when she had nothing to do but rest. She knew children grew attached, and Fletch was particularly vulnerable since he'd lost his mother. She wondered about the wisdom of her deepening relationship with Eli, because as good as it seemed right now, it might not work out.

The idea that Fletch could be hurt troubled her deeply. The idea of not being a part of Eli's and Fletch's lives, however, filled her with grief.

Once she returned to work, she was so busy she didn't have time to dwell on painful possibilities. Her first day back, Andie connected so many tubes to her new two-year-old patient she wondered if it were possible to add any more.

If only people would be more diligent about securing their children in car seats. This little guy's injuries were extensive. He was on a ventilator, and they'd used meds to keep him deeply sedated. If he started coming up from that sedation, he would inevitably try to pull out his tubes. Still worried about his head injuries, she gave the tow-haired boy one last glance before she nodded toward the nurse who'd just returned from lunch.

After she entered everything into the computer, she stopped by the nurses' station. "I'm gonna grab something to eat," she told Missy, the PICU day shift supervisor.

"Fine," Missy said with a quick smile and handed her a slip of paper. "Here's your phone message. I took it myself. He's got a nice voice."

Andie glanced at the name and smiled. "Yes, he does." Eli had never called her at work. Growing more curious with each passing moment, she want to the staff lounge to use the phone and had to get past three professional screeners. As soon as she told them her name, however, they put her through.

"Sorry," Eli greeted her, sounding out of breath. "I was away from my desk, so your call went back to the switchboard."

Andie twisted the phone cord. "No problem. It's nice hearing from you. Having a good day?"

"Pretty good. And you?"

Thinking of her newest patient, she sighed. "Automobile accident. The kid wasn't in a car seat, so he bounced around like a Ping-Pong ball. I've got a very sick two-year-old."

"I'm sorry."

His sincerity washed some of her tension away. "Thanks." She pushed her hair behind her ear. "So what's going on in the world of chromosomes and genes today?"

"Same thing—still looking for a bad gene." His hesitation was brief, but full. "There's this research award. It's fairly prestigious, and they announced the winners today."

Andie heard the restrained excitement in his voice and smiled. "They did?"

"Yeah, they did." Eli paused again. "I was one of them."

"Terrific!" she said, loud enough to turn the heads of the other staff in the lounge. "Congratulations. You've worked hard, and you deserve it," she told him emphatically, wishing she understood his work better. "Can you tell me what it's for?"

Eli laughed, clearly pleased with her enthusiasm. "It's an award based on research papers presented at a national conference. Why don't I tell you more about it tonight?"

"I'm on a twelve-hour shift, so I can't get off early. Can we make it a late dinner at my place?"

"I'll be there."

They hung up and after Andie finished her shift, she stopped by a Chinese restaurant and a specialty store Sam had recommended. Every time Andie looked in her shopping bag, she groaned aloud and considered going back, but Eli deserved a celebration and she was damn well determined to give him one he wouldn't forget.

Andie opened the door before he could knock twice. Eli simply stared.

She must have just gotten out of the shower, because her hair was wet and combed back from her face, making her eyes look huge enough for him to lose himself in them. She smelled of apricots, and she wore a full-length, belted ivory satin robe that bared the soft skin of her throat and her pink toes. It was the kind of garment that made a man want to touch—the robe and the woman beneath it. Eli's pulse shot up to the second story of Andie's little Cape Cod.

He might have been fooled into believing she wasn't the least bit self-conscious if he hadn't noticed the color of her cheeks and if she hadn't been asking him questions, then answering them before he had a chance to open his mouth.

"Do you like Chinese? It's not gourmet cuisine, but at least we won't have to wait for it. Cashew shrimp, sweet 'n' sour pork, sesame chicken, stir-fry vegetables and rice." She waved toward the table, set with a crisp white cloth, flatware, china and candles. "Have a seat, and I'll light the candles. Were your co-workers excited about your award?"

Andie struck the match, but it didn't catch. She tried a second match, then a third. "I bet your director was patting himself on the back for hiring you."

Eli saw her hands tremble and felt his chest grow tight. Andie was uneasy. He stepped closer and covered her hands with his. "I like Chinese. My co-workers were pleased and a little envious. Dr. Berylman was borderline nauseating. Sweetheart, look at me." She finally met his gaze. "Why are you so nervous?"

She took a deep breath, then bit her lip. "Give me a break. It's my first night as a courtesan." She smiled slowly. "At least in this century." Leaning forward, she kissed him. Quick and soft, the caress was a delicious taunt. "Would you light the candles while I pour the wine?"

"Courtesan," he echoed in a rough voice. He barely restrained the urge to take her back in his arms and finish that kiss. For that matter, he wouldn't mind taking her on the kitchen table.

She poured the wine and nodded. "That's right and I'm practicing on you." When she leaned forward to put the glasses on the table, the robe gaped to reveal the slope of her breasts and the shadow of her nipple.

Stifling a groan, Eli tugged at his collar. "Are you going to tell me what you have planned?"

She shook her head. "That would spoil the fun."

Distracted as hell, he lit the candles. It took him three matches and a few muttered curses to do the job. He wondered what she was going to do to him.

He sat down and watched her serve an assortment of the food on his plate, and start on hers. "It just occurred to me that you're going to be entirely too far away if you sit there."

She looked confused. "Then what do you sug—"

Eli pulled her onto his lap. "We can share." Then he kissed her the way he'd wanted to since he'd walked in the door. Tasting her, drawing out her response, he ran his hands over the cool satin of her robe, feeling the warmth of her skin beneath it.

Pushing against his chest, she pulled back and took a couple of deep breaths. "This is going to go much faster than I'd planned if you don't stop that."

"Is that a promise?" he asked, his interest caught by the way the satin slipped loose from the belt of the robe.

Before he knew it, she popped a bite of cashew shrimp in his mouth. "Tell me more about the award."

He swallowed the bite. "Token money," he said with a shrug. "But it looks great on the resumé, and when they're deciding on grants it doesn't—" He stopped when she began to unbutton his shirt. "What are you doing?"

"It doesn't take a genius to figure this out," she told him. "I'm helping you get more comfortable."

He felt the brush of cool satin on his chest and his gut tightened. "Well, don't stop there," he muttered when she undid the button closest to his pants.

Giving him a chiding look, she handed him the wine. Eli downed the glassful in three swallows.

"When they're deciding on grants," she prompted, lifting the fork to his mouth.

He took the fork and served her instead. "These kinds of awards don't hurt at all. Corporations like them. The National Institute of Health likes them. Everybody—" He broke off. "Just out of curiosity, you are prepared for everything, aren't you?" He was referring to his dwindling supply of contraceptives.

Andie poured more wine in his glass. "I got something from my doctor, so we won't need any more..." She waved her hand and sipped the wine.

"Condoms," he finished in a rough voice. She couldn't have known. He'd never told her, but one of his most vivid fantasies was to make love with Andie with nothing between them. That tore it. He stood with her in his arms. "Let's go."

"But we haven't finished dinner."

He strode toward her bedroom. "I'm not hungry anymore."

"I've got Black Forest cake from the bakery."

"Later."

"You're not sharing," she told him, her voice faintly accusing.

His heart pounding against his rib cage, Eli stopped and took a deep mind-clearing breath. "You're right," he muttered, and allowed her to slide down to her feet. He wondered if his pressing desire to make love to her had something to do with his fear that she was going to slip away from him. Losing Andie would be like losing his center, he realized. Nothing would ever be quite right again. Clenching his jaw with the effort, he tried to rein his thoughts and emotions under control. He wondered if she had a clue how important she was to him.

She put her hands on either side of his face so he would meet her gaze. "You're very tense. Can you tell me what's going on?"

He thought about it, thought about trying to extract a promise, beg for a vow, all the while knowing he couldn't extract or beg to get what he wanted. She had to be ready to give it. "I'm wondering when you're going to have your way with me," he said instead.

She smiled. "Trust me. You're going to like this."

She was so earnest she nearly broke his heart. "Okay, I'm in your hands."

Her smile broadened. "Let's finish dinner in the bedroom."

She returned to the table to get his plate and wine, and Eli closed his eyes. It was going to be a long night.

She played a CD, something soft and sultry, then turned off the lights and lit more candles. Between bites of Chinese food, she massaged his neck and back, chasing the tension from his neck to another demanding part of his anatomy. She charmed him with harmless bits of gossip and got him to talk about his job. He stole a few kisses and when he mentioned he was warm, she helped him out of his jeans. She wasn't being deliberately provocative, just friendly.

Eli had never realized friendly could be so damn sexy.

After a couple of glasses of wine she gave up fighting with her robe and let the lapels hang open, exposing her small uptilted ivory breasts. Eli gave up fighting and pulled her into his arms.

Andie melted into Eli's hard strong body and offered her open mouth to his. His tongue slid inside and the room began to tilt from side to side. Her mouth kept getting dry from a combination of talking and nerves. Now she was suffering the effects of a little too much wine and not enough of Eli. Her heart pounded against pulse points in her temple and throat and deep inside her secret places.

He kissed her voraciously, taking her, coaxing her to take him. Neither seemed able to get enough. His mouth alternately sucking her lower lip and tasting her with deft strokes of his tongue, he slipped the robe from her shoulders. In a distant corner of her mind, she felt it whisper down her back.

Her nude body clearly sent his libido into overdrive. Everything about him said how much he wanted her, from the way he strained against her to the way his hands sought every intimacy. He squeezed her breasts and plucked at her nipples, then skimmed his restless hands down to her waist and hips. Pushing her thighs further apart, he thrust against her and she felt his bare masculinity rubbing in her most sensitive places.

Then she remembered.

She tried to pull away. "One more thing," she managed between broken breaths. "Just one more," she said as she untangled her legs from his, accidentally brushing his erection in the process.

"Oh, God," he muttered, still holding her.

"Please," she urged, fighting her own desire to have him inside her.

Making a sound of raw need, he allowed her to slip from his arms. "You're killing me," he told her in a rough, husky voice.

Andie looked at him and her chest ached. His eyes, hooded and darker than the green of the forest, glinted with sexual intent. He lay sprawled on the bed, his muscled chest rising and falling with the force of his breath, and so aroused his erection pushed out of his briefs. She sensed the dark, demanding need driving him, yet he was obviously determined to hold it in check.

On trembling knees, she scooted off the bed and pulled out her purchase from the novelty store. For a moment, she wondered if she was crazy to do this. In the same moment, she decided she wanted to know what it felt like to go a little crazy. Taking a deep breath, she sat on the edge of the bed, holding the bit of insanity behind her back.

Eli's unrelenting gaze locked onto her. "Well?"

Forcing a smile, she lifted the wispy feather for him to see.

Eli stared at it. "Oh, my God."

"I wanted to do something really special to celebrate your winning the award."

His eyes still trained in horrified fascination at the feather, Eli swallowed hard. "Dinner is special.

Champagne is special. This is—'' He shook his head, unable to finish.

A twinge of uncertainty pulled at her. "You said you were curious about feathers."

He nodded. "Yeah, I said that, but..."

She bit her lip. "You don't want me to—"

"I didn't say that," he said quickly. His chest lifted on a full breath and he met her gaze again. "You're enjoying this."

With the devil licking through her veins, she twirled the feather between her fingers. "I know how I could enjoy it more."

If possible, his eyes darkened further. "Okay. Here's the deal. If you use it on me, then I get to use it on you."

"Deal," she said immediately. This was Eli's fantasy. She suspected it wouldn't have nearly as much of an effect on her.

Spreading his arms out on either side of him, he closed his eyes. "Okay. I hope my life insurance is paid up," he muttered under his breath.

Her heart swelled and she swirled the feather under his chin. When he flinched, she kissed him. There was a method to her madness. She bent over him and twirled the feather down his chest to his abdomen. Watching a shudder ripple through him, she smiled and kissed his belly button.

His stomach was rigid with tension. "What are you doing?"

"Relax," she whispered. "Everywhere the feather goes, I'm going to kiss you." She skimmed the feather over his toes and planted a soft kiss there.

He twitched and his eyes flew open. "You're going to—''

"Shh. You're breaking my concentration." She brushed the downy fluff over his knees and thighs, then pressed her lips there, too.

He gave an injured growl of protest and pleasure. His nostrils flared. "This is one hell of a celebration," he said through gritted teeth.

"Let's slip these off," she said in a voice that was husky to her own ears. She eased his briefs down his hips.

Andie took the fantasy a little further and swirled the feather up his fully aroused masculinity. He shuddered, arching toward her, his green eyes telling her he'd reached his limit. "Andie—"

Before she replaced the feather with her mouth, she whispered, "Congratulations, darling. I love you."

Chapter Fourteen

An hour and a half later, Andie lay as still as possible, waiting for her heart rate to approach normal. The satin sheet cradled her body in softness while Eli's arm rested heavily around her waist. A few of the candles still glimmered, and the room smelled of sweet vanilla and sex.

Andie stared at the man beside her in amazement. Like an indolent lion, he'd indulged her even though she'd tested his patience.

Then he devoured her.

Although he was now sleeping like the dead, an hour earlier he had turned the tables on her, alternately seducing her with the feather and his mouth. Who would have thought something as unsubstantial as a feather could make her scream? She closed her eyes and covered her burning cheeks at the thought. She'd been so embarrassed she'd tried to crawl under the covers, but Eli, unable to suppress his gentle amusement, hadn't allowed her to hide.

Something more profound than love play, however, had transpired between them. He had endured her need to pleasure him and his own need to claim her. For all her teasing, through Eli's giving, she had become his. Through the sharing, she had been completely taken.

It had started almost the moment they'd met. In the past, the men in her life had been content to take. Eli had instead insisted on giving—understanding when she'd needed it, care when she was sick.

She looked at his face, his lips swollen from kisses, his eyelashes shielding the fire in his eyes, the hard line of his determined jaw unsoftened by sleep. Her chest squeezed tight with tenderness. She shook her head in wonder. He had been persistently attentive, and it had been the everyday attention that had conquered her, she realized. Not grand gestures or big promises.

No pretending anymore. He hadn't actually asked, but she was committed in a way she'd never been before. If something hurt Eli, it would hurt her, too. If he was happy, she would feel his joy. She sensed it was the same way for him.

Exhilaration and fear battled for dominance inside her. She loved him so much she thought she would burst with it, yet Andie had learned the hard way relationships could fall apart with no warning. There could be no easy parting between them, now. Her heart twisted with the bittersweet knowledge. They'd shared too much.

"Chicken pox," the pediatrician confirmed as he surveyed the telltale spots on Fletch's trunk. He chucked Fletch under the chin and smiled encouragingly, then scribbled some directions on the blue prescription pad. "If he gets uncomfortable you can purchase both of these over the counter," he said to Eli. "Discomfort is usually the main issue with chicken pox in children. It can be a little more troublesome with adults."

"What about fever?" Eli asked, pulling Fletch's striped shirt over his head.

"Children's Tylenol. No aspirin." He scribbled some more on his chart, then handed Eli the bill and gave Fletch another quick smile. "He should be fine. The chicken pox virus is very contagious, though, so you'll want to keep him away from other kids until his lesions get crusty." He opened the door and slid the chart in the wooden slot. "Call me if you have any problems."

Eli paid the bill, then hustled Fletch into the car.

Fletch remained unusually quiet until they'd nearly reached home. "What does contag—contag—"

"Contagious," Eli said. "It means that it's very easy for other people to catch your virus and get sick."

"Virus?" Fletch's voice rose anxiously.

Hearing the thread of panic in Fletch's tone, Eli gave his son's stiff little shoulders a reassuring squeeze. "Chicken pox is a virus. You'll itch a little bit, then you'll get over it. You probably caught it from one of your friends. Has anybody in the neighborhood got it?"

Fletch paused. "Jennifer," he finally said in a ominous tone. "I'm never playing with her again."

Eli pulled to a stop in the driveway and regarded his son curiously. "Why not?"

"'Cause she made me get sick!" So upset he looked ready to cry, Fletch unhooked his seat belt and pushed open the car door.

Eli's heart gave a hard jerk at Fletch's distress. He caught him just as he rounded the corner of the car. "Hey, hey. What's going on here?" He pulled his little boy up into his arms, and Fletch fastened himself around Eli like a rubber band.

Eli's heart gave another jerk. He closed the car door, then ruffled Fletch's hair. "You're gonna be okay. I think you're feeling bad because of your fever. After we get inside, I'll give you some medicine to make you feel better. Then you can go upstairs and take a n—" Eli made a quick modification. Fletch didn't respond well to the *N* word. "You can relax. I'll even let you have grape Kool-Aid in your bedroom if you promise to keep the sipper seal on your cup."

Fletch glanced up at him. "Mrs. G. won't like that."

Pushing the door open, Eli laughed. "Yeah, well, since Mrs. G. is off for the whole weekend, maybe we won't tell her. If you're feeling better tonight, you can watch a Three Stooges movie with your uncles and me."

"When are they gonna be here?"

Eli glanced at his watch and winced. "Sooner than I'll be ready for them," he muttered. He let Fletch slide to the floor and urged him upstairs. "C'mon, you need to get a little rest."

After Eli bribed Fletch into bed by allowing the puppy to stay with him, he came downstairs to prepare for his brothers' arrival. The most obvious reason Eli had invited his brothers for the weekend was that he was trying to give Fletch more of a sense of family. There was more involved, however, than the obvious. Being with Andie had made Eli aware that he'd let his relationship with his brothers fade to nearly nothing. Now, he was beginning to realize how important those brotherly bonds were.

He figured they should be able to fumble through a weekend as long as he had plenty of cold beer, pizza and a few Three Stooges videos.

He had beer. Unfortunately, the refrigerator was broken. He made a quick call to a twenty-four-hour repair service and was told the repairman would show by nine o'clock. He put the beer in the refrigerator anyway.

After making a call to the pizza delivery, he learned they were in the process of moving and wouldn't be delivering against until September.

"Dad. Brownie peed on the floor," Fletch called from the top of the steps. "Can I have some more Kool-Aid?"

"Just a minute." Ignoring the phone, Eli grabbed the paper towels. He'd hoped Brownie was finally trained, but the puppy just couldn't seem to contain his excitement or control his bladder. After cleaning up the puddle, Eli put Brownie in the kennel downstairs, gave Fletch a refill and ordered him back to bed.

The first thread of uneasiness ran through him when he punched the button on his answering machine for messages and heard Andie apologetically inform him that she had to work late.

Then the doorbell rang.

"Dad, all my Kool-Aid is gone, and I gotta go to the bathroom," Fletch yelled from his room.

"Go ahead, I'll be up in a minute," Eli called as he opened the door.

Drenched, Ash stood in the doorway. "Hey, bro."

Eli took in the sight of his two-hundred-pound baby brother, and his heart gave an odd clutch. "You always did ignore weather reports."

Ash pushed his damp hair from his face and strode through the doorway. Water dripped from his duffel bag and boots. "It was a great day to ride my bike—sunny in Florida, Georgia and South Carolina. The sky opened up when I hit the North Carolina border."

Eli shook his head. "I'm checking the date. It's got to be Friday the thirteenth. Come on in." He put his hand on Ash's shoulder and urged him down the hall.

Ash, who had been persistently cheerful since birth, grinned through his dampness and cocked his head to one side. "Rough day, Oh Great One?"

Eli felt himself respond to Ash's good-natured jab despite the chaos. Throughout his growing-up years, both his brothers had razzed him with the nickname to keep his head from swelling. Funny how it used to annoy him. Now it made him feel connected. "Do you know how long it's been since someone called me that?"

"You mean they don't call you Great One in the lab?"

"No. The neighbors call me Dr. Frankenstein when they think I'm not listening." His lips twitched. "Andie nearly skinned one of the men alive over it."

"Andie's the babe next door," Ash recalled with a nod and stopped at the stairs. "Wasn't she a nurse? I may need someone to tend to my wounds," he said waggling his eyebrows. "I think I got a scratch when I put down my kickstand."

Eli's gut instinctively tightened. Ash was just teasing, he told himself, but he knew his baby brother had turned into one hell of a flirt. On the off chance that Ash wasn't needling him, Eli set the record straight. "Andie doesn't tend to other men. I keep her busy."

Ash's grin glinted with mischief. "Just checkin'."

Eli relaxed and nodded. "Glad you could make it. You want to take a shower?"

Ash nodded. "Dinner afterward?"

"I'm working on it."

For all his joking, Ash had never possessed much of a sense of humor about food. He gave Eli a worried glance. "Working on it?"

"Got a little problem with the refrigerator, and the pizza delivery place is temporarily closed, but—" The doorbell rang again. "That's either the refrigerator repairman or Caleb."

"Where's Fletch?"

"In theory, he's taking a nap," Eli said and opened the door to his other brother.

Laptop computer in hand, Caleb regarded Eli with a familiar glazed expression as he stood there silently.

Eli immediately knew Caleb hadn't cut down on his hours in the lab. Behind those wire-rimmed glasses, his brother was in a different world. But that discussion was for a different time. Sighing, he waved Caleb through the door. "How was your trip? Did the rain slow you down?"

Caleb's brows knitted together. "Rain?"

Eli stifled a groan. It was worse than he'd thought.

"Have you got somewhere I can set up?" Caleb asked, looking around. "I had a few ideas on the way and wanted to key them in before I forgot."

"My study's the second door on the left. I'll try to rustle up some dinner...." Caleb was already walking down the hall.

The irony struck him and he shook his head. While Caleb probably wouldn't think about food until midnight, Ash would start gnawing on the woodwork if Eli didn't find something in five minutes. Glancing out the door, he noticed Caleb's headlights were still on and ran to turn them off. At least he'd turned off the engine.

The refrigerator guy showed, and just as Eli had decided to feed Ash a peanut butter sandwich, Andie swept through the door with bags from a local restaurant.

He was so glad to see her he took her in his arms, bags and all. She felt like heaven. "How did you know we needed food?"

She pulled back and looked at him with knowing humor in her eyes. "I had a feeling you might wait until the last minute to order pizza."

"Just a feeling, huh." Eli kissed her thoroughly, tasting her lips and soaking up the pleasure of holding her.

Ash cleared his throat loudly. "Excuse me, but—"

Eli reluctantly ended the kiss. "What?"

"Food."

Andie's cheeks turned scarlet. She wriggled away. "Oh, here," she said, thrusting the bags on the table. "I stopped by this little place right here in Cary called Serendipity. There are plenty of sandwiches and they make the best gazpacho soup and chocolate chip pecan pie with whipped cream." Taking a quick breath, she glanced around and self-consciously pushed her hair behind her ear. "Where's Caleb?"

Ash had already unwrapped a sandwich. "Having an intimate experience with his laptop."

Andie looked confused.

"He's working in my study," Eli clarified.

She nodded. "And Fletch?"

Eli groaned and wiped his hand over his face. "He's got chicken pox." He swore. "I was supposed to take him some Kool-Aid. It's been almost an hour."

"I'll do it," she offered, stepping around the table. "You go ahead and eat."

"No, I—"

Andie shook her head. "Really," she said, waving him off. "Spend a few minutes with your brother. Let me see if I can make Fletch feel a little better. I do this for a living. Remember?" she asked in a pseudostern voice, then quickly filled a cup and left.

Eli watched her go and felt his heart squeeze with emotion. God, he was in love with her.

"So, the Great One has finally fallen," Ash said.

Eli met his brother's considering gaze and nodded. "Yeah. All the way."

Ash slid a sandwich across the table. "Well, she won't let you starve."

His brother was speaking of food, but Eli remembered sipping wine from her skin. He gave a rough chuckle. "So true."

For the first time today, Eli eased back in his chair and relaxed. He asked Ash about the construction business in Florida and took some ribbing when he told him about his recent award. He was just about to take some food to Caleb when Andie returned to the room with a worried expression on her face. He immediately stood.

"I looked under his bed and in his closet. I checked your bedroom and the bathroom."

Eli's heart plunged. "What are you saying?" he asked hoarsely.

She shook her head helplessly. "I can't find Fletch."

Within seconds Ash set down his second sandwich and Caleb cut off his computer. They searched the house. Andie grabbed her slicker, but Eli had already gone outside.

Stepping into the rainy night, she heard Eli calling Fletch. Her stomach twisted. The night was black as pitch, but she could still picture the rigid anguish on Eli's face when he'd realized Fletch was missing.

She ran to catch up with him and squeezed his shoulder. "We'll find him, Eli," she told him.

He swore. "I should have checked on him sooner, but I swear the whole damn house went nuts. Fletch was freaked about getting chicken pox." He shook his head. "I still don't understand."

His words nudged at something in the back of her mind. She couldn't put her finger on it, not with the rain pouring down, not with Eli so worried she could feel it standing next to him. Not with Fletch missing.

They split up after they searched Eli's yard and garage. Eli went down the street calling out Fletch's name. Andie checked her yard again and again. Desperation edged in and she began to make bargains.

"Come on, Fletch. I brought pie and you haven't had any."

Silence.

"You can have frozen yogurt."

Silence.

Huddled beneath Andie's porch, Fletch clutched his llama closer to him. It was wetter and darker than he'd thought it would be. He missed his Flintstones nightlight. He'd gotten scared when the doctor said he had a virus, but his dad made him feel a little bit better. When he was in bed, though, he started thinking about the virus that killed his mom. He got so scared his stomach started hurting. He didn't know what else he could do but leave. Now Andie was calling and Fletch wanted to go home, but he knew he shouldn't.

"Fletch, honey, chicken pox isn't that bad. It'll be gone before you know it."

Her voice sounded as if she might be crying. Fletch swallowed over a hard lump in his throat.

"Fletch, your daddy and I love you. We want you home, so we can take care of you."

He squished his eyes closed. All his insides hurt.

"Fletch, your father is worried. He's so sad."

A sob squeezed through his tight throat, and Fletch started to cry.

"Fletch—"

Andie heard a muffled broken sound and froze. Her heart seemed to stop. She waited agonizing seconds and heard the heartrending sound of a child crying helplessly beneath the porch steps.

"Fletch!" She nearly stumbled in her haste. "Eli!" she screamed. "He's here." Dropping to her knees, she reached toward him in the dark, but he shrank backward.

"No," Fletch said, shaking his head. "I got a virus, and you might get sick."

Although he fought her, she pulled him out. "No, I won't, sweetheart. I've had chicken pox before."

His small frame rigid with distress, he continued to cry. "But the doctor said I'm very contag—contag—"

"Contagious?" Andie wiped her own tears. "That doesn't mean—"

"Fletch!" Eli rounded the corner of the house. "Oh, thank God." He had died a thousand deaths in the past fifteen minutes. Sweet relief ran through him when he saw Fletch and Andie. Walking closer, he extended his arms. "Come here."

Fletch shook his head and started screaming. "No! No! Go away!"

Eli froze in shock, glancing at Andie, who looked as confused as he was.

"I'll make you sick like I made Mommy sick, then you'll die," he wailed.

His heart breaking, Eli shook his head. "You didn't make your mother sick."

"Yes I did," he insisted. "She died 'cause I gave her a virus I got from day care."

Fletch's words echoed between the three of them for an endless moment. Horrified that Fletch thought he'd been responsible for Gail's death, Eli slowly walked closer. "No." When Fletch started to protest again, Eli lifted his hand. "You must listen to me. I won't get chicken pox."

"But—"

"You've got to trust me, Fletch." Eli shot a quick glance to Andie and felt her support clear to the bone. He just wished he deserved it.

Kneeling, he took one of his son's small resistant hands in his. He looked at the child who'd come to mean the world to him. "Your mother caught a virus in South America. She was very sick when she came home." He tried to think of a way to simplify the explanation. "The virus made her heart sick and that's why she died. You don't have the same virus."

Fletch's face crinkled in confusion. He sniffed. "But I got one in day care right before she went to the hospital."

"That's right. You got a bad cold and sore throat. Your mom didn't catch your virus. She got sick in South America."

He sniffed again and swallowed. His eyes were wide with tentative hope. "Does that mean I didn't make her die?"

Eli's eyes burned. His heart ached. Although it took all his strength, he kept his voice steady. He wanted to brand these words on Fletch's heart and mind. "You absolutely, positively did not make your mother sick. And you absolutely, positively did not make your mother die."

Eli watched the truth sink in.

Fletch stared at him and took a big, shaky breath. His young face remained solemn. "I'm glad I didn't make her sick, but I still wish she hadn't died."

Andie reached for Eli's hand, and he spotted the tears falling heedlessly down her cheeks. Again, he drew comfort from her presence. "I'm sorry she died, too," Eli murmured and held out his other hand to Fletch.

Fletch threw himself against Eli.

Closing his eyes to compose himself, Eli took a careful breath. "Let's go inside now."

"But won't I make everybody get sick?"

Eli glanced at Andie and suffered again.

"Usually people only get chicken pox one time," Andie explained. "Almost *always*, you can't catch it a second time. I've already had it," she said. "And I bet your dad has had chicken pox, too."

"That's right," Eli said gruffly.

"What about Uncle Caleb and Uncle Ash?"

Eli smiled through his pain. "We all had it at the same time."

Fletch gave a big sigh and snuggled against Eli. "Can I have some pie now?"

Andie gave a wry smile. "One of my promises."

Eli stood and carried him home.

He dried off Fletch and changed him into fresh pajamas. Then the uncles gave Fletch a big welcome and regaled him with tales of their own bouts with chicken pox. After Fletch got his pie and everyone was reassured of his safety, Eli tucked his little boy into bed and came back downstairs.

While his brothers watched a video, Eli stood in the kitchen and stared into a shot glass of whiskey. He felt Andie behind him. He downed the glass. "Thanks for your help. I don't know how long it would have taken me to find him."

She didn't touch him, but she stood close. "You would have found him."

His lips twisted bitterly. "For the past four months, my little boy thought he had killed his mother."

"He doesn't now."

"For four months," he repeated, shaking his head. "Can you imagine how guilty he felt? I should have known. I should have done something."

"Oh, Eli, you did everything you could." He stiffened when she put her hand on his arm. "You can't always know what's going on in a child's mind, especially at a time like this."

Eli shook off her soft hand and sweet comfort. He didn't deserve it. "I'm his father. It's my job to know."

"Eli," Andie began.

"No." He forced himself to look at her and lifted his hands. "I appreciate everything you've done, but we'd better call it a night."

"I think," she said quietly, "it would be better to talk about this."

"I don't." Just the thought of talking about it turned his stomach. All Eli wanted to do was crawl into a cave. Through the thick haze of his guilt, he thought he saw a flicker of hurt in her eyes, but the expression passed so quickly he couldn't be sure.

She knitted her fingers together. "I don't want to leave you right now."

He balled his fists in his pockets to keep from reaching for her. Too much defeat and confusion roiled inside him. He sucked in a painful breath and narrowed his eyes. "It's best."

Chapter Fifteen

Andie struggled to focus on the conversation at hand, but it was like swimming against the tide. Torn between hurt and anger that Eli had turned *away* from her instead of *to* her, she took out her energy on the weeds trying to choke the last of her Big Boy tomatoes. He had pursued her and caught her, and now it was almost as if he were pushing her away. It was enough to make her scream. As a matter of fact, she'd done just that after they'd finished another stilted conversation last night.

"I don't see the attraction to this gardening stuff," Samantha said as she stood over Andie. "Especially when there's a perfectly good produce stand right down the street."

Pushing aside her preoccupation with Eli, Andie turned her attention to Sam's question and yanked out another weed. "It's the idea of starting with a seed or a little plant and helping it grow, seeing it bear fruit." Andie plucked a ripened tomato from the vine. "See?"

"Yeah," Samantha said in a noncommittal tone. She had been trying to talk Andie into joining her for a movie. "It sounds a little like raising kids to me."

Andie hadn't thought of it that way, but she supposed Samantha had a point. "True. Speaking of kids, how's your sister?"

"Better. She dumped her boyfriend, so she's around to take care of her kids more now." Samantha grinned. "I guess you could say I'm back in the saddle again."

"Good for you." Andie picked a few more of the ripe tomatoes and put them in her basket.

"You haven't said much about your Viking explorer lately."

Andie was more worried about Eli than she had admitted to anyone, worried and powerless to change the situation. "He's still upset about what happened with Fletch."

Samantha crossed her arms over her chest and leaned against the maple tree. "So, he's not calling you anymore?"

"I didn't say that." Andie turned on the sprinkler and quickly moved away. "He calls or sees me once a day." They talked about nothing important for a few minutes, enough for her to know that he still felt guilty over Fletch and that he still cared about her. Enough to frustrate the dickens out of her. She brushed the dirt off her palms and picked up her basket to carry it inside. "Don't get me started on Eli. I'm so confused I don't know if I'm coming or going."

Samantha followed her out of the late-afternoon sun and through the back door. "If he's causing you this much grief, then why don't you just dump him?"

Andie stopped midstride.

Her heart squeezed tight. She'd had her share of doubts during the past few days. She was afraid Eli would shut her out again, yet she could see that he was doing his best not to. She sensed it was his natural inclination to pull away when he was in crisis. Despite his natural inclination, he was *trying* to reach out to her. The fact that he was trying bound her to him.

Realization flooded her, and her doubts were squashed. "I don't want to dump him. When he didn't understand everything that was going on with me, he hung in there. I want to do the same for him."

Samantha raised her eyebrows. "Sounds serious."

"It is." Serious enough to break her heart. She set the basket on the counter and washed her hands.

Sam sighed. "Sometimes love sucks."

Andie chuckled, despite her worry.

"As much as it goes against my grain to encourage you, I think you should remember that your past life experience centers around French kings. A Viking explorer is a different animal."

Wiping her hands dry, Andie looked at Sam in complete confusion. "I have no idea what you're talking about."

Sam gave another long-suffering sigh and leaned against the counter. "A Viking explorer requires a different approach."

"Than a French king," Andie concluded, wondering if she was going nuts, because Sam was starting to make sense.

"Exactly."

"Sam, he's really hurting. He holds himself completely responsible for Fletch's mistaken belief that he made his mother die."

"And part of the reason you love him is because he cares so much."

Her heart felt bare and raw. "Yes. But it frustrates me that he keeps holding on to his guilt. It's like he's stuck in a dungeon."

Sam nodded. "Which means you may have to help him get out. You may have to talk about Fletch even if he doesn't want to. Sometimes you have to hit a man over the head with the truth." She cocked her head to one side and thrust out her chin in characteristic defiance. "And if that doesn't work, as my daddy says, 'You might just have to kick a little.'"

Andie considered Sam's advice, not the kicking part, the talking part. Mulling it over, she decided it was time for Eli to hear another side to this story.

Eli opened the door to Andie at the same time Fletch yelled. "Da-ad, Brownie peed on the floor again."

"I'll be up in a minute," he called. "Some things never change," he muttered to himself. "Please come in. Mrs. G. left dinner for us."

Andie smiled and he felt it clear to his gut. She wore a white sundress and smelled of apricots, and looking at her made him ache.

She kissed him full on the mouth. "I've missed you.

His heart swelled and his body responded. He wrapped his arms around her. "I've missed you, too."

"There's something I need to tell you," she said, an undertone of determination in her voice.

Eli absorbed a jab of wariness and braced himself. The last time a woman had said that to him, she'd told him she wanted a divorce. "Okay." He hugged her tight, then released her. "Give me a minute or two. I've got to mop a puddle." Then he escaped. He knew he wasn't giving Andie what she wanted, and with a sickening sense of dread, he wondered how long she would hang on.

The past several days he'd been consumed with determining how he could have prevented Fletch's suffering. Through it all, Andie's words haunted him. *You did everything you could.* But it was difficult for Eli to accept that he couldn't have protected his son from unnecessary pain. God, how he wanted to believe that he wasn't a rotten father, that he wasn't a failure because he hadn't figured out the basis for Fletch's fears sooner.

The sense that he'd caused irrevocable damage wouldn't last forever, he told himself as he cleaned up the puddle. It couldn't. Despite his chicken pox, Fletch was as happy as a clam. Eli would get past this. He had to. In the meantime, though, he didn't want to lose Andie because of it. Determined to devote the evening to restoring his relationship with her, Eli joined Andie at the dinner table followed by Fletch.

Before he took two bites, the lab called. There was a problem with some missing data, and they needed him to come. Andie immediately offered to stay with Fletch.

Thwarted by the disruption, Eli grabbed his keys and swore under his breath. The timing couldn't have been worse. Andie followed him to the foyer just as he was about to leave. "It shouldn't take long," he said.

"If it gets late, you can call Mrs. G. or Mrs. Grand-view."

"Are you saying you don't want me here when you get back?"

The uncertainty in her voice took him by surprise. "Hell, no. I don't want you to think I'm taking advantage of you."

"Oh," she said, comprehension dawning on her face. Her lips twitched, and a teasing light glinted in her eyes. "It seems to me you haven't taken advantage of me nearly enough the past few days."

Eli took a careful breath. Maybe things weren't as bad as he'd thought. "Then I'll definitely have to rectify that situation as soon as possible." He kissed her thoroughly enough to bring a dazed expression to her eyes and a rush of heat to his own body. Reluctantly leaving, he spent the entire drive to the lab thinking about all she'd said the night Fletch had run away.

Three hours later, Eli returned home. His brain felt like scrambled eggs, but he'd located the missing data on a computer disk. He stretched to relieve the kinks in his neck.

From upstairs he heard a soft humming sound. He followed the noise to Fletch's room and pushed open the door. The light from the hall bathed the room in a soft glow. Andie was rocking his son in the rocking chair. Fletch's head rested on her chest, his cheeks sleep-flushed, and his hair lovingly tousled by Andie's fingers. She was humming a lullaby.

Eli's heart squeezed tight. The sight filled up all the empty places inside him and healed his hurt.

She glanced up and met his gaze. "Hi," she whispered.

Eli had the odd sensation of seeing all his tomorrows in her clear brown eyes. Swallowing over a thickness in his throat, he walked to her side and stroked his little boy's cheek. "Out like a light," he murmured.

"He had a bad dream," she said softly. "But he's better now. You want to put him to bed?"

Eli nodded, and Andie brushed a soft kiss on Fletch's cheek before he tucked his son under the covers. He looked at Fletch for a moment, absorbing a fresh sense of completeness.

Taking Andie's hand in both of his, he led her down the hallway to his bedroom. "What was the bad dream?"

She shrugged. "Something about cavity monsters. I told him to brush his teeth again, then rocked him for a while."

Flicking on the lamp, Eli shook his head. "Cavity monsters."

"Before he went to sleep, he told me not to worry." She gently tugged his hand to make sure she had his attention. "You'd be back by morning."

He met her gaze. "He really trusts me."

She nodded. "He really does. I do, too. One of the reasons I love you," she said, looking like a woman with a mission, "is because you're such a good father to Fletch."

Eli rubbed the back of his neck. "Right now, I'm not sure— "

Andie stopped his protest with another kiss, then pulled slightly away. "I want you to be sure. But for now, maybe you should just listen."

Eli blinked. He felt as if she'd shifted from second gear to fourth and skipped third. "Listen?"

Her gaze earnest and intent, Andie nodded. "To the truth. The truth is Fletch is one happy, well-loved little boy. He's crazy about his father."

Torn between hope and an ebbing sense of failure, he sighed. He wondered how he'd lived his whole life without her. "Andie, I—"

She pressed her finger over his mouth. "Not finished. The truth is you've helped him adjust under incredibly difficult circumstances."

"Maybe," he conceded, "but—"

She gently pinched his lips closed. "The truth is, as soon as you found out about his mistaken belief that he'd caused his mother's death, you immediately took care of it. Immediately," she emphasized.

Eli stared at her, and his protests stalled like a rusted engine. His sweet Andie had turned into a bully, a wall breaker.

Her healing words seeped through a crack in his heart, soothing his private agony.

She bit her lip. "You once said you needed me to believe you," she whispered. "Now I'm asking the same of you."

Something broke free inside him. "I do," Eli said and drew her closer. "I got stuck on the guilt, but you shook me loose. I don't want to do without you anymore, Andie. Next door is too far away. Sometimes the next room is too far away. I love you so much it's scary." He felt her tremble and was amazed that she felt the same way about him.

"Is there any way," he asked in a husky voice he couldn't do a damn thing about, "I could talk you into marrying a guy the neighbors *still* call Dr. Frankenstein?"

"Yes." She slipped her arms around his neck and met his gaze head-on with her honest brown eyes. "I don't really understand it. You're a genius and I'm not, but for some strange reason, we're right—together."

His heart full, he took her mouth in a kiss that gave and took, but mostly promised. He'd given her his heart and she would keep it safe, just as he would protect hers with his life. She was soft and sweet, and she was his.

He swept her into his arms and laid her on his big bed where she belonged. "I have another theory about why we should be together," he told her as he lay beside her. "It involves genes."

"Oh, really?"

Eli grinned at her skeptical tone and fingered one of the straps of her sundress. The pretty white garment would be history soon. "Really. I have a faulty gene, and faulty genes can cause a multitude of problems."

She looked at him curiously, her lips twitching. "Is that so? And exactly what do I do for your faulty gene?"

"You have an enzyme that makes my faulty gene function properly."

Her smile broadened, but her eyes grew soft as if she knew he was telling that he needed her desperately. "Well, that's amazing. And here I just thought I loved you."

*   *   *   *   *

Silhouette®

SPECIAL EDITION™

COMING NEXT MONTH

#985 D IS FOR DANI'S BABY—Lisa Jackson
That Special Woman!/ Love Letters
Eleven years ago, Dani Stewart had no choice but to give up her
baby for adoption. Now she was determined to find her son—and
the last thing she expected was a reunion with Brandon Scarlotti,
the father of her child.

#986 MORGAN'S WIFE—Lindsay McKenna
Morgan's Mercenaries: Love and Danger
Everything was at stake when Jim Woodward accepted a dangerous
mission to rescue his closest friends. Pepper Sinclair was along for
the ride to ensure he got the job done—and to melt the ice around his
enclosed heart....

#987 FINALLY A BRIDE—Sherryl Woods
Always a Bridesmaid!
Katie Jones never expected a proposal of marriage from the man
who was once her best friend. She'd always loved Luke Cassidy,
but once they said their "I do's," Katie learned a few secrets about
her new husband....

#988 A MAN AND A MILLION—Jackie Merritt
A newly rich woman like Theo Hunter attracted her share of roguish
attention—and town bad boy Colt Murdoch made no secret of his
interest. Talk around town predicted Colt stealing Theo's land, but
the only thing she was sure of losing was her heart!

#989 THIS CHILD IS MINE—Trisha Alexander
Eve DelVecchio and Mitch Sinclair hadn't seen each other in years,
but the attraction between them still smoldered. Mitch was elated
to find his lost love, but would Eve's secret jeopardize their second
chance?

#990 AND FATHER MAKES THREE—Laurie Campbell
Premiere
Despite the wild attraction between them, Sarah Corcoran knew
Nate Ryan was not her type. After all, she was single-handedly
raising a teenager—but maybe footloose and fancy-free Ryan
could be convinced to settle down....

Take 4 bestselling love stories FREE

Plus get a FREE surprise gift!

Silhouette

SPECIAL EDITION™

It's our 1000th Special Edition and we're celebrating!

Join us these coming months for some wonderful stories in a special celebration of our 1000th book with some of your favorite authors!

Diana Palmer   **Nora Roberts**
Debbie Macomber   **Christine Flynn**
Phyllis Halldorson   **Lisa Jackson**

mini-series by:

Lindsay McKenna, Marie Ferrarella, Sherryl Woods, Gina Ferris Wilkins.

And many more books by special writers.

And as a special bonus, all Silhouette Special Edition titles published during Celebration 1000! Will have **double** Pages & Privileges proofs of purchase!

Silhouette Special Edition...heartwarming stories packed with emotion, just for you! You'll fall in love with our next 1000 special stories!

Become a
Privileged Woman,
You'll be entitled to all these *Free Benefits.* And *Free Gifts,* too.

To thank you for buying our books, we've designed an exclusive FREE program called *PAGES & PRIVILEGES™*. You can enroll with just one Proof of Purchase, and get the kind of luxuries that, until now, you could only read about.

BIG HOTEL DISCOUNTS

A privileged woman stays in the finest hotels. And so can you—at up to 60% off! Imagine standing in a hotel check-in line and watching as the guest in front of you pays $150 for the same room that's only costing you $60. Your *Pages & Privileges* discounts are good at Sheraton, Marriott, Best Western, Hyatt and thousands of other fine hotels all over the U.S., Canada and Europe.

FREE DISCOUNT TRAVEL SERVICE

A privileged woman is always jetting to romantic places. When <u>you</u> fly, just make one phone call for the lowest published airfare at time of booking— <u>or double the difference back!</u>

PLUS—you'll get a $25 voucher to use the first time you book a flight AND <u>5% cash back on every ticket you buy thereafter through the travel service!</u>

PROOF OF PURCHASE

Offer expires October 31, 1996

SSE-PP56